MAKE YOU LOVE ME

Also by LaTonya Y. Williams

MIXED MESSAGES

MAKE YOU LOVE ME

LATONYA Y. WILLIAMS

URBAN BOOKS
www.urbanbooks.net

Urban Books
10 Brennan Place
Deer Park, NY 11798

ISBN-13: 978-1-893196-81-0
ISBN-10: 1-893196-81-X

First Mass Market Printing March 2007
Printed in the United States of America

10 9 8 7 6 5 4 3 2 1

This is a work of fiction. Any references or similarities to actual events, real people, living, or dead, or to real locales are intended to give the novel a sense of reality. Any similarity in other names, characters, places, and incidents is entirely coincidental.

Submit Wholesale Orders to:
Kensington Publishing Corp.
C/O Penguin Group (USA) Inc.
Attention: Order Processing
405 Murray Hill Parkway
East Rutherford, NJ 07073-2316
Phone: 1-800-526-0275

Dedication

This book is dedicated to my mother, Avis, for encouraging me to set high goals for myself, and making me believe each one was attainable.

Acknowledgements

There are so many people to thank for their help, generosity, and continued support. *Make You Love Me* was written for readers to find their purpose in life and pursue it, no matter what challenges and hardships they may face.

My Lord and Savior, Jesus Christ; for with You, I am able to do all things!

My husband and sons, whom I love dearly. I cherish every day I spend with all of you. You're worth every single sacrifice.

My mother; I treasure our friendship most of all. Everything that is good in me, came from you, and I am so blessed to have you in my corner.

My family and friends; your continued support means the world to me.

My Sista Team: Cabrina, T'Ronda, Nat, Shatia, and Ashley—I appreciate your help so much as baby-sitters, traveling companions, promotions crew, and anything I asked you to do at a moment's notice. I couldn't have gotten this far without any of you.

My Urban Family: Carl Weber, Roy Glenn, Arvita Glenn, and the rest of the staff, thanks for rallying behind this project. It is a wonderful family and I am very honored to be a part of it.

My author friends: Trista Russell, Tina McKinney, Lexi Davis, and Keisha Bell, I appreciate the emails, calls, advice, and sharing of ideas. We are all in this together! I wish each of you much continued success.

My review team: Michelle Davis, Michelle Knight, Shauna Cooper, and my sis T'Ronda, I appreciate your input. I hope you are proud of the finished product.

Book clubs; for reading, loving, and sharing *Mixed Messages*. I really enjoyed attending the meetings, sharing in on the conversation, and eating the food! A special thanks to PSSST! Book Club (Richmond, VA) for throwing me the surprise baby shower.

To all the readers, may the words in this book inspire romance, laughter, insight, and most of all the motivation to reach higher in life.

God bless!

Be sure to check out my website at:
www.latonyawilliams.com

Chapter 1
(Tate)

Who said in life you can't have your cake and eat it too? I adopted that motto while in college. Only thing was, there was no cake. There wasn't even any sweetbread. Unfortunately, my college years were an exact replica of my high-school years. No popularity, no parties, and, for damn sure, no women. By many standards, my classification fell under the category of "Greek." Typo, I meant "geek." In a thesaurus, other appropriate adjectives would be "nerd," "retard," or just plain "Oh, he's so gross." I'm a mama's boy and proud to be one.

My parents never blessed me with a knowledge of social skills, something they never lacked. Repeatedly, I would hear from relatives and potential friends, "You must've been switched at birth."

This question always popped in my mind over the years. Dan and Myra Gibson were both social icons in our black neighborhood on Jacksonville's north side of town, referred to only as The Northside. Mama, a city bus driver, and Dad, a factory worker for Maxwell House, were known for throwing the best parties, back in the day when afros, dashikis, bell-bottoms, and platform shoes were the "thing."

I can still remember sneaking downstairs to the family room, where the white light bulb was replaced with a yellow one. Marvin Gaye's *What's Goin' On* played on the record player. The air filled with cigarette smoke, and couples slow danced on the temporary dance floor. Back then, women folk stayed to make sure the house was cleaned, furniture put in place, and the house looked back to normal before leaving.

I tried to hang out as long as I could, before Mama or Daddy would say, "Boy, get back in the room!" and send me back upstairs. Once, my Uncle Byron actually let me have a sip of his "spirit-filled drink" before escorting me to my room. Yep, I'm sad to say that my only party experiences were at my parent's house when I was just a little boy.

That drastically changed, when I turned ten. Mama got saved and made the whole family join Calvary Baptist Church. Myra Gibson traded her short dresses for long dresses, her platforms for more conservative pumps, and all of the liquor was given away to the other so-called sinners in the neighborhood. It wasn't long before Dan Gibson followed suit and began to serve on the Deacon Board. Needless to say, I never had a chance.

I was the type of brotha whose mama still bought and picked the clothes I wore in high school. My early credits included: class treasurer of the senior class, loyal member of the National Honors Society, and I even played an instrument in the band. I graduated from high school with a 4.0 GPA and attended Jacksonville University, majoring in business. I continued to live at home with my parents, held a job at Wendy's at night and weekends, and worked my ass off to get the best grades. I graduated with honors in three years and received my first job working as a claims adjuster for American Income Life Insurance. A few short years later, I was promoted to senior management and earned a $70,000 income to go with it.

Drastically, my life changed in a matter of moments. As soon as my first direct deposit was automatically wired into my checking account, my adult status changed. I went from "dweeb" to "successful bachelor," living in the 3,000-square-foot condo and driving the white 525 BMW to prove it. Not bad for a guy who wasn't even 30 years old.

Now when Mama took me shopping, she helped me buy tailored suits for my new look. I know you're probably wondering why my moms picked out my clothing even though I was a grown man, but she still had good taste. She even decorated my new condominium, along with the assistance of the sisters from the church. Twenty thousand dollars later, I was living in my own little private paradise on the beach.

So here I was, cruising in my BMW on JTB (J. Turner Butler Boulevard) to downtown at dawn and looking very sexy (if I must say so) in my Perry Ellis sunglasses I picked up at Dillard's in the mall the week before. I pulled my car into the parking garage, grabbed my briefcase, and walked toward the elevator.

My cell phone rang. "This is Tate. Talk to me."

"Hey, baby. I wanted to wish you good luck with your meeting today." It was LeQuisha.

"Thanks. Look, I have to—"

"I know you're gonna be busy all day and all, but I wanted to know if I could stop by your place later tonight, you know, so we could celebrate."

(I wanted so badly to say no. As of late, I began to think with my other head. I'll tell you about that later.) I stepped into the elevator. "You can come by around ten."

I could hear the sudden sound of delight in her tone. "Okay. Bye, baby."

"Bye, LeQuisha."

Just then the elevator doors opened on the ninth floor. I walked down the hall to spot my assistant, Gladys, speaking through her headset to a client.

"Mr. Gibson."

"It's Tate, Gladys." I don't feel comfortable being on a last-name basis with Gladys. She was old enough to be my mother, and it just didn't seem right for her to call me Mr. Gibson, like I was one of her elders.

"Right." She smiled. "Tate, don't forget your staff meeting at nine, and lunch with Mr. Thomas at twelve."

I saluted her. "Thanks, Gladys. Oh, and hold my calls until my first meeting; I need time to review my notes for the other adjusters."

"Yes, sir."

I closed the door behind me, not surprised to see my vertical blinds already opened, and a hot cup of coffee on my desk. *I must remember to give Gladys a sizable bonus at Christmas.* I took off my jacket, placed it on the back of my leather chair, and sat down. *What the hell was I going to do about LeQuisha? What the fuck was wrong with her . . . calling me this early in the morning?*

It's only been six weeks, and she already thought she was my woman. I met her at the mall one evening when I picked up a suit and tie for a conference I had to attend in Los Angeles. (LeQuisha was the sales associate in the men's department at Dillard's.) I felt an immediate attraction to her enormous J-Lo ass and thick thighs. Her platinum-blonde hair pulled back in a long ponytail left some horse running around without its mane, but a brotha still wanted to holla.

I got them digits, and the rest was history. She asked me to pick her up from work the next night. I took her to Olive Garden for dinner and back to my condo for dessert. Possessing soft skin that complemented her honey-colored complexion tempted me to taste all of her sweetness. She rocked my fucking world all night. Straddling her huge thighs on mine, she rode me as if I was the Hulk roller coaster at Islands of Adventure. I wasn't disappointed with the merchandise either. Along with a tight ass, came a succulent pair of breasts with large nipples always standing erect.

Now, you know a woman with a clit as good as hers had some baggage. And I mean her luggage was stacked. Three pieces she neglected to tell me about. Turned out, LeQuisha had three kids! I wasn't ready to be nobody's daddy. Just being at the top of my game, ain't no-way-in hell I was about to sit on the bench. Not this soon. Problem was, as soon as LeQuisha could sense I was about to kick her ass to the curb, she started laying the pussy down for a brotha. Sucked my rod until the juices flowed all over her mouth. She would leave her kids with her no-man-having-sister and stay at my crib all night. I always sent her ass packing before sunrise.

A buzz from Gladys interrupted my thoughts. "Your staff is arriving for the meeting. I'll go ahead and direct them to the conference room."

"Thanks, Gladys." I grabbed my jacket, notes, and a pen. I walked toward the conference room and bumped into Glen Thomas on the way.

"Hey, are we still on for lunch today?" Glen asked.

"You bet."

"See ya then, man. All right." Glen patted my shoulder.

The meeting only lasted forty-five minutes because now, business was good. I managed to bring in two more adjusters to lighten the heavy caseloads of my bogged-down team. Everyone put in lots of overtime hours, and all reviews were above satisfactory. My performance record looked good in my new position as the leader of this very committed team.

Carmela Singleton, senior accountant at American Income Life, stopped me as I exited the conference room. This was one fine sista all the brothas in the building wanted to holla at. Tall and thin with a nice cocoa-brown complexion, very classy, mid-thirties in age, career-minded and driven, and not interested in pursuing any serious relationships.

"If you don't mind, Tate, I need to go over revisions made to next year's fiscal report."

"Sure, I'm free right now." I opened the door for her and followed her out.

Carmela clutched her clipboard. "I'll only be a few moments." Her gaze lingered for a moment.

I followed Carmela as she entered my office and walked over to the chair in front of my desk. I had always admired her sexy-ass sashay, you know. The one when the sistas think they are modeling on a runway or something. She sat down, crossed her legs, and began to review her notes on the clipboard.

I closed my door and confidently strutted toward her.

Her leg shook nervously.

I massaged her shoulders, hoping she wouldn't jerk and ask me what the hell I was doing. I mean we were friends; at least I considered her to be one and wanted to help her relax.

I bent down to whisper softly in her ear. "Now, you wanna tell me what this meeting is really about?"

"I told you." She freed herself from my grip and turned around to face me with her look of death I was all too familiar with. "I need to go over a few things with you first."

I wasn't in the mood to play any games with Carmela right now. I glanced down at my watch and realized Glen would be waiting for me in the lobby in less than an hour. Plus, my penis swelled, just eyeing her in that short skirt, so I simply pulled it out and lay all nine inches in front of her.

"Check this out, Carmela—I don't have time to play your little games. Now, either you're going to suck my dick, or you can take your narrow ass back to your big office upstairs and finger your coochie until you cum all over yourself."

Since she shut the fuck up, I knew I needed to get this party started. I pushed both of her shoulders down and proceeded to sit her ass back down in the chair. As she opened her mouth, her tongue slowly licked the head of my dick. I rubbed my hands through her short brown hair, and she sucked it with all intensity.

Just before I was about to reach an all-new high, she stopped and stood up. Carmela quickly undressed right in front of me, revealing her tiny little breasts and hairy pussy.

I lay her down on the floor and nibbled on her right breast. While I slipped on a condom, I massaged her clit. Then I glided in, hard and fast as I could . . . just the way she liked it. Her slender body contracted and then pulsated. I tore her stuff up, probably better than I had in the past three months.

Forty-five minutes later, I met Glen in the front lobby for lunch at our favorite sandwich shop, within walking distance. The day was very sunny and humid, caused by the short rain drizzle earlier that morning. As we exited the building, we immediately put on our sunglasses to block the sunrays from our eyes. Glen took off his olive-green blazer and rolled up his sleeves while carrying his jacket on one arm.

Glen was one of those smooth Kappa guys from FAMU in Tallahassee. His childhood differed from mine. Having grown up in a family of college-educated professionals, he became quite accustomed to having women and money. Meeting Glen had to be the best thing that happened to me. I knew he was someone who didn't see me as a nerd, but solely as a co-worker and friend. Now, I officially had a partner to frequent the clubs with and hook up with women. Until he met Terri Ransom.

On this particular Saturday night, we hung out at Jim's Place enjoying a few drinks at the bar. Terri strolled in with two of her stuck-up friends, acting as if they owned the place. Actually, I would never admit this to my boy, but Terri was one stuck-up bitch too. One look at her and my boy was strung. I mean, I should have handcuffed and placed his ass in a jail cell.

For months after the chance encounter with Terri, I never saw Glen unless he was at work. He never stayed late, no matter how high his paperwork was piling up, choosing to spend his time with Terri from sun up to sun down. Whenever we talked, it was "Terri said that I . . ." or "Terri thinks that I . . ." Suddenly, I felt like I was fucking Terri. Oh and that was another thing—he wasn't even getting any because "Terri didn't think it was a good idea for them to become intimate right away." I constantly tried to figure out what they did with all the time they spent together. Talking, I guess.

Before I knew it, my best friend was reduced to masturbating over dirty magazines and porno flicks as if he was in high school again. I don't know how he resisted sexing his woman. Terri was beautiful, if you were into black girls who looked and acted white.

Me, personally, I needed a woman with a little color, ass, and attitude. Oh, and she needed to be able to cook, too . . . just like my moms. You know Mama didn't have a problem with giving cooking lessons. Every Sunday, I drove over to my folks' place for a nice soul food dinner after church, and I never left without packaged leftovers to eat for the rest of the week.

Lucky for us, there wasn't a line at Korbich's Sandwich Shop, so we were seated immediately. After placing our orders, I went to the restroom to wash my hands. When I returned, the waitress served our drinks.

I gulped down my raspberry iced tea. "Man, you wouldn't believe what me and LeQuisha talked about last night. I mean that crazy smack she was talking."

"What? She still wants to get married, right?" Glen raised his thick eyebrows. "I tell you, single mothers these days are looking for a man with a good job to take over and be their baby's daddy. With three kids already, Tate, I don't think you want to do that. I'm telling you."

"Yeah. I mean what's wrong with that girl? Sometimes, I think women are just living in some kind of fairytale. LeQuisha has to know by now I'm only interested in the sex and nothing else." I sat up straighter in my chair. "I don't even take her out in the public anymore. Ever since she's been kicking those outrageous ghetto hairdos, I'm just too embarrassed to be seen with her. I usually ask her to drive over to the crib in the dead of night, and she does it." I shook my head. "Man, I'm telling you, she's hot for this dick."

Glen almost spit up his drink from laughing so hard. The waitress placed our plates of deli sandwiches in front of us.

"I especially can't stand to even look at those freak nails. Yesterday, they were neon-green and fuchsia." I shook my head. "Man, I ain't taking her to meet my moms; she would have a fit."

"It's like Terri said, 'If a woman doesn't respect herself, then she is susceptible to anything.' And that even means bad taste in fashion." Cautiously, he took another bite of his Italian sub, and some of the sauce and lettuce spilled out from the bottom onto the plate.

I nodded. "Guess so."

"Man, if you feel that strong about it, then you know what you gotta do."

"What's that?"

"Drop that chicken head and hook up with a real woman. A woman with some class and a real job. A sales associate—that's not a real career choice." He took another bite and wiped his mouth with a paper napkin. "I mean, I'm not knocking her . . . because a woman's gotta do what needs to be done to take care of her kids. At the same time, you are a successful executive and you work for an excellent insurance firm; don't even go out like that."

I scratched the back of my head. "Right. It's not like I could take her to the Christmas party. I'd never hear the end of it if a co-worker saw her in that red leather skirt with the matching boots."

"I know I'm right—that's why I make more money than you." Glen pumped his fist in the air.

I knew Glen was right; I just wanted to keep hitting that G-spot, at least for a little while longer.

It was Glen's turn to pay for lunch, so I excused myself to the men's room while he waited for the check.

On our way back to work, I listened to him talk nonstop about Terri. "Yeah, man, I think it's time for me to pop that big question and ask Terri to marry me." Glen smiled. "She's the one. Man, I mean she's everything I've ever wanted in a woman. She's smart, has a good job. She listens to me, supports me in everything I do, and believes in me. My parents love her."

"No, it's too soon."

"I'm telling you, man, if I don't get some pussy soon, my dick is going to fall off from all the hand action." Glen motioned with his hand. "I'm finding myself doing it like three or four times a day. The other day, I woke with cum all over my balls."

No, this muthafucka didn't just say that. Never let him handle my drinks or food again. If a brotha was that desperate to tell me some personal shit like that, then he must actually be a lot worse than I thought.

I pretended to be supportive. "If you need me to help you shop for rings, then I'm there. Just name the day and time."

"Awww, thanks, dawg." Glen grabbed my shoulder, beaming from ear to ear.

I was happy for him, even if I did feel like Terri held his ass by puppet strings. *Maybe that was what love was like—knowing the woman got you by the balls and not caring or giving a damn anymore.*

I decided to bring this up at dinner with my parents on Sunday. Get a real perspective from a couple married for almost thirty years. Hell, the way they acted around each other you would think my folks were still on their honeymoon.

Sitting back at my office I began to think that maybe LeQuisha was keeping me from meeting someone special in my life. Maybe she was just a distraction. I took in two deep breaths. I felt a strong twisting in my stomach as I made the call. *No sense in putting it off.*

I dialed her number at work. The receptionist answered and I asked for the men's department. Some guy answered.

"I need to speak with LeQuisha Stocks. Is she there?"

"Yeah, man, hold on a minute."

A few seconds later, "LeQuisha speaking."

I cleared my throat. "Are you busy?"

"Never for you, boo." She giggled.

"Well, I'll be brief. This thing between us just isn't working. We've had some good times, but I'm not feeling it, LeQuisha. I don't think it's a good idea for me to keep leading you on like this when—"

"So, what you sayin', Tate?" She sounded like she was about to go off.

"I'm saying it's over." I wasn't going to prolong this conversation and get cursed out, even though I deserved it. My throat suddenly went dry. I reached over on my desk for my bottled water.

"Oh, so just like that—you decide, and it's over?"

I took a sip. "Well, isn't that the way it works? One person wants out, and it's over?"

LeQuisha said nothing.

The silence killed me. I wanted to get back to work.

"Why don't we get together and talk about this? I mean, you're special to me." Her tone was patient and persuasive. "Whatever I did or said, I'll make it right; I don't want to lose you. I'll meet you at your place tonight."

"Hell no. There's nothing to talk about. Have a good life." I hung up the phone.

Damn, that was fucked up! I didn't have to call her at work. If I'd waited to call her when she got home, then she would have jumped in that beat-up Honda of hers and driven clear across town to my place.

I didn't need her; I already had Carmela. Not that I'm the only guy she was fucking, but who cared?

I always used a condom. Like my boy said to me at lunch today, *I need to be a little more selective.*

I finished up on my paperwork, looked at my watch, saw it was long after seven, and decided to call it a day. There was pitch blackness and dead silence on the rest of the floor.

Gladys took off a few hours earlier. Her husband was scheduled for back surgery, and she requested two weeks personal leave to help him recuperate at home. *The next couple of weeks would be pure misery without her.* It was like having moms on the job to take care of me. She knew Carmela and I did more than discuss business in my office, but never said a word.

See, when you have yourself those young gossiping assistants, they put all your business out on front street. Then they want to try the goods for themselves and call Johnny Cochran's ass, screaming sexual harassment. Yeah, that's why I listened to my moms and hired me an older, respectable, church-going woman.

On my way home, while listening to "Contagious" by the Isley Brothers on 101.5, I realized I'd done the right thing where LeQuisha was concerned. You see, sometimes you have to act like an ass to get what you want—it's all about the result. I don't give a damn if that trick was mad at me; I'm not the right man for her, and she wasn't the right woman for me.

She needed one of those niggas with a mouth full of gold, so he could pawn it in a grill for a sista, help her out with the bills . . . because I never gave LeQuisha any of my hard-earned money to support her baby daddy while he was on lockdown. *She'd better find her a dealer.*

Chapter 2
(LeQuisha)

No, he didn't. The thought kept running through my head like a tape recorder for the rest of the night. I was so upset that I couldn't wait to close the store and get home. I had a long day . . . since seven this morning.

After I left Tate's at three—he liked to get up early and meditate alone—I drove home to my apartment ready to get some sleep. My sister, Rhonda, had her latest tired-ass man, Tip, over there. That bitch had the nerve to put her two kids and my three kids all up in my bed to sleep. And where the hell did that put me? On the couch.

I was tired of having her negative ass up in my small cramped two-bedroom apartment anyway. My kids needed their room back because I was sick of sharing mine and having Lil' Donny sleep on a twin mattress on the floor. Rhonda didn't mind sharing a bed with her two sons—having a bed lately was a step up from the way she'd been living this past year.

Her dumb ass moved in with her baby daddy, Brutus, right out of high school, thinking he was going to marry her. Two kids and five other women later, he threw her out in the streets. His no-good, trifling ass moved in his new double whopper size of a Mexican girlfriend with her eight kids. Of course, a woman with that many damn kids got a larger check and food card than my sister!

I finally decided, out of the goodness of my heart, to let her move in with me after she'd been sleeping in a homeless shelter for a month. You know I loved my two nephews, Pee-Wee and Tank. Problem was, me and that bitch didn't halfway get along when we had to live under the same roof. She had the nerve to move up in my apartment and start trying to regulate shit by telling me how I should be handling my business.

Now you know I wasn't having that, so I had to get her ass straight about a few things. Then we were cool like Kool-Aid. Then she went and brought a nigga up in my place without so much as a day's notice.

She done put her kids out on the living-room floor to sleep, just to make room for this deadbeat. That muthafucka didn't have no job, 'bout six kids from seven baby mamas (you do the math!), and been locked up for every crime you could think of. And she wanted him? What for? Let Dee-Dee, from across the hall, tell it—'the nigga got a small dick too.'

See, I can't be going out like that. My man had a good-ass job, okay. He was college-educated and worked for an insurance company. A brother got paid very well. He drove a BMW and lived in a phat-ass condo on the beach. He said he couldn't get enough of me—you know I can put it down for a brotha.

We got along well and everything too. Had real serious discussions about our future. He was just the kind of man I wanted my kids around . . . instead of they fucked-up-ass daddy. Unlike my sister, I knew to leave Big Donny alone; he wasn't good for me or my kids. The only time he bought something for the kids or gave me money (and that was very rarely!) was when he wanted to taste my cherry again.

And as for me, well, you know I took care of business. I worked for Dillard's at the Regency Mall, and as a nail-tech on the side. I made out all right. My sister helped out with the rent, and so did Kenny. I had a nice apartment, and it was going to be even nicer when I got my new living-room suite on lay-away. Of course, that's when my sister was getting the fuck out. Her kids wasn't fixin' to be messing up my new furniture; you see, I got my kids trained, and they kept my house clean.

Lil' Donny was the oldest. I was teaching him how to cook; Daneisha was my middle child; then there was Dante, my baby.

I was so proud of my kids and wanted nothing but the best for them. That's why I worked so hard. I never had a damn day off. It took a lot of money to feed three kids, buy them clothes and sneakers (you know I get hooked up with my discount at work), and take them places, too. I tried to spend time with my kids, unlike my mama did with us. She did her best though, working three or four jobs to take care of us and never got mixed up with those drugs either.

Well, I know my hard work had paid off, 'cause

my kids were all on the honor roll at school. Like I said, I was very proud of my children. That's why I was so glad I met Tate. I finally done went off and hit the jackpot! *When we get married, my kids will have a father to love them, and able to financially provide for me and my kids, as a real man should.*

Anyway, I got in this morning and tried to sleep on my old broke-down couch. I woke up to call Tate on his cell phone before he made it to his job. You know, I wanted to show him I could be the supportive corporate wife and everything. Then I woke up the kids, made them breakfast, and walked them to the bus stop. A few minutes later, I jumped in the shower and got ready for my first job, down at the nail salon. That's when I heard my sister in the kitchen—she finally got her sorry behind up to cook breakfast for that joker.

No, she didn't!

I walked in the kitchen to find his dirty behind sitting at my table, eating grits, scrambled eggs, bacon, and sausage. I mean a big ass breakfast at that. Might I add, my sister hadn't paid for any of the food in this house. I didn't even see a plate for my sister. And the pots and pans were already in the sink. A few seconds later, my sister came up from under the table, after giving him a blowjob to say good morning.

Disgusting! I folded my arms. "Well, good morning. Looks like the only one having a good morning in my apartment is Tip."

"Don't start." Rhonda twirled her fingers in the air.

"Don't start what?" I cocked my head to the side. "You could've at least helped get your kids ready for school and cook them breakfast, instead of cooking for this tired-ass nigga you call your man!"

Tip turned around in his seat and twisted his face real ugly style. He waited on his woman to put me in my place.

Rhonda rose up from the table and walked up to my face. Of course, she was two inches taller than me so I stepped back.

"I was tired." Rhonda snapped her fingers. "Shit . . . your ass was up."

"And your point is what? They're your kids, not mine. You ain't doing shit for them. Just this sorry-ass man getting all your attention."

"Quit talking about my man." Rhonda waved her hands in frenzy. "I loves him, okay; he is there for me. We both lookin' for jobs."

"Where the hell you looking?" I asked. "From the damn window after you finished fucking him in my son's bed!"

"That's enough." Rhonda pointed her finger in my face. "I'm going to pack my shit and go. I'm tired of you judging me, walking around here like you Judge Judy or somebody." She sucked her teeth. "Just because you got a man making a lot of money. He just fucking you. Soon as he gets tired of you, he going to drop your ass like a bad habit—just wait and see."

Oh, I was mad then. She did not have to go there with me. I balled my fists, stormed out of the kitchen, and finished getting ready for work. I didn't want to have to be responsible for what I might have said or done at that point. Even though I was already tired as hell, I dragged myself on to the shop and worked for four hours. Then I went back home, got dressed in black dress slacks and an indigo blue silk blouse for my real job, and headed for the mall. I wasn't scheduled to get off until nine-thirty. Then I planned to head over to see my man, Tate, after that.

Yep, that was the plan—until he called me from work, saying he wanted to break up with me. For no reason. Just because, he claimed, things weren't working out. *He had a lot of damn nerve.* (I tried to reason with him, but he didn't want to hear it.)

I dreaded my drive home. I parked my car and stopped by the boxes to get the mail. On my way upstairs I stepped over three dudes sitting there smoking a joint. Lil' Donny peeked out the window and met me at the door. My son was so handsome with his beautiful green eyes. He got his looks from his daddy. I don't mess with no ugly men.

Now, Tate, that's one fine brotha, but short, though. He's light-skinned, with green eyes too. People wouldn't have a hard time believing him to be the father of my children. He's cut in all the right places, because he worked out at the gym. Sporting a fresh, lowly trimmed cut every week and professional on the job, brotha was talented in the bedroom. He had a lot to work with, if you know what I mean.

Lil' Donny's big eyes grew wide. "Mama, what's wrong? You look weak."

I kissed my son on the cheek. "That's because I am."

He closed the door behind me.

"That's why I can't wait to get a job, so I can take care of you."

"I know, baby, but you have to go to college first." I turned around to face him. "Getting your education is most important. Then you won't have to work so hard like me." I sat down on the couch and Lil' Donny followed.

He took off my shoes and began to massage my feet. My eyes rolled to the back of my head as the pain slowly subsided. My lips slowly curled to a smile. Hmmm.

From the day my son was born, he made it his personal mission to take care of his mama.

"Thank you, baby." I leaned back on the couch. "You finished with your homework?"

"Been finished. And Dante and Daneisha already took their baths and in bed, 'sleep. They finished their homework too. I left it on your nightstand if you wanted to check it."

"I will, first thing in the morning." I looked around for my nephews. "Where's your cousins?"

"Oh, when we got home, Auntie Rhonda said she was leaving. All their stuff was already packed and they left. We cleaned up our room, and I put the twin mattress back on the bunk bed."

I guess my sister wasn't lying. Ma must've felt bad for her. I grabbed the cordless and called over there.

Rhonda picked up on the second ring.

"Hey, sis."

"Hey, yourself." Rhonda's voice sounded cheerful.

"You didn't have to get up and leave. I was just tired and tripping."

"Me too. You were right. I've overstayed my welcome anyway. Ma told me to bring the kids. You know how she gets lonely and needs company."

"So, what about Tip?"

"I told him he had to go—he ain't shit anyway."

I decided not to say anything.

"Anyway, I gotta get up early if I'm gonna go look for a job."

I switched the phone to my other ear. "You should come put in an application at the store. They're always hiring."

"Maybe I will." She yawned in the phone. "Bye, chica."

"Bye. Kiss my nephews for me." I put the cordless on the glass end table.

"So, is Auntie okay?" Lil' Donny plopped down on the couch beside me.

"Yeah, she's fine." I looked up at the clock and realized it was almost eleven. "Lil' Donny, you need to get ready for bed yourself." I walked over to the kitchen and poured me a glass of grape Kool-Aid.

"I will. Right after I finish watching *Smack Down.*"

Then I went in my room and sat down on the bed. I picked up the phone and pressed "1" on my speed dial.

Tate answered on the first ring.

"'Sleep?"

"Do I sound 'sleep?"

"I was trying to be thoughtful . . . unlike you, calling me on my job to dump my ass. You're so considerate, Tate. Thank you for that."

"Bye, LeQuisha—"

"No wait." I held the phone tightly with both hands. "Just listen to me for one minute."

"One minute and then I'm getting off the phone; I got a long day ahead of me tomorrow."

"I'll be quick, 'cause I know you have a lot on your mind and everything. It's just that I thought things were heading in the right direction. I thought things were cool between me and you."

"Forty seconds."

"If you have to act like that, then bye, Tate." I kicked my foot in the air.

"No. I'm sorry, LeQuisha. Don't hang up. I did act like an ass today. I shouldn't have called you on your job. I'm not ready for anything serious and you are. I don't want to keep stringing you along."

"You're not stringing me, baby. I never ask you for anything. I just want to be there for you. I had a real fucked up day today. First, I got in a fight with my sister, and she moved out. And then for you to call me at work just made a bad situation even worse."

"Look, I don't want to hurt you."

"I know. Tate, you're a good man." I chewed on my bottom lip. "We're friends, right?"

Tate hesitated. "Right."

"And friends kick it from time to time, right?"

Tate took a deep breath. "What's your point?"

"My point is—" I closed my eyes and thought for a long second; I needed to choose my words carefully—"I've had a stressful day. I need someone to kick it with, to help clear my head. After that, if you don't want to see me . . . then . . ." I squeezed my eyelids tightly and held my breath. ". . . then, I won't bother you no more."

I knew how desperate I sounded. Still I didn't care; that was my only chance at having me a good man.

We talked for a little while longer, and then Tate agreed to see me that night. I arranged for Dee-Dee from down the hall to bring her little girl and stay over to watch the kids for me. I gave her twenty dollars, packed up my lingerie, and took off.

I arrived at his place a little after midnight.

He came to the door with a towel around his neck, wearing the blue silk boxers I bought him.

"Hey, boo." I kissed him on the lips.

He grabbed my ass and kissed me back. "Baby, you smell good."

I licked my lips. "So do you." I opened my mouth to invite his tongue inside.

Tate started to tongue me hard, just the way I like to be kissed.

I changed in his bathroom and slipped into my red see-through teddy. When I came out he was lying on the bed, his big dick standing up at full attention.

"Did I take too long?" I stood at the foot of the bed, crawled on top of him, and slowly slid on a condom with my mouth.

"What do you think?" He pulled up my teddy, squeezed my breasts. "You got some fat-ass melons, man." Tate laughed and began to ravish on both of them.

I then pulled the teddy off and exposed my red thong.

My man turned me over and started biting my ass. He didn't even wait for me to pull my thong off, just slid it to one side. He grabbed my hips, parted my thighs, and went in for the kill.

I held onto the backboard to brace myself from all the hard thrusts.

His muscular thighs slapped hard against mine. Tate panted as he plunged deeper, and I groaned with satisfaction as I sucked on my index finger.

He squealed as his penis swelled inside, and collapsed on top of me.

A few minutes later, he was sound asleep. I had a sudden case of insomnia, so I turned on the television.

Tate pushed me in the fold of my back.

I glanced at the clock—5:00.

"LeQuisha, get up."

I turned over on my side.

He nudged me again. "LeQuisha."

"What?" I didn't move.

"You need to wake up and get your kids ready for school."

I poked my lips out. "Since when are you so concerned about my kids? You ain't never even met them." I placed the pillow over my head.

"One day, I will." Tate sniffed. "Now get your ass up." He pushed me off the bed.

"Damn, Tate!" I yelled. I can't stand him when he acted like that.

He grabbed my pillow and went back to sleep.

"Fuck you, Tate. Either you gon' start respectin' me, or I ain't comin' all the way over here no more to see you."

He looked up. "You're still here?"

My eyes slanted. "Aaaawwww!" I threw my hands up in the air. "I hate you!"

"You weren't saying that a few hours ago," He mumbled; "you loved my ass then."

"I hate you now."

I grabbed my stuff and left.

On the drive back home in my old Honda, I realized I overreacted. I knew Tate had to get up early, and I needed to get home. It was important to him that I'm home before my kids woke up to notice I wasn't there. I guess that was important to me, too. *My kids would understand. They know mama's gotta have a life too. Plus, I don't want to ruin a good thing.*

My neon-green Nokia rang. I reached in my purse and looked at the caller ID before answering.

"Hey, Kenny." I chewed on my bottom lip.

"Where you comin' from this time of morning?"

I took a deep breath. "Don't question me about my whereabouts—where's your wife?" I plugged in my headset.

"She's out of town with the kids. I don't expect her back until Thursday. Can I come see you today, take you out to lunch?"

"Depends on where you takin' me." As I drove up on the I-95 ramp, I yielded for oncoming cars. I sped up to ease through the early morning traffic.

"To that Chinese restaurant you like."

Now, I really shouldn't even be fooled up with Kenny's tired ass. "Pick me up at twelve."

"Well, I was thinking maybe I could come when the kids left so we—"

"So, we could what? I already told you—I got a man; and you have a wife." I gripped the steering wheel.

"Since when did that make a difference?"

"You comin' at twelve or what?"

"Yeah, I'll be there," Kenny said in a breathy voice.

I got the kids ready for school, and then called the shop to let Karen know I wouldn't be coming in that day.

Kenny showed up a good fifteen minutes later. "You're early." I folded my arms.

"I had to see you." Kenny's smile looked like a kid's at the damn candy store. He pinched my ass as I turned away from the door, and I smacked him hard.

"Don't be so hostile. I missed you." Kenny looked at me strangely.

"Really?" I sucked my teeth and rolled my eyes.

"Yeah." His dark-brown eyes hungrily fixed on my breasts dangling out the top of my robe.

I covered my babies up. "How much?" I held out my hand.

He reached in his wallet and placed a stack of hundreds in it.

I counted five hundred dollars—just what I needed to pay my rent, since my sister moved out.

He followed me in the bedroom as I put the money in my purse.

"Get out, Kenny." I pushed him toward the door.

He grabbed my arm. "Why you gotta act like that, LeQuisha?" His eyes blinked rapidly. "Especially, since I'm trying to look out for you and your kids. You know I care about you." He let go of my arm and sat down on my bed, like his black ass was at home or something. "I wanted to see you. I missed you, baby. Don't you think about me anymore?"

"I told you I got a man now."

Kenny grabbed my waist and pulled me over to him. He tried to put his slimy hands on my breasts.

I pushed his hands away. "I told you, Kenny, I don't get down with you like that anymore."

"Come on, LeQuisha. Don't be like that." Kenny started to stroke my breasts, and my coochie tingled. He pulled the sash on my robe, and it fell to the ground. Then he lay me down on the bed, slid my panties down, and stretched my thighs up in the air.

I let Kenny eat my precious jewels out until he

sucked it bone dry—oral sex was his thing. He had a nice size and all, something a sister coulda work with. I just wasn't getting down like that no more, especially since I started sexing Tate. Kenny had nothing on my man.

I showered, combed my hair up in a ponytail, dressed, and met Kenny in the living room.

We went to eat at my favorite Chinese restaurant, and he talked about his ongoing problems with Linda, his wife and mother of his two daughters. Of course, the girls took after their white mama . . . , 'cause Kenny was butt-ass ugly. I mean, he didn't have one good thing going for him—except his body.

Me and Kenny been kicking it off and on for about two years now. He helped me out with the bills and used to hook me up with a little dick action every now and then. *You know I gotta have me a friend now. Don't even act like you don't know what time it is.*

I started to get tired of his sporadic ass, so I was overjoyed when Tate came into the picture.

Kenny only called me to talk about his problems, and he still wined and dined me every now and then. He always hooked me up with that money. Kenny worked for UPS, so you know he made a little grip. He knew how it was—to get with this big ass, you had to come correct with the cash! Unless you was my man, Tate.

Now, with Tate, I was looking at the big picture. I wasn't going to mess that up. I wanted him to see me as an independent woman who didn't need his money. Tate never put his hands on me and he never would. He treated me like a lady. Myra Gibson taught her son better. That's what made him worth keeping.

So, I was going to keep satisfying my man, not pressure him, and wait for him to marry me.

I know what you're thinking—why would Tate marry a mother of three children? Well, I don't know. However, what I did know was, me and my kids were a package. If you couldn't accept my children, then you couldn't be with me. It was only a matter of time before Tate would meet my kids. And he would fall in love with them and vice versa.

Chapter 3
(Tangy)

"You know I love you, girl."

"I know, I know," I said.

"Well?"

"Well, what?" I fidgeted with my hands nervously.

"Don't act stupid; I can't stand stupid-ass girls."

"I'm not acting stupid." I slid over to my side of the car and folded my arms.

"Okay, see, now you wanna get upset." Vince tried to put his arm around me, and I pushed it away.

"You're the one getting upset," I said with an attitude. "You called me stupid."

"See, there you go." Vince tossed up his hand. "I didn't call you stupid. I said, 'Don't act stupid.'"

"Whatever."

* * *

From the first day I'd met Vince, he was constantly trying to get in these panties, even though he knew I was saving myself for my husband. I was nothing like the girls he usually went for. In high school, I was never thought of as a real beauty queen, but in my senior year I put on a few pounds in all the right areas.

Being the center of the basketball team certainly had its privileges. Vince had probably slept with every girl at JU, including the cheerleaders, female athletes, and, yes, the white girls too. I guess it could be said—Vince was an "equal opportunity lover."

"Don't you think I deserve a little booty action by now?" Vince asked.

"I guess if I was any other sista you probably would." I looked out the window as I uttered those words.

"I can date any girl I want." Vince hit his chest. "But I chose you."

"And what do you expect me to say?" I asked emphatically, "that I'm going to change my mind for you? Vince, I already told you the only man I plan to have sex with is the man I marry." I slammed my hand at the door.

"Yeah." Vince chuckled. "You plan to follow your parents' rules for the rest of your life? You're a grown woman, Tangy; you need to act like one."

"My parents taught me to love and respect myself." I cleared my throat. "Why do you have such a problem with that?"

"I don't." Vince shook his head. "I'm not going to wait forever."

"Then don't." I glanced down at my watch. "It's getting late. Just take me home."

I was a freshman and when I got here, the first two people I met was Sharon, my roommate, and Vince.

I moved here from Alabama to attend college and partly to break away from my strict parents. Second, I needed to establish myself as a new person, you know, "reinvent myself."

Ever since I was a little girl, I've had dreams of being on television, but not as an actress, though. I was way too smart to pretend to be someone else and speak through someone else's words. Being an intelligent Nubian princess with my own voice, I had something to say in a big way. My mama said I was going to be the next Oprah. I intended to fulfill my dreams, and no way was I going to let a man stop me.

Vince and I were at his parents' home for dinner a few hours ago. He was supposed to be taking me back to my dorm when, all of a sudden, he decided to stop near the landing to talk. Of course, talking leads to kissing, kissing leads to feeling, and then he tried to slide in for the kill. I stopped him dead in his tracks.

He was pissed, and drove like a maniac to get me back to my dorm. As far as I was concerned, I couldn't get there fast enough. To tell the truth, I was trying to avoid being alone with Vince, because it was getting harder to say no to him.

Lately, I was getting in after our dates with my panties soaked. I had to take long hot showers just to cool off. Vince kissed like a dream. His hands felt like warm silk all over my body. He was so fine, and I was weak for tall men.

Once, at his apartment, I let him finger me. His entire hand was covered with my cream. I was so embarrassed. At that point, he knew he had me.

Vince pulled his Maxima in the circular entrance of my dorm. He looked straight ahead without bothering to glance over in my direction.

"Good night." I tried to make eye contact as I put my purse strap on my shoulder.

Not a word.

I opened the car door slowly, trying to give him the opportunity to say something. I wanted him to realize he was ruining this relationship by continuing to treat me this way.

Still silence.

"Well, call me." I gave one final effort.

Vince sped off in a hurry.

I rushed in to tell Sharon what happened.

"Men are different from women," I told her; "they don't equate emotions with sex."

"Therefore, it's impossible for them to commit," Sharon explained, "until the dog in them is completely gone."

"And they decide to be real a man."

Sharon nodded. "Some of them never reach that point of maturity."

I pulled off my brown knit top and matching shorts. I grabbed a towel and put a plastic shower cap on my head.

Sharon followed me into the bathroom. "That's why I can't be fooled up with these knuckleheads around here. I need me a man that can be faithful. It's too many diseases out there. I'm not ready to die."

I tossed my underwear on the floor and stepped in the shower. "I know you're right. Sharon, can you hand me that bar of soap?"

She tossed the soap over my head.

"Dang! I said hand me the soap, not throw it. You almost hit me in the head."

"Oops." Sharon giggled. "My bad."

"Oops my ass!"

Sharon was supposed to majoring in finance, but if you asked me, it was men's sexuality. Her mother died when she was little, so her stepmother was the only mother she knew. She came to JU because her older sister, Terri, went to school here.

Terri had a nice apartment over on the Southside. Sometimes, we went to her apartment for lunch or dinner. When we didn't have any food in the fridge, we would crash in on her private evenings with her boyfriend. Even though Sharon's sister acted like a bourgeois princess, I agreed with her strong beliefs about having sex before marriage.

Sharon and Terri were like night and day. Raised in Miami, Sharon had the trashiest mouth. With her tiny petite frame, I knew she couldn't harm a fly. Her sense of style was like the sexy, fly women you saw in the videos on BET. When my girl went back home, she came back with high-priced clothes you couldn't find in any of the malls in Jacksonville.

Sharon and I hung together most of the time. We were like sisters. Very rarely did you see one without the other. We did have a small clique—Josie, Brina, and Kat—that we exclusively hit the town with on weekends.

When I met Sharon, I was ready to change my appearance and attitude, and I found it easy to adapt to her lifestyle. It must have worked, since I was able to snag Vince in the process of my transformation. The only problem was, Vince expected me to put out like Sharon did. I quickly realized I needed to stop acting like someone else and be myself.

When I got out of the shower, I wrapped my hair in a scarf and slipped into my pink silk pajamas.

Sharon sat on her bed reading Mary B. Morrison's latest novel.

"How is it?" I plopped down on the edge of her bed.

"Girl, it's better than the second one. I'll give it to you when I'm finished."

I could tell by the way her eyes were glued to the book she wasn't going to put it down anytime soon. "Okay." I picked up my sociology book and notebook. I thumbed through until I found my notes for Monday's test. "Looks like I'm pulling in an all-nighter."

"Yeah, I know. Professor Tookes is kicking my ass too. You have to give it to the sista. She knows her stuff," Sharon said as she slid on a pair of socks.

"She certainly does." I scratched the back of my head. "It's hard to keep up with her, though."

Sharon pointed her finger. "Then take a tape recorder. Write your notes when you come back to the room. That way you won't leave out anything."

"I guess I'll try it. I just have to find the recorder my mom bought me. I know it's in one of those boxes in the closet." I put on my headset and started to bob my head to Mariah Carey.

Meanwhile Vince never called, but I wasn't surprised though.

Chapter 4

(Tate)

"That's what I'm talking 'bout."

"The Jags are gonna take it!"

"Touchdown!"

I haven't been around guys this happy in a long time. That's probably because this was the first game the Jags was winning all season. I tried to get together with the boys every Sunday during the football season, mostly to watch the Jags play.

"Hey, man, toss me a beer from the cooler," Sherman ordered.

I obliged, since this was Sherman's house. Today, it was his turn. I know Sherman liked having the fellas over, but not his wife, Peaches. She made you take your shoes off as soon as you entered the door. And we couldn't even enjoy the game without her tipping her big, hippo ass in the room, complaining about us being too loud. Never mind the fact that their four bad-ass boys ran around and screamed in the house too. Yeah . . . I said four. Looked like every time Sherman tried to make a clean break from the marriage, Peaches cried about being pregnant again. And again. And again.

Now, her ass was pregnant again, talking about trying to have a little girl. I think it had more to do with Sherman's latest girl, Hannah, if you ask me. Don't even ask me about the race. How many black girls you know named Hannah? Let the truth be known, Sherman slept with any and everything he set his eyes on. He didn't care what race, size, or class. As far as he was concerned, "a pussy looked and felt the same."

I remember when he and Peaches first bought this house. It wasn't much to begin with, but after having four kids, every damn piece of furniture was broke the fuck down. My moms said, "Peaches' kids don't have no home training." That's why I didn't want to meet LeQuisha's kids. *They for damn sure won't be coming over to my crib to fuck up my shit. I paid good money for my stuff.*

I reached inside the cooler filled with ice and pulled out a Heineken. My hand damn near froze. I kept shaking it until I could feel some warmth again. I passed a beer over to Sherman, who stood in the doorway of the den arguing with Peaches.

Glen popped me on the back of my head. "Man, you shakin' your hand like a little bitch."

"Ha, ha." I swung back at his ass.

He tried to dodge my swing, but it landed on his chin.

"Oh, all right. Man, you tryin' to mess up this pretty face?" He held up his fists and pretended to throw Muhammad Ali jabs in the air.

I held my up mine too, and we began to shadow box.

"Sit y'all black asses down."

We crossed the line by stepping in front of the television during the next play.

Everyone slowly rose out of their chairs. "Oh, oh, ohhh!" Fred Taylor was about to score a touchdown. Just then, he was tackled down to the ground. "Damn," they all said in unison.

My cell phone rang. "Hello."

"Hey, booooo," LeQuisha sang.

"Why you callin' me? I told you I'm at my boy's house watching the game."

"Isn't that game almost over?"

"Yes. What's your damn point?"

"I thought you might want to hook up after the game."

"Naw. You thought wrong."

LeQuisha sucked her teeth. "Why the hell not?"

"This is the night I hang out with my boys. No females allowed."

"Peaches there, ain't she?"

"Yeah . . . that's because this is her house." I took a sip of beer.

"Well, then I'm coming over there too."

I swallowed hard. "Don't do that."

"Why shouldn't I? It's a free country."

"You know Peaches don't like your ass."

Where I grew up, everybody knew everybody. I figured out Sherman must have messed around with LeQuisha back in the day. I just couldn't prove it. Something about the way his head jerked when I told him I was messing with LeQuisha. Glen picked up on that shit too and was riding me even harder to get rid of her.

"How you know that?"

"I know, because she told me."

"Awwww, that's because she think I want some damn Sherman. Don't nobody want his tired ass."

"Well, I'm not going to get into that with you. So you—"

"Wait. Come on. I miss you. Don't you miss me?"

My voice went up an octave. "I just saw your ass!"

"It's been over a week, Tate."

I thought about it. Shit, the plan wasn't working. The more I distanced myself from LeQuisha, the harder she pushed her way back in, leaving messages on my cell, at work, and at home. The woman was relentless. People were beginning to think she was my girl. *Fuck!*

"You can come by around midnight," I said through clenched teeth, "and not a moment sooner." Obviously, I was thinking with the wrong head again. *Why do I keep doing this shit repeatedly?* It's as if LeQuisha had some kind of voodoo on me or something.

"Okay. Bye, boo." She giggled. "Enjoy the rest of the game."

I hung up.

"Who was that?" Glen asked.

I slumped in the chair. "You know."

"LeQuisha. Man, I thought you got rid of her."

"I know." I hung my head down.

"Well, that's you. I do know this—" Glen moved in closer—"While you're messing around with LeQuisha, you're missing out. Think about that." He walked away to claim his seat and finish watching the game.

That thought stayed in my head all night. For the rest of the week I devised various plans to get LeQuisha out of my life for good. I ignored all her calls and deleted any message she left.

Of course, the following Saturday I gave in to her sexual whims. I hit it again. And again. And once more for old time's sake.

I couldn't sleep. I tossed and turned. LeQuisha's snoring in my ear was partly the reason. I tried to figure out how things were so mixed up, how I let things drag on like that. LeQuisha really thought she was my woman now. I even bought her something for her birthday. That was it—I had to be a man, say good-bye to the coochie, and end things with her.

The next morning, I awoke to smell an aroma of breakfast in the kitchen. Damn! I was supposed to have kicked her ass out by now but was too tired to get up any earlier. I walked in the kitchen and drank straight from the orange juice carton on the counter. Trying to act like the dog Glen told me I had to be, I didn't even look in LeQuisha's direction.

Damn, not a pot of grits. LeQuisha cooked just like my moms. Were those biscuits? Fuck!

"Well, aren't you going to say good morning?" She folded her arms across my Lakers Kobe Bryant jersey.

"Morning," I said flatly.

"Are you hungry? I cooked eggs, sausage, grits, and I baked some biscuits too." She stepped aside and pointed like Vanna White.

"I didn't have all that in my fridge."

"I know. I got up and ran to Winn-Dixie." She smoothed grape jelly on a biscuit.

I went in my room, got dressed in my workout clothes, and I walked back in the kitchen. "Look, I'm headed to the gym. Lock up the place on your way out." I put a twenty on the counter and left before she could say a word. This took a lot of will power, because my damn stomach was growling.

Chapter 5
(LeQuisha)

No, he didn't.

I just got up early this morning and went to Winn-Dixie, spent my damn money, cooked breakfast for his ass. *Forget that!*

I know I didn't drive over here late last night to give him the time of his life, real freak-style too. And this is the way he gon' treat me?

I dialed Tate's cell phone.

No answer.

Shutting my eyes, I took a deep breath and dialed again.

Still no answer.

I was about ready to throw everything away and leave—Hold up. I ain't stupid. I got on the phone and called home.

"Hello," Rhonda answered. She stayed over last night to watch the kids for me.

"Are the kids up?"

"Yeah, they're in the living room watching TV."

"Feel like driving?" I juggled the phone on my shoulder as I buttered the warm biscuits from the oven.

"Driving where?"

"Out here to Tate's. We can enjoy this big breakfast I just cooked. Then the kids could play out on the beach. Girl, we can lay out like these white people do." I giggled.

"Hey, I'm there. Shoot, you ain't gotta ask me twice."

"Hurry up . . . before this food gets cold."

About an hour later, we were seated at the table and bar eating breakfast.

"Mama, this place is nice." Daneisha got up from the table to check out Tate's condo. Her eyes were glossy as she looked out of the big windows to see the view of huge waves crashing along the sandy beach.

I rested my hands on her narrow shoulders. "Yeah, it is. This is where we're going to live when me and Tate get married." I showed her the rest of the place.

"Oh, Mama," she said clapping her hands together, "I can't wait. Let me see which bedroom I want."

"Go ahead, baby." I watched Daneisha disappear down the hallway.

"You know that ain't right to put those thoughts in her head like that," Rhonda said from behind.

I turned around to face her. "Why not? It's the

truth." I put my hands on my hips. "It's getting serious."

Rhonda rolled her neck. "What kind of relationship is this? He hasn't even met your kids. Tate don't give a damn about you." She looked me up and down like I was garbage.

"Mind your damn business." I pointed my finger in her face. "You're my sister, and I love you—stay out of my business; you don't know nothing."

"I know plenty and the way you—"

The phone rang. *Just what I needed—an interruption to keep me from putting my sister back in her damn place.* I assumed it was Tate finally calling me back after I left several messages on his cell. "It's about time you called me back."

The phone on the other end hung up suddenly. I put the phone back on the receiver. It rang again. This time I looked at the caller ID before answering. "Good morning." I smiled a toothy smile.

"I thought I had the wrong number."

"No, you have the right number, Mrs. Gibson. This is LeQuisha."

"Who?" Mrs. Gibson's voice resembled Florence's from *The Jeffersons*.

I took a deep breath. "LeQuisha Stocks—I'm Tate's girlfriend. I had the kids over this morning for breakfast."

"Breakfast? At my son's place? What did you say your name was again?"

"LeQuisha. You mean Tate hasn't told you about me?"

"This is the first I've heard of this."

I rubbed the back of my neck. His own mother didn't even know me. Maybe Rhonda was right—I had been fooling myself all this time; I didn't want to continue to push the issue. "Well, I'll let Tate know you called."

"You mean he isn't there?"

This was starting to get worse. I didn't like the tone Mrs. Gibson used. I thought any minute the police were going to show up at the door to arrest my ass. With the way Tate had been treating me, I wasn't sure what he would tell the cops. He would probably act as if he didn't even know me.

"No . . . uh . . . Tate went to the gym." I held my breath.

"Well, I wanted to know if he was coming over for Sunday dinner, since he didn't make it over last week."

"I don't know for sure, but I'll let him know you called."

"You do that, honey. And LeQuisha . . .?"

My eyes rose. "Yes."

"Why don't you come over too? You're more than welcome. Baby, can you cook?"

I smiled. Before I hung up the phone, I agreed to make macaroni and cheese and a dessert for Sunday dinner. *This would be my way to impress his parents.* Tate already told me I could cook almost as good as his mama. I had to stop by the store again today to get what I needed to make a slamming dish for my future in-laws. I rubbed my sweaty palms on my lap. I couldn't stop thinking about what I was going to wear. I wanted to impress Tate's parents and, of course, look good for my man. Maybe things weren't as bad as I thought.

Chapter 6
(Tate)

Spending the morning at Glen's apartment, I stayed away from my place to make sure LeQuisha got the hell out. Barely giving myself enough time to get changed and ready for Sunday dinner, I decided to dress up for the occasion, considering I had missed a few dinners. Choosing a pair of navy dress slacks and light-blue shirt, I finished the look with navy dress shoes. I shaped up my hair in the mirror and splashed on my favorite cologne.

I managed to arrive in front of my parent's house by five. I couldn't wait to enjoy some good cooking. Plus, I wanted the chance to have another serious discussion with my parents about where I was headed in my life.

I was getting older, almost closing in on thirty. I wasn't necessarily ready for marriage but at least I needed to be involved with someone who had similar interests. What I had going with Carmela was all right, but I wanted more than just someone to fuck every now and then. I could sense she was starting to get tired of me. Probably, because her latest man was Latino and all buff. Apparently, he had a bigger dick than me.

I had to thank Shatia, Carmela's gossiping assistant, for that little bit of info. She walked in on Carmela giving the man a blowjob in the office. I guess she must have been so excited about getting laid, she forgot to lock the door. Before the day ended, the news spread all over the entire building.

You'd think Carmela would've been embarrassed, you know, taken a few days off. Not that ho. She was bragging about it with the girls the next day in the hall by the vending machines. Then, them stank bitches laughed at my ass when I passed by. It didn't matter; I know I still had it, 'cause Carmela was still coming back for more.

As I strolled up the driveway, I noticed a beat-up car like LeQuisha's parked on the street. Greeted by the mouth-watering smell of greens and fatback from the kitchen, I entered the living room and saw my dad sitting in his brown Lazy-Boy, watching the Jets game.

"Hey, son. Why don't you get me a Pepsi from the ice box?"

Just like my dad. I hadn't even put my other foot through the door, and he was already bossing me around.

"Sure. Anything else?"

"Yeah, get me some chips too. The bag is on the counter."

I patted my dad on the shoulder as I passed him. I could hear loud voices from the kitchen as I walked down the hall, so I assumed Mama must've invited one of the sisters from the church. My mom leaned in the refrigerator, and LeQuisha sprinkled paprika on my mom's potato salad.

LeQuisha. What the fuck?!? Was this crazy-ass bitch stalking me?

Mama closed the door to the refrigerator and opened her arms wide. "Hey, baby, give your mamma a kiss."

I obliged and kissed both plump cheeks.

"Hey, boo." LeQuisha eased over and landed a big, juicy kiss on my lips.

"Can I speak to you for a minute?"

"Sure, boo." She blushed and followed me out to the patio.

"What are you doing here?" I balled my fists in anger.

"Your mom invited me—what's the problem?" LeQuisha stretched her eyes wide. "I thought you'd be happy to see me."

"I just saw you last night."

"And then you left this morning without giving me a second glance after I went out of my way to prepare a delicious breakfast for you." LeQuisha folded her arms. "I'm trying to show you that I'm the woman for you, and you keep taking me for granted."

"I don't want a woman right now." I lowered my voice, not wanting my mom to overhear. "Besides, you know we're just kicking it."

LeQuisha closed her eyes. "If you say so." She grabbed my hands. "Tate, I want more; I thought you did too. When your mom invited me over, I was thinking this was my chance to prove to you I'm worthy of your love."

I pulled my hands out LeQuisha's tight grip. "I'm not ready for this."

LeQuisha reached for my arm. "Tate, please . . ."

I slightly pushed her away. "No." I straightened my shirt, then entered the kitchen.

Lifting the lid to the largest pot, I inhaled the aroma of collard greens soaking in smoked neckbones. "Smells good in here. What else is for dinner?"

"Get out of my pots and out of my kitchen." Mama smacked me in the back.

I closed the lid and tried to duck from another hit. On my way out, I grabbed the bag of chips off the counter.

"Where's my Pepsi?" my dad asked as I handed him the bag. His frown revealed wrinkles around his mouth. (I favored my old man—short and stocky, red-skinned, and green eyes.)

"You gotta get it yourself—moms just kicked me out." I sat down on the couch. "Would you mind explaining to me how LeQuisha ended up here?"

My dad offered me some of his Ruffles potato chips. "Myra called over to your place looking for you, and LeQuisha answered the phone." He switched positions in his leather recliner. "Next thing I know, your mama was inviting her over for dinner."

Damn. If only I had gotten rid of her ass. This shit was fucked up! LeQuisha was not the kind of girl I wanted to bring home to meet my mom and dad.

"Now, why you wanna hide LeQuisha from us, son? She seems like a nice woman, raising three kids all by herself. That woman has been through a lot. It's good she has you to look out for her and be a role model for her kids, especially to them two boys."

"Well, uh . . . actually . . . I don't know her children."

"You don't?"

"No. Dad, it's complicated."

"What is?"

"This thing goin' on between me and LeQuisha. It's not exactly what—"

"Oh, I see." He grinned. "You're sampling the goods with no intention of buying."

I smiled back. "Yeah, something like that."

I knew my dad would understand. I mean, I know my mom wasn't the first woman he had sex with.

Then my dad's grin turned into a frown. Suddenly, I had a feeling this conversation would turn into an hour lecture. It did. My dad started talking about how a man should respect a woman, especially a woman with children. How I was wrong to continue to sleep with LeQuisha if I did not intend to be serious. Then, he even went on to scrutinize me for having sex before marriage.

I was suddenly happier for more reasons than one to hear my mom announce that dinner was ready.

My dad slowly stood up. "We'll finish this talk when dinner is over."

Oh, hell no!

I followed him into the dining room.

The next day at my office I couldn't wait to tell Glen what happened. With each detail he cracked the hell up.

"So tell me how it went."

"Oh." I shrugged. "We ate dinner, and then LeQuisha went home. She claimed she had to run home to see about the kids. Funny, I've never seen her run off like that before—I think she wanted to impress my folks."

"Think so? Man, that's wild." Glen leaned back in the chair where he sat in front of my desk.

"I know, man." I slapped my hand on the back of my neck. "It's like a damn nightmare; I kept hoping it was all a dream."

Glen opened his hands. "So that's it? You mean LeQuisha didn't say anything stupid? What did your parents say when she left?"

"Man, that's the craziest part—they actually liked her. My dad was harping on my ass bad, telling me I shouldn't be sampling the goods without any intention of buying."

Glen laughed.

"That shit ain't funny. This is fucked up for real, man."

Glen stood up slowly, doubled over in laughter. "Hey, dawg. I had better head back to work if I'm going to get out of here early. I got a big night planned." He rubbed his hands together.

"Oh yeah, what's up?" I placed both elbows on my desk and leaned forward.

"I'm going to propose to Terri. It's our two-year anniversary, and I'm taking her to Crawdaddy's. I picked up the ring Saturday." Glen pulled the small box out of his suit jacket and he popped it open to reveal a two-karat ring.

My eyes opened wide.

"What do you think?" Glen flashed a huge dimpled smile.

It's not as if he really needed my opinion; he'd

checked out every jewelry store in town to find the perfect ring. "I think you did good, man." I walked over to give my boy a hug.

"Thanks." He stepped back. "Whew. Just think, tomorrow, I'll be an engaged man."

"Hey, Terri didn't say yes. Not yet anyway."

"Right. Suddenly, I'm getting nervous." He put his hand on his forehead.

"You nervous?" I put my arm on Glen's shoulder as I escorted him out. "She loves you."

"You're right."

"I know I'm right—that's why I make more money than you." I smacked him in the back of his head.

I had to admit for one moment I felt a little envious of my boy. Not that I'm ready for marriage or anything, but I mean finding the one true love. I wondered if it would ever happen for me.

Carmela strutted by in a red wrap dress.

I walked up to her as she approached Gladys' desk. "Hey, girl." I smiled.

"What do you want, Tate?" she asked dryly, her nose turned up.

I would've backed off, but I was used to it. *An orgasm would put a smile on her face.* Now that I thought about it, she hadn't done it in awhile. Suddenly, I felt a little insecure. "So what you doing tonight?"

Carmela scowled. "Washing my hair."

"Oooh," I said, "you should let me do that for you."

Carmela suddenly stopped. The twinkle in her eyes let me know she was interested.

Chapter 7
(LeQuisha)

The phone rang.

"What?" Tate asked.

"Hey, boo."

He sighed. "What do you want?"

"Nothing. I just called . . ." I paused. "Just got in from work, got the kids off to bed, and I wanted to talk."

"About what?"

"Anything. How was your day?"

"The same as any other day, I guess. Look, I got nothing to say."

"Well, I was wondering—"

"No. Not tonight. I'm tired."

He hung up.

"No, he didn't! I can't believe this shit." I rushed home from work to put my kids to bed and got all dolled up to surprise my man, to reward him for working so hard. I got my nails done at the shop this morning, picked up a new bottle of Donna Karan perfume. (Tate loved how it smelled all over my body.) I went to the Body Shop and bought me a fiery-red catsuit. Then I called him on my cell phone when I parked in front of his place. Now he wanted to hang up the phone on me?

I let out a deep breath. *No problem. He was probably just sleepy.* I gathered my overnight bag and was about to get out the car, when the door to Tate's condo opened, and some bald-headed, wannabe Halle Berry bitch came out the door.

I got out of my car and stepped to her. "What the hell are you doing coming out of my man's place?" Halle Scary looked me up and down and scoffed.

"Your man?"

"Yes, bitch. Did I stutter?" I snapped my fingers and swung my head back.

She laughed.

"Hee, hee, hee. What's so damn funny?" *This bitch picked the wrong one!*

She gripped the strap of her purse and let out a deep sigh. "Look, Tate's inside. Talk to him, since he's your man." And she casually strutted off.

I ran my hands through my hair and paced back and forth, trying to figure out what to do next. I wanted to kick her ass—No, I wanted to go in there and kick Tate's ass. *Why would I do that? And risk going to jail?* Then my kids would have both parents locked up. No man was worth that.

I decided the best thing for me to do was get back in my car and drive home. I tapped my fingers on the steering wheel. I couldn't even see straight, let alone think. I was pissed off to the nth degree, picturing Tate in bed with that bitch and talking to me like I was shit. I can't believe he disrespected me for her. I know I'm way better than that skinny bitch. Humph!

Lil' Donny was lying on the couch sleeping when I got home. I turned off the TV and told him to go to bed. Then I made myself a cup of hot tea while listening to my Alicia Keys CD. "Ouch!" It burned the tip of my tongue.

Staring at the wall, I started to think about my life. It seemed as though it wasn't getting any easier. I grabbed a pillow and punched it.

As soon as I made a right, life seemed to make a left turn. Always one thing after another. I hit it again, this time pretending it was Tate's face. "Muthafucka!"—Another punch.

I didn't know why I was so upset. It wasn't like I should've been surprised. He'd been treating me as if I don't mean nothing, and I ate all the bullshit he served up. I took another sip of my hot tea.

The phone rang.

"Hey, girl," I answered after checking the name on the caller ID.

"I wanted to let you know I made it home," Rhonda said.

"Oh, okay." I cleared my throat. "Thanks for watching the kids."

"Uh huh. What did Tate do now?"

"I goes over there and he had someone already in bed with him." I struggled to catch my breath.

"You caught him?" Her voice went hoarse.

"No, but I confronted that bitch when she was leaving."

"Well, what did Tate do?"

"Nothing." I let out a deep sigh. "I never saw him."

"What!" Rhonda screamed. "You let that mutha-fucka off the hook!"

I rolled my eyes. "Look, I'm not trying to go to jail. And, that's exactly what would've happened if I stayed another second. Somebody was going to get their ass kicked, and it wasn't going to be me!"

"Quish, you're better than me . . . because it would've been on!"

"Whatever!"

"Oh, you know me. I don't give a damn! Now, I hope your dumb ass finally sees the light."

I gritted my teeth. "See, that's why I don't like to tell your ass nothing. And you need to stop lying. You ain't nothing but a doormat when it comes to them no-good men you be messin' with."

"Oh, so now it's about me," Rhonda said in a defensive tone. "See, you ain't right. Well, don't ask for my advice then."

I laughed. "You're the last person I would go to for advice."

"You know what—" Rhonda breathed heavily in the phone—"I know I have my share of problems. We all have our own demons to deal with. I'm doing my best, but—"

"Wait a minute. I'm sorry, Rhonda." I sat up on the couch. "I shouldn't have said what I did."

"Forget it, Quish!" Rhonda sniffled. "The next time you need a babysitter at the last minute, don't call me." She hung up.

I shook my head. Something was up with my sister. The way she snapped like that. I was so caught up in my own problems, I never realized my own sister was going through something too. I whispered a prayer. "Lord, help her."

Chapter 8
(Tate)

"She was like *this close* to my face. I mean she wanted a fight. I mean, I don't know what her intentions were exactly."

Carmela paced back and forth. "I mean, what were you thinking becoming involved with a tramp like that?" She laughed. "She was dressed in a red cat-suit, for Christ's sake." She slowly rubbed her temples. "Oh, I just had a visual. It was such a disgusting sight."

"Carmela, are you finished?" I continued to work on my computer, pretending to be busy. I glanced over in her direction.

Carmela cocked her head. "Yes, I am." Her voice was stiff.

"Oh really? I guess I'm a little tired of your ass too." I sighed.

"How dare you!" Carmela quickly turned her

back, and then paused. "You'll be back—" She smiled—"begging for more of this."

I sat back and rested my hands behind my head. "Don't count on it."

Carmela slammed the door shut.

Damn! I was glad the incident took place last night. I hoped LeQuisha would be out of my hair for good. Women usually walked away after shit like that happened. Finally, that girl was out of my life, but I didn't want to lose Carmela in the process.

I heard a knock at the door, and Ginger stuck her head in. One of the best adjusters on my team, she was always willing to put in the extra hours without complaining.

"Have a minute?" Ginger's dark, black hair bounced around her shoulders.

I motioned with my right hand. "Sure."

"Well, I need to talk to you about a few things." She nervously fidgeted in the chair.

"Okay." I folded my arms.

"There's no easy way for me to tell you this, so I'll get straight to the point." Ginger cleared her throat. "I haven't been happy for quite some time now. Tate, the workload has more than doubled, and I'm having a tough time balancing my caseload and my personal life. Having two little ones at home, I can't keep up anymore."

I nodded. "I see. Well, I'm glad you came to talk to me about it. I have a meeting with Dan first thing tomorrow morning to discuss hiring more adjusters to lower the caseloads." I shook my head. "To tell you the truth, I'm starting to get bogged down by it too."

Ginger's gaze drifted downward. "It's good to hear you're going to do something about the amount of mounting work for the others. As for me, I'm here to put in my two weeks notice." She handed me the resignation letter.

I took a deep breath. "I can't accept this. Ginger, you're the best adjuster on the team. What can I do to get you to stay?"

Ginger ran her hands through her hair. "Nothing. I've thought about this long and hard. I have to make the decision that's right for me and my family."

I shifted in my seat. "You're going to be missed around here."

Ginger smiled. "Thank you so much for understanding."

I held up my hands. "Of course. Don't hesitate to use me as a reference. You know I would give you a glowing recommendation."

Ginger stood and stretched out her hand. "It's been a real pleasure working for you. You've been a great boss . . . especially under the circumstances."

"What circumstances?"

"You know, with all the charges."

My eyes widened. "What charges?"

Ginger backed up. "You mean you don't know the real reason why you're meeting with Dan tomorrow?"

I placed my hands on my hips. "I guess not. Why don't you tell me?"

She lowered her voice. "Okay, you didn't hear this from me—Valerie claims you came on to her.

And when she wouldn't accept your advances, you had her terminated."

I rubbed my chin. "I see. Only problem is, I had nothing to do with Valerie's termination. But that will all come out tomorrow." I forced a smile.

Although the accusation appeared out of left field, I pretended to play it cool. *Anyone could look at Valerie's fat ass and know I wouldn't be the least bit interested.* "Anyway, I know you want to get out of here. I'm going to really miss you."

"Likewise." Ginger slowly exited.

I took a deep breath. Word traveled fast around here, but this time it never got to me. I can't believe this shit—Valerie claiming I tried to have sex with her. Not in a million years. Now, I couldn't concentrate on my work. I shut down my computer and left.

In my car, crazy thoughts entered my head. *What if Dan believed her? My career would be ruined. Should I hire a lawyer? No, that would only make me look guilty.*

I pulled up in front of my parent's driveway. Using my key, I unlocked the door. Seeing my mom's face brought an instant sense of comfort.

"Hey, baby." Mama kissed me on the cheek. "There's some smothered pork chops left on the stove." She rested her hands on her wide hips. "You want me to fix a plate?"

I rubbed my stomach. "Sure." I looked over her shoulder. "Where's Dad?"

She pointed. "He's out there on the patio."

"Well, I need to talk to him."

"Okay, baby. I'll bring your plate out there to you. You want lima beans too?"

"Yes, and load it up."

My dad was seated in a lounge chair, drinking

grape soda from a Big Gulp cup. "Hey, son. What brings you this way?"

I sat down beside him. "I got something to talk to you about. It's kind of serious."

My dad scratched his graying hair. "Serious, huh?"

"Yeah." I searched my dad's eyes for support, just as I had ever since I was a young boy. In the same backyard where we sat, my dad taught me how to play football and baseball. Not having any friends, many afternoons were spent here with him. Just the two of us. As an adult, I know my dad must've been exhausted when he got home from work. Never did he say it or show it. He was always there for me, and there was no one I respected more.

I told him everything. Even the stuff I was ashamed of, about my affair with Carmela, and why it would be easy for my co-workers to believe I came on to Valerie. With all the water cooler gossip, Dan would be left with no choice but to ask for my resignation.

"Son, this is easier than you think."

I smirked. "It is?"

"Uh huh." He gestured with his hands. "See, you didn't do it. You didn't even have anything to do with her termination. Didn't you say it was the accounting department that found out she was stealing from the company?"

I rubbed the back of my neck. "Yes."

"So it's simple; one has nothing to do with the other."

"I know that. Somehow, Valerie is trying to use this as a way to get her job back, or money or something. I really won't know until tomorrow."

"Let me tell you what you need to do. You go to

that meeting and answer all of their questions. Even if they ask you about Carmela, just tell them the truth. They just want to get your side of the story. If you don't hide anything, then my guess is this thing won't go any further."

I finally took a bite of my pork chop. The juices seared through my tongue. "This is good." I took another bite. "Dad, you're probably right. It's clearcut."

"If this goes any further, then find a good attorney. You said so yourself, you had nothing to do with that woman being fired. No sense in the big dogs trying to drag you into the fight now."

"You've never steered me wrong before."

My dad patted me on the shoulder. "I'll let you enjoy your dinner, while I catch the Lakers."

"Okay. I'll be in there as soon as I'm done," I said, chewing on a mouthful of lima beans and rice.

The next day, I rested my head in my hands. I was so glad when the interrogation ended. Never had I felt more humiliated than giving details of my sexual relations with Carmela.

Dan reassured me the investigation would be over soon. There was no evidence to support Valerie's claims, but the issue with Carmela had to be cleared up.

Carmela stormed into my office. "I can't believe you told Dan and the rest of those smug bastards about us!" She twisted her tiny lips.

I raised my thick eyebrows. "I'm surprised. Since you told half the women who work here. You should've known those yakking hyenas would spread it all over the building."

"I did no such thing." She pointed her bony finger in my face.

I leaned back. "Kindly remove your finger from my face."

Carmela obliged. "But now you've managed to put the intimate details of our affair in a formal deposition! Now, Dan is requesting a meeting with me first thing after lunch."

"I did what I had to do," I said; "it wasn't your ass on the line."

"What!"

I grabbed her by the arm. "I wouldn't even be in this shit, if it wasn't for you. You're taking your bony ass in that meeting and tell the truth. Then you're never coming to my office again. The only time I want to see you is when I have to."

Carmela snatched her arm back. "No problem."

I had to hand it to her—she had fire, and I was going to miss her.

Chapter 9
(LeQuisha)

"**A**nyway . . . I'm glad you called me, LeQuisha," Kenny said. "It's been a while since I last talked to you or even seen you."

"Yeah. I've been busy working and taking care of my children." I took a sip of wine from my glass as my eyes scanned the restaurant. An old couple stared right at us, all up in our business. I gave them the look of death. They fidgeted and went back to eating. *Sometimes, white people act like we ain't got no business in nice places, like we made the place dirty or something.*

"I respected what you said the last time I saw you, you know, when you said you had a man in your life. I just chilled, stayed out of the picture." Kenny smiled to reveal his front gold tooth. "I knew you would come back, though. It's not easy for a woman like you to find a man when you already got three kids. Men, these days, ain't looking for no already-made family." Kenny ate a forkful of shrimp and lobster.

When was he going to shut the fuck up? I came here to enjoy a nice seafood dinner at Red Lobster, not listen to him talk the whole time.

It had been three weeks since I cussed that bitch out in front of Tate's house. He hadn't even bothered to call me to apologize, and I know she told him what happened. I finally decided I didn't need his tired ass anyway. He hadn't even met my kids yet. I mean, what kind of shit was that? Like my children weren't good enough for him or something.

I wasn't even mad at Tate. I couldn't blame him. A man could only get away with what a woman was willing to allow. But that was Tate's loss. He missed out one hell of a woman!

"And that's ridiculous," Kenny said with a mouthful of food. "How she gon' tell me I need to make more money. She needs to get her lazy ass up and get a job too, help me out with some of these damn bills."

"Uhh huh." I nodded. "Yeah, you right, Kenny." Here he was going on and on like a victim. I pretended to understand, to care about his problems.

I did care about Kenny. Hell, we went back a long ways. However, I loved Tate, and I wasn't going to be able to give my heart to another man for a very long time.

Kenny grabbed my hands and hungrily kissed them. "See that's why I need a woman like you, baby. A real woman who's not afraid of a hard day's work. A woman holding down two jobs and still keeps a

clean house. I'm tired of paying for a house cleaner
. . . when Linda's ass is home all the damn time. Fuck
that!"

"Yeah, I hear you." I sat up straighter in my
chair.

"You hear me, baby?"

"Yeah." I forced a smile and batted my thick eye-
lashes.

"You wanna feel me too, don't you?" Kenny's
voice was barely above a whisper.

"You know it," I said, licking my full glossy lips.

Kenny raised his eyebrows. "Let me get the
check. I already reserved a room. Oh, and I got a surprise for you too."

I can't believe I'm back to my old tricks again,
but I had to do something to take Tate off my mind.
I spent a lot of time with my kids and working. I got
desperate for some male attention, even if it had to
be Kenny—at least he gave me some money.

All that time I wasted with Tate. He hadn't done
shit for me. I hoped he would help a little, especially
when he knew I was having a hard time getting
money to buy my kids stuff for Christmas. That
muthafucka never offered me a dime, never asked to
meet my kids.

That was one good thing about Kenny—he
spent time with my boys. He would take them to play
basketball, to the movies. He even called every now
and then just to talk to Lil' Donny. Gave them money
for making good grades on their report cards.

* * *

"Oh yeah, baby." Kenny howled. "That's the way I like it." He squeezed his eyes shut.

I was on top. He placed both hands on my waist to steady me. I slowed down, gyrated in small circles. He gasped for air like an asthma patient. I wondered if there was anyone trying to sleep in the room next to ours, Kenny was making so much damn noise.

"Do it, baby. Yeah."

I looked over at the clock. Almost 9:00. I had to get this over with. I picked up the pace. Sped up rotations, rode faster. Then that nigga let out a high-pitched shriek and came.

He threw me over and lay on top of me. He kissed me all over, working his tongue all the way down to my clit. *Does this man ever get tired?* I'm guessing his wife at home don't know how to fuck, 'cause Kenny be wanting to fuck my ass hours straight without even taking a break.

Kenny made sure I experienced two sweet orgasms. Suddenly, he was rock hard again, and he wanted to hit it from behind. I obliged, figuring it would be weeks before I would get some dick action again.

Kenny dropped me off around eleven in front of my apartment building. I carried my leftovers and jewelry box upstairs. Kenny bought me a diamond tennis bracelet as a Christmas gift, and I knew he would be spending more time with his family, because it was the holidays and all.

It was nice to receive gifts from a man. The only thing Tate had ever bought me was perfume for my birthday. I thought he was so sweet, at the time. Sure,

Kenny had given me nicer things than that. But, I just felt a gift from Tate meant something.

The next day, my sister and I decided to take the kids to the Regency Mall to see all the pretty Christmas decorations. Decorated with glass ornaments, and satin and candy ribbons looking delicious enough to eat, a fifteen-foot glittering tree centered right in front of Dillard's took my breath away. Oversized boxwood wreaths, bells, and holly went all the way down from the ceiling. We took turns snapping pictures, standing next to the tall toy soldiers.

It amazed me how white people actually spent all they damn money putting up this type of stuff in their houses for Christmas. All I could afford was a fake tree and a few icicles and ornaments. Dante and Tank were anxious to stand in a long line to take a picture with Santa. Rhonda agreed to go around with Lil' Donny, Daneisha, and Pee-Wee to do some more shopping.

The line stretched long, with children running around and babies crying. At the pace we were moving, we would have to wait at least close to an hour. I shifted from side to side.

"Mommy, Mommy." Dante pulled on my sweater.

I knelt down. "What, baby?"

"Mommy, there's Kenny." Dante pointed.

I squinted as I searched for a familiar face. Sure enough, Kenny was holding his oldest daughter in his arms while his wife, Linda, pushed a plaid Eddie Bauer stroller with their youngest daughter. They looked like the picture-perfect family, with all those shopping bags. *All that complaining he was doing last night. He didn't look so miserable to me.*

"Let's go over there," Dante said with a huge grin.

"No, baby," I said nervously. "We're not getting out of this line."

When the happy couple came closer, Dante and Tank jumped up and down. "Hey, Kenny!" The boys screamed in unison.

Kenny never saw us, so he was surprised to hear his name being called out in the crowded mall. He glanced over and jerked his head when he saw me standing there. Trying to play it cool, Kenny fixed his collar and picked up his steps.

"Kenny, did you hear those little boys calling you?" Linda made eye contact with me as they passed us.

"They must have me confused with someone else." He turned and tried to walk away.

Linda pulled on Kenny's shirt. "Kenny, stop this instant. Those boys know your name. You obviously know them too. Now, who are they?"

Oh, shit, it sounded like Kenny had some explaining to do. That's good for his ass for trying to ignore my son, knowing good well he was just tickling and playing with him last night before eating my coochie out as if it was a buffet at the hotel.

Kenny took a deep breath and fidgeted with his collar once more. He stared at me like he remembered who I was.

"Is that?—Yeah, it is." Kenny stepped closer.

I stood there waiting, anxious to see what he was going to say next. I curled up my lips.

"Yes, I do know her. This is LeQuanda, right?"

"It's LeQuisha. LeQuisha Stocks, remember?" I smiled coyly.

This was better than *Young & the Restless*.

He cringed.

"Yeah, right. Linda, LeQuisha used to date my brother Larry. And this is her son and nephew. Hey, boys." He patted Dante and Tank on their heads.

Linda shook my hand. "It's very nice to meet you."

I quickly snatched my hand back. "Same here."

Linda clapped her hands and smiled. "Forgive me. Where are my manners? I didn't introduce my family. Of course, you already know Kenny." She knelt down. "Here are my girls, but I'm sure Larry has told you all about them." Linda removed her daughter's hat and turned her around to face me. "This is Amber and my fourteen-month-old in the stroller is Jasmine."

I reached down to play with her.

She giggled and tossed her little hand toy, and Dante picked it up and handed it to her.

I forced a smile and nodded. "Your daughters are beautiful."

Linda laughed and tossed her hair off her shoulders. "Thank you. You know they keep me so busy these days. That's why we tried to fit in some last-minute shopping, before my parents get here to-morrow." She grabbed my arm.

Linda went on and on about what they planned for the holidays. Then she even went so far as to in-vite me to their New Year's Eve party if I didn't have any plans.

Kenny seemed more dumbfounded than ever, and I just played along with the stupid act, cracking a big, fake smile on my face.

This shit was funny to me. I pretended to be interested in everything she talked about, like I was doing the same things for my kids too. *Damn! She talked more than Kenny did.*

Now, I didn't want to admit this, but Linda was actually pretty. Blonde hair and blue eyes and nothing like the fat cow Kenny made her out to be. And her skinny behind complemented her clothing very nicely, that is if you like the "white-girl-casually-dressed-in-khakis prep look." Her red sweater around her shoulders finished off her suburban, at-home-mom look.

After endless conversation on Linda's part, Kenny told her they needed to get going. She gave me a big hug like we were old girlfriends, as we said good-bye. Just like that, they were off to their perfect life. Leaving me to feel empty and barren like a dried-up well.

It was finally the kids' turn with Santa. I couldn't wait to find Rhonda and the kids. After that latest incident, I felt drained and ready to take a nap. Too much excitement for one day. Seeing Kenny's lying ass at the mall with his wife and kids made my ass mad, while all the shoppers were so happy and joyous.

Now, I had an attitude. I wanted that life. It was supposed to be me strolling in and out of expensive stores with the great husband and kids, not that bitch! Shit!

Why do I continue to do this to myself?—Let men just use me and walk all over me. Focusing on finding a decent father for my kids caused me to miss opportunities to improve my own life. All these broke-down men. I wanted and needed more. My kids deserved it. I had to do better, even if I died trying.

I tried to hold back my emotions while in search of my sister. When I finally caught up to Rhonda, she was as tired as I was. We both called it a day and headed home.

I collapsed in my empty king-sized bed. I cried hard. The ugly cry. Refused to hold onto the pain. This would be the last time. Tomorrow, everything was going to change.

Chapter 10
(Tate)

I'm never going to make it. I checked my watch for the second time. Already six. Glen and Terri's engagement party was set to start in an hour.

My cell phone rang. I knew it had to be Glen, waiting to see if I was on my way. We were supposed to ride over to the Marriott together to help set up. When he stopped by my office, I was swamped with last-minute calls to return. I told him I would be there as soon as I finished.

A second ring.

I answered. "Yeah, man. I'm on my way."

"Excuse me?" It was a woman's voice.

"Who's this?" I raised a brow.

"Tate, this is LeQuisha."

Fuck! I felt a yank in my stomach. I hadn't heard from her in over a month. *What in the hell did she want?*

I cleared my throat. "Look, I'm busy."

"I'm sorry to bother you, but I need you to come pick me up."

"What? Look, LeQuisha, I don't—"

"My car broke down, and I can't get in touch with anyone else. Could you please do this for me? I won't ask you for nothing else. Please? I need to get home; my kids are there alone."

Shit! I was going to be late. If I didn't make it, Glen would never forgive my ass. "Where are you?"

LeQuisha gave me directions. She canceled her AAA membership because she could no longer continue to pay the fees. On my way to Soutel Boulevard, I called for a tow company to pick up her beat-up, old Honda. I passed her car as I drove up to the grocery mart where she waited inside.

LeQuisha made eye contact and waved at me. I almost didn't recognize her; she wore very little make-up. I actually had to do a double-take. She appeared so different from the ghetto queen I used to know. Sporting a new, short, brown hairdo, she wore jeans and a long, brown leather jacket with matching boots. I certainly did like what I saw.

I pushed the heavy door open to the loud cowbell used to alert the owner of a new customer entering. As I approached LeQuisha, I thought back to how this woman used to please me better than any other woman did. "Hey, LeQuisha," I said awkwardly.

"Hello." LeQuisha folded her arms and held an intense gaze.

I glanced around the store. "You want me to get you something out of here?"

"No. I just need to get home." LeQuisha held up her cell phone. "The battery died."

"Here." I handed her my phone.

LeQuisha swallowed hard. "Thanks."

As she used the phone to check on her kids, I purchased a bag of chips and soda. She climbed in my car, and I parked behind her car waiting for the tow truck.

I paid the driver cash and handed him my business card with instructions to call me if there were any other expenses. I followed LeQuisha's directions to her place.

"Make a right here on Edgewood, Tate." LeQuisha rubbed her hands together.

"You cold?"

She nodded.

I turned up the heat. Warmer air blasted out of the vents.

LeQuisha sat back. "Much better."

Out of the corner of my eye, I watched her cross her legs. Those thighs were slicing. I remembered what it felt like to run my hands along them. I turned away.

"I moved, you know," LeQuisha said casually.

"Naw." I never even knew where her first place was. I sat up straighter in my seat. "I didn't know that."

LeQuisha nervously adjusted her position. "That's right. Well, I moved to a better place." She tugged at her ear.

"Oh yeah?" I turned the heat down. It was starting to feel like a sauna.

"I wanted more room for me and my kids."

We pulled into Park Place Apartments, and I parked in front of the townhouse she was renting. A tall and rather good-looking boy peered through the blinds and came outside.

LeQuisha rolled down the window. "Lil' Donny, it's me. Go back in the house. It's cold out here."

"That's your son?"

"My oldest. You sound surprised." She smiled. Then she started to go on about how he was a great ball player, how all of her kids made good grades in school and wanted to go to college. LeQuisha told me she wanted to set a good example and enrolled in college herself.

That caught me by surprise. She was always so proud of the fact that she'd earned a certificate to do nails from cosmetology school.

"Why don't you come in and meet the rest of my family?" She smiled nervously, waiting for me to answer.

I told her that I could only stay for a few minutes, because of my plans. I went in, and she introduced me to her kids. They seemed polite and well-behaved, not at all like I'd imagined.

Her place was nicely furnished and immaculate. Shit, LeQuisha's crib looked better than mine did. She took me on a quick tour, engaged me in some small talk, and then I said good-bye.

Just as I opened the door of my BMW to get in, LeQuisha ran back out. *Oh, here we go!* I knew she was up to something.

She tapped on my window, shivering uncontrollably. "I wanted to thank you for picking me up, Tate. That was really nice of you." She rubbed her hands together. "And also for meeting my children. That means a lot to me."

"No sweat." We locked eyes for a moment. "LeQuisha, let me take care of the car for you. I know you're probably all spent out from Christmas."

"No, you don't have to do that, really." She leaned on the window. "I'll manage."

"I'm sure you'll manage. But, let me do this for you. I already gave the driver my card. If you need me to take you to pick up your car, just call."

"Okay." LeQuisha pecked me on the lips softly.

We were silent for a moment, taking heavy breaths. As she ran back inside, I stalled for a few minutes, trying to gather my thoughts. *Was I actually starting to feel something? Hell no. Maybe a hard on.*

I arrived at the party well after nine. Glen's tight-lipped grimace let me know he was pissed off. I pretended not to notice. I greeted the happy couple and proceeded to mingle with the rest of the guests. There were a few people there from the office, Glen's parents, and, I assume, Terri's folks, the people who looked like they had something stuck up their asses. Her father was slightly bald, tall with a nice strong build. He wore a black tuxedo, while Terri's stepmother modeled a gold floor-length evening gown.

Damn! Glen should have told me I needed to dress up for this shindig. Our co-workers from American Income Life were dressed as if they had just left the office and looked out of place as well.

Regardless, everyone seemed to be having a nice time in the elegantly decorated banquet room. I swung over to the buffet and fixed a plate of small stuffed mushrooms and some chicken wings. Suddenly, I felt a strong grip on my shoulder.

"So, you stood a brotha up?"

I turned around to face Glen. "See, what had happened was—"

"That's right, make it good." Glen nodded his head pretending to listen, gesturing with his arms. "Come on with it."

"See, man—" I took a deep breath. I could no longer keep a straight face.

"Just tell me who she was, and I'll let you off the hook." He leaned over closer, so I could whisper it in his ear.

I hesitated. "LeQui—"

"Man, tell me you didn't. Tell me you didn't stand me up at my own engagement party for that trick-ass LeQuisha." Glen stroked his mustache.

"Let me explain. See, her car broke down right, and I had—"

"You had to what? What? I'm listening. Really, I am. Let me tell you something, man-to-man." Glen searched over his shoulder to make sure no one was within earshot. "Leave her alone." He put his arm on my shoulder to escort me away from the buffet.

Glen formally introduced me to Terri's parents and Terri's sister, Sharon. He was pulled away for a moment to meet some future in-laws, and I conversed with Sharon for a little bit. We had a lot in common, since I graduated from the same college.

A tall, thin, gorgeous beauty in a red silk slip dress walked up to Sharon. I couldn't help staring. Shit, I drooled. For real. I mean, damn! This girl was fine.

"Oh, I'm sorry." Sharon grabbed my hand. "Tate, this is my roommate, Tangy."

I grabbed her hand and kissed it. "It's nice to meet you, Tangy. I'm Tate Gibson."

Tangy smiled. She had a great smile.

I gazed into her big, baby-blue eyes. Just like Vanessa Williams. I'd never seen a black woman with blue eyes in person. Even though she was young for my type, I had to have her. I totally forgot Sharon was beside me, or anyone else for that matter.

"Can I have my hand back now?" She asked, still smiling.

"Well, it depends." I moved in closer.

"Depends on what?"

"Whether or not I can have your number."

Tangy cocked her head. "Why do you need my number?"

"To call you, of course. I want to take you out, spend some time with you, get to know you."

Her eyes danced in circles. "Humph."

"So?" I gazed in her eyes a little harder. No way was I going to let go of her soft hand without a fair exchange. I could tell she was actually considering my offer.

"Okay. I'll give you my number."

"Uhhmmm. Hummm. I can see that you two would like some time alone."

"Tate?"

"Yeah."

"I need my hand back now." Tangy's tongue parted her delicate lips. "You know, so I can write down my number."

"No need."

"Come again?"

"No need. Just tell me; I won't forget." I winked.

Tangy smiled flirtatiously. I had her attention. Right then, I knew there was no boyfriend either. At least not a man I should be concerned about.

We spent the rest of the evening getting to know one another. Tangy left a strong impression. She was a smart woman with a good head on her shoulders, interested in pursuing a degree in journalism. Articulate, beautiful, and funny. Everything I've ever wanted in a woman. Did I mention her body? The girl had a body that wouldn't quit.

I convinced Tangy to let me take her back to her dorm on campus. It took some prodding on my part to win her trust. I was a perfect gentleman. No hidden agendas. I enjoyed the conversation on the way. I told her I would call her the next day, and we parted.

On my way home, I thought about the chance of meeting the woman of my dreams. I knew this was definitely God's way of letting me know that there were better women out there for me. Not that LeQuisha was all bad; she just wasn't the woman for me. I wasn't the right man for her. Hell, you never know. Tangy could be the next Mrs. Gibson. All I knew, this could be the start of something new. It felt so damn good.

Chapter 11
(Tangy)

One more mile to go. Sharon lost me back in her tracks. No sight of her. I ran past two homeless guys on the corner and made a right. At least I'm back on Merrill Road. I saw Sharon slowing down at the next street. She jogged in place, and I picked up my pace knowing she was waiting on me. A five-mile run was a cakewalk for her, so I know she couldn't possibly be tired.

As soon as I caught up to her, I feverishly trembled because my gray sweats felt like ice. People don't realize how low the temperature actually drops in Florida. This morning, the temperature dropped down in the twenties. When Sharon woke me up at six, I declined at first, but changed my mind. I needed the exercise. Staying healthy and fit was important to me.

We ran another block down to Smoothie King

and entered through the double-doors. I anticipated having a strawberry-banana smoothie.

"So, you got in late last night," Sharon commented.

"I know. Tate and I lost track of time. We talked for hours."

Sharon cackled. "You know, you're better than me. There's no way me and Craig would stay up for hours talking."

I turned up one eye. *I guess she and Craig must be more serious than I thought. Dang, they just started dating three days ago.* Not wanting to appear to be judgmental, I decided not to say anything. I know most people my age, are not virgins. Most of them were probably engaging in some morning sex as I spoke.

"Sounds like you really dig Tate."

I spoke softly. "Yeah." I slurped on my drink. I didn't want it to sound like I was in love with him already.

"Uh huh. I knew it." She pointed at me. "Not Ms. 'I don't need a man, because all they do is get in the way and I'm all about the books to further my career.'"

I dropped my eyes in embarrassment. "I know. I know. I'm serious about all that still."

We sat down at the booth near the window.

I rearranged my ponytail and fanned the back of my sweaty neck.

"Have you explained to Tate your situation?"

I frowned. "What situation?"

"I mean . . ." Sharon leaned in closer and spoke in a whisper so that the older couple sitting behind us couldn't hear. ". . . have you told "Prince Charming" you're not interested in a relationship involving sex?"

"No, not yet." I shifted from side to side. "We've only been out once, Sharon, dang. Plus, I don't even know if things will go any further than that; I'm going to play it by ear."

Sharon held up her hand. "Okay. All I'm saying is, the way he was eyeing you at the party"—She sucked her teeth—"It made me think he wanted to do more with you than just cuddle. Plus, I know for a fact that Tate—"

"Tate what? Go ahead, say it."

"Nothing." She folded her arms on the table and took another sip.

I snatched her cup from her. "Nothing, huh?" I pretended like I was going to throw the cup at her.

"Okay, okay, okay." Sharon reached out for the cup.

I handed it back to her reluctantly.

"All I was going to say was Terri told me that he's into freaks, that's all." Sharon shrugged.

"And you're sure that's it? I mean, Terri didn't say anything about a girlfriend, did she?" I studied her.

"No. Nothing. He was seeing some ghetto-fabulous freak who loves to have sex all the time, but it's been over for a while now."

"Oh," I said flatly. Sharon knew me better than to drop things so quickly. Talking about issues or concerns was what I did best. I was going to school to be a voice in the community, to society, and hopefully to the world. I knew this wouldn't be the end of the discussion about Tate. Soon Sharon would reveal all the women he's been with in the past. She knew eventually, Tate would pressure me to have sex with him.

I did too. However, my answer would be no, and I was willing to lose any man that didn't respect that.

After almost running five miles, I didn't have the energy to finish this conversation. Tate was no different from any other man. I liked Tate. Fine, educated, and the perfect gentleman. It was nice that an older man could come down to my level and share the same interests as me. Of course, I was only basing my opinion on one date, meaning a lot could happen, and a lot could change. Whatever happened, I was ready for it.

We both agreed walking instead of running back to campus was a good idea. Due for a meeting with my study group in an hour, I jumped in and washed my nasty hair. When I got out of the shower, I could hear Sharon on the phone talking with her new man. I dressed, grabbed my Jansport backpack, and dashed out the door. *If I paced myself, I would make it to the library in time.*

Chapter 12
(LeQuisha)

A large crowd of students stood outside of the classroom. I couldn't believe with all the running around this morning I actually showed up fifteen minutes early. I peeped in the glass door window and saw a class seated. Looking around I decided to stand along the outside hallway. I chose a spot a little ways down away from everybody, to have a minute to myself. Shit, I needed to relax.

I observed the way the students talked to one another, like they already knew each other. Suddenly, I felt out of place. Surprised to see there was not another black person in sight. The ones I passed in the parking lot on my way here sounded like a bunch of white girls. And they had the nerve not to speak to me either. One look at my ten-year-old Honda Accord, and they didn't feel like I was worth even a hello.

Girls like that thought they were better than me. But, I wasn't going to college to make friends and I for damn sure wasn't trying to be like those fake-ass stuck-up bitches. I was trying to better myself, get a good job, and take better care of my children. *Forget the rest.*

My stomach felt all jittery on the inside. Didn't sleep much the night before. It had been so long since I'd been in school. I mean, I went to school to be a nail-tech, but that wasn't the same. Most of my hours were spent in a shop working and getting experience, not sitting in a classroom all day.

My kids were so excited for me this morning. Lil' Donny cooked breakfast. My mother brought a gift over last night. She bought me this real nice leather carry bag to tote my books in. Rhonda even bought me a new outfit, a brown knit top, and some loose-fitting dark blue jeans I was kicking. Rhonda said she figured the way I usually dressed wouldn't fit in with these college kids. With all this booty and breasts, I still looked damn good though. Some of these white people didn't even wear jackets. One idiot actually had on cut-off shorts and a T-shirt—in thirty-degree weather!

Finally, the door opened and a large crowd of students came rushing out like a stampede of animals. I looked down at my watch. Five more minutes until my class was set to begin. I maneuvered my way through the crowd. No one seemed thrilled to be there. A girl with auburn-colored hair held a flat expression, and a few kids laughed and told corny-ass jokes. That nervous feeling came back again.

When I walked into the cold and plain room, I spotted a few seats available in the front row. I sat down and just kept looking straight ahead. I felt all eyes in the room were on me. Pretending to straighten my new hairdo, I quickly glanced around the room. Not one person paid attention to my black ass, even though I was the only spot in there. Wanting the other students to think I was a serious student, I opened my bag and pulled out a pen and my spiral pad. I also grabbed the psychology book I would need for the class.

A fat white guy with a full beard entered. The room sat so still, you could've heard a penny drop. No one spoke a word. He wrote his name, Robert Dean, and Psych 101 on the board. He passed out the syllabus and explained it. I scribbled notes on paper and tried my best to keep up with him. Professor Dean lectured the entire time, and I wrote down everything he said. I must've written six pages of notes.

Fifty minutes later, the class ended. That was it! This wasn't hard at all. I wanted to kick my own ass for not doing this sooner.

I didn't have the workbook I needed for the class, so I stopped by the bookstore to pick it up before I headed for my next class. Assigned to read three chapters, I had one more class to go. Then to the shop to do nails. I planned to stop by my place first to check on the kids.

My new schedule was going to be hard to keep up with—do nails in the morning, then go to two classes on Monday, Wednesday, and Friday afternoons. On Tuesday and Thursday, I had two more classes to attend in the mornings. I was going to finish the day at the shop until it closed. I had to put in a lot of hours, since I had cut Kenny loose for good, which put even more pressure on me to take care of business completely on my own. Karen was flexible enough with the schedule to help me out. She even volunteered to take the kids for me if I needed time to study.

That was the only thing I hadn't even had time to figure out yet, when to study. I hoped it wouldn't be as hard as everybody kept telling me, especially knuckleheads that ain't never even been to college. Everything was happening so quickly, I really hadn't had a chance to sit back and think my plan all the way through.

I don't know how to describe it, but it was sort of, like, I was being led to go through with plans I'd made for myself years ago, before I even met Big Donny, but never acted on for whatever reason. It seemed like once I made up my mind I wasn't going to keep serving myself up shit for breakfast every morning, better things started to happen for me. All this only confirmed God is real—there wasn't anything He couldn't handle or do for me, or anyone else for that matter.

"Hey, Karen. How you doin'?" I asked as I dragged myself into Fabulouz Nailz.

"Hey, yourself, college girl." Karen had a mouthful of food. She was wolfing down jerk chicken and rice out of a white container from the Caribbean take-out place next door.

I grabbed a plastic fork out of a small box in the bottom drawer.

"How did it go today?" She handed over the white box of food for me to finish all by myself.

I was so damn hungry from not having had anything to eat all day long. I didn't have any money to buy something to eat. I probably had enough change to buy a soda, but nothing else. All of my money paid bills. I was still waiting on my financial aid check to come in.

"Fine."

I couldn't wait to pay Lil' Donny's basketball coach back for buying the shoes he needed to play on the team. I didn't even ask him to, but he offered. He told me I didn't owe him anything. Every time I went to Lil' Donny's games, Coach Peterson would be giving me these looks as if I owed him a favor, like I issued him a coochie coupon to cash in for a good rump in the bed—his old married ass needed to stop.

"Has it been busy in here?" I noticed only one customer sitting at the table letting her nails dry.

"Slow as hell—you know how it is on Mondays." Karen picked at her teeth.

"True," I said, chewing on a tough piece of meat.

I had worked at Fabulouz Nailz for about five years. It was an old and shabby place in front of the Gateway Mall, and Karen was doing the best she could to keep her business going, considering the cheap-ass oriental shops were stealing all of our customers. We tried to provide quality service and that didn't come cheap.

A young girl wearing a silver, tight-ass outfit came in the shop. My eyebrows rose. I had the same outfit in my closet. I guess I never realized I probably looked as stank in it as she did. And her hair, oh my God, it had silver streaks in it to match. Dang. I traded in all my fresh stylish hairdos for my new conservative cut with golden highlights.

"What you need today?" I said as I motioned her over to my table.

"A fill in," she said in a husky drawl.

I placed my food container on the counter to finish later. "All right. Sit right here." *Gotta make my money.*

Chapter 13
(Tate)

"I love you," Tangy whispered.

"I love you too." Tangy kissed me. Even harder than the first time. Something else got hard at the same time, and it was in between my legs.

We lay on the small single bed in her dorm room. I unbuttoned her green plaid shirt, and Tangy was breathing heavily. We began to grind back and forth. Tangy held me so tight.

I pulled her breasts out of her bra and began to suck on one, my other hand on her ass.

Tangy's closed her eyes and moaned as if she enjoyed it. I know *I* did. I slipped my hand underneath her skirt and eased her panties down her legs. I fondled her wet clit. *Ooohh, so warm.* I'd never gotten that far before. I quickly pulled my pants down and massaged my penis. I decided to slide on a condom and go in for the kill.

"Tate, no . . . no . . . no . . . I'm not ready for this." She struggled to push me off her.

I picked up on her vibes and moved away from her as fast as I could. I shook my head. *Here we go again with the innocent little girl routine.* My body jerked. "Not ready? You get me this worked up, and then you say you're not ready?" I pulled my pants up.

"No, I'm not; I got caught up in the moment. My eyes were closed, and I didn't realize what you were doing."

"What the fuck! Tangy, you actin' like I was trying to rape you or something." I stood over her on the bed while she continued with her act. "I don't have time for these childish games," I said through clenched teeth. "You knew damn well what I was doing."

"My eyes were closed; I didn't know." Tears streamed down her face.

If I didn't really know how crazy her ass was, I would have actually believed her. "Oh, so I was trying to rape you?" My stare was intense. "Seriously, I was trying to rape you, right? That's what you sayin'?"

Tangy started crying.

My fist opened and closed. "Are you going to say anything?"

I heard the door unlock and Sharon rushed in. Her head jerked left to right, first at me standing at the foot of the bed, then at Tangy sitting on the bed, her clothes still hanging off her. It didn't help that she appeared disheveled like someone was trying to kill her ass.

"What the hell is going on in here? I heard your voices all the way down the hall." Sharon placed both hands on her hips. "Why are your clothes all torn up? What just happened here?"

Tangy said nothing. She didn't even try to defend my ass. She sat on the bed in a daze or something.

"Not a damn thing happened here," I said in a hostile voice and stormed the fuck out. In the hallway, students stood in their doorways, glaring at me like I was a serial rapist. I decided to pick up my steps and exit quickly. No doubt, in a matter of minutes a couple of police officers would show up in response to all of the commotion. I drove home as fast I could without the risk of being pulled over by a cop.

That's what I get for hanging around in a college dorm. I don't even know why I was still fooled with that young-ass girl.

I was mad as hell. Fuming. Crazy bitch! Her eyes were closed. What kind of a game was she running? Six months, I've been messing around with her crazy ass. And nothing. I should have ended things when she told me she was a virgin. I actually had respect for her. She was different. What I soon learned, different didn't necessarily mean better. Childish was more like it.

Tangy's jealousy got on my nerves too. At a friend's party, she got mad at me for talking to another woman. The woman was a co-worker, and she still wanted to trip even after I told her. She always accused me of sleeping with someone else. The truth is, I wasn't. I hadn't had sex in so long, my balls felt like they were about to fall off.

I figured Tangy would give in and give it up eventually. It wasn't as if she led me to think otherwise. Every chance she got, Tangy rubbed her hands on my chest, even in front of her friends. When we were alone, she would rub my dick until it got rock hard. When I touched her, she would stop me and say, "Not yet." Not yet. That meant, "I'm going to let you hit it, but not yet." Come on, it didn't take a brain surgeon to figure that shit out. Therefore, I was cool about it, taking my time, and being patient, thinking eventually it was going to pay off. Not that I intended to marry her, but she didn't know that.

Tangy was too damn crazy for me. She would be fine one minute, and then pissed off the next, then, beg me not to break up with her. This whole relationship was a joke, if that's what you want to call it. It amazed me how women can be so beautiful and fine, and so fucked up in the head.

My thoughts drifted off to the worst day of my life in high school. Felicia Anderson stood outside of my class talking with Timothy Harris, the quarterback on the football team. Felicia lived next door, and we grew up together. Having pretty much the same advanced classes, Felicia asked for after-school help for our trigonometry class. As fine as she was, and me being a skinny, little guy, I jumped at the chance.

Felicia's auburn-colored hair danced around her shoulders, and her full breasts bounced perfectly in low-cut sweaters. Every time she came over, she let me finger her, leading me to believe I would finally get a chance to stick it in. As hard as I tried, Felicia never let me tap that ass but agreed to be my girlfriend. Secret woman sounded more like it. I never got to hold her hand or show her any affection at school. It bothered me. I fantasized about her during the day, while she teased my emotions with fake promises of letting me tap the coochie in the privacy of my bedroom.

"Can I speak to you for a second?" I asked in a voice barely above a whisper.

Felicia's jerked her head. "Excuse me?"

I clutched the straps of my backpack. "Can I speak to you for a second?" This time my voice sounded more like my father's. *No, this girl wasn't trying to embarrass me in front of old boy.*

"Am I interrupting something here?" Timothy grinned. "I mean, is this supposed to be your man or something?"

Felicia pointed at my chest. "Him? No, Tate's just a friend."

I wiped my nose and shook my head in pure disbelief. Trying to control my anger, my fists balled up tightly. I mean what was I going to do?—Start a fight with this man? Hell, no. No woman was worth that ass kicking.

"Hey, man." Tim pushed me back. "Why you blockin'?"

I looked at him strangely and faced Felicia. "Do you still want to get together after school?"

Felicia twisted her lips. "No, I don't need your help anymore. I didn't tell you—I got an A on my last trig test. So, see ya!" Felicia waved her hand. As soon as I was out of earshot, I heard a wave of laughter behind my back.

Alone in my bed that night, I decided I would never be made to look like a fool again. The stunt Tangy pulled gave me the same feeling of stupidity.

My stomach rumbled. I went in the kitchen to fix a sandwich and pour a large glass of Chek grape soda. I picked up the cordless and dialed Carmela's cell number. Her voice mail picked up. I thought about dialing her home number but changed my mind. Big-dick Hector might answer the phone and ask a lot of questions. I took in a deep breath. It wasn't as if Carmela was even interested in me anymore.

I dialed LeQuisha's number instead. *What the hell, I had nothing to lose.*

"Hello," a young boy answered. There was a lot of noise in the background.

"Hello, is LeQuisha there?"

"Yeah, hold on for a minute. Ma, the phone."

I sat there nervously trying to think of what to say.

"Yes, LeQuisha speaking."

I scratched the back of my head. "Are you busy?"

"As a matter of fact, I am," she snapped. "Too busy for you anyway."

I cocked my head. *No, LeQuisha wasn't trying to front on a brotha.* Now, you know me. I don't back down so easily. "Is that the way you want to act?"

"It's not an act, Tate—Now what do you want?"

"I wanted to call and see what was up with you." I cleared my throat. "I hadn't heard from you in a while so I assumed you were busy with school."

"Ooohh. No, you didn't. Tate, you know my damn number. And the last time I seen or heard from you was months ago—I don't have time for this."

"Wait. Girl, you know you need to stop." I sat straight up.

"Stop what? Stop what? Tate, you ain't shit, never been shit, and never gon' be shit, so good-bye."

Dial tone.

Pacing back and forth in the living room, I decided there was no better time than the present and got in my car.

Thirty minutes later, I approached Park Place Apartments. I couldn't believe I remembered where it was, since I'd only been there once.

I knocked on the door. No response. It was very quiet and dark inside. *Maybe, she wasn't there.* I knocked again.

LeQuisha opened the door slowly, dressed in a pink robe, her hair tied up in a scarf. She let out a snort of disgust. "What are you doing here?"

"I came over here to talk to you. I tried to talk to you on the phone, but you wouldn't listen."

"Tate, you weren't trying to tell me nothing."

"I was, but you never gave me a chance." I gazed into her eyes, and she reluctantly looked back into mine. If I could get her to listen, then she would leave herself open.

At the time, I knew that night would possibly lead to other nights with LeQuisha, but I really wasn't concerned about that. All I knew was I needed her right then. It didn't matter where. Being close to a woman was all I wanted. *I would deal with later, later.*

LeQuisha rolled her eyes then smacked her lips. "I really shouldn't let you in, but . . ." She held the door open wider. ". . . Come on."

I fought hard to suppress my smile as I followed her to the couch. "Where are the kids?" I asked, observing the quietness.

"Lil' Donny's staying the night with Travis, and Daneisha and Dante went with Rhonda." LeQuisha crossed her legs and folded her arms.

I looked up. "Rhonda's your sister, right?"

She nodded.

I clapped my hands together. "So, how's school going?"

LeQuisha rubbed her thighs and smiled. "Very well. I'm maintaining all A's so far."

"Really?"

LeQuisha nodded and licked her full lips. "Yep."

Inching my way closer, I grabbed her hand and squeezed it. "That's great."

LeQuisha snatched away. "Do you want some tea?"

Picking up on her nervousness, I surrendered. "Yeah."

LeQuisha rose from the couch to go in the kitchen and came back a few minutes later with two mugs.

I waited for the most opportune moment, so when she leaned over I reached for the mug. I put it on the table, reached over, and pecked her on the lips.

LeQuisha sat down and rested her arm along the couch.

I reached over and kissed her again.

She opened her mouth and invited my tongue inside. I savored the taste of her strawberry lip-gloss.

Next thing you know, I was licking on her supple melon-sized breasts.

"Uuuhh," she moaned. LeQuisha lay down on the couch, and I continued to lick down to her navel and down a little lower. She grabbed my head as I sucked and licked her sweet juices.

She squirmed wildly. "Damn, Tate."

After she climaxed, I undressed completely and slipped on a condom. For the first time, I wanted the sex to be different. Better than the times before. My manhood worked her slowly but vigorously.

I sighed when I was about to release. "Aaawww, man."

We lay there breathing heavily. I actually had to admit—I did miss her.

LeQuisha led me upstairs to her bedroom to finish what we'd started.

Chapter 14
(LeQuisha)

"**M**ommy."

"Hey, Dante." I reached down and gave my son a big hug and kiss. Rhonda dropped off the kids this morning after their overnight stay at her apartment. They filed in and went upstairs to empty their bags. I stood outside to wave bye to my sister while she headed off to work at the mall. (I helped her get a job at Dillard's, before I quit.) Finally rid of that no-good-ass nigga, my sister worked hard to support Pee-Wee and Tank, and they moved in a two-bedroom apartment not too far from me in Arlington.

"Are you guys hungry?" I asked, my hand on my hip.

"Yes," Daneisha answered from her room upstairs. "Starving!"

"Well, come back downstairs so you can eat."

I went in the kitchen to fix Daneisha's and

Dante's plates. Lil' Donny was big enough to fix his own.

Tate strolled in the kitchen rubbing his eyes.

My man looked so damn fine in his black silk boxers, all his muscles cut in all the right places.

"Is there something for me?" Tate asked as he sat down at the table.

"Uh huh." I flung my head up. "I'm sorry, but my kids are here. So you need to go upstairs and put on some clothes. My children don't need to see you in your boxers, Tate, no matter how good you look." I smiled.

Tate shrugged. "Okay, my bad." He rushed back upstairs.

This was the first time a man had spent the night at my place since Big Donny, and I wasn't sure how my kids would react to another man being here.

After seeing them this morning, it seemed as though I was worried for nothing. Everybody, including Tate dressed in jeans and a T-shirt, stretched out at the table and bar to chow down on my cheesy grits, eggs, and sausage. Dante entertained Tate with an arm-wrestling match, and Daneisha talked my ear off about the girls at her summer day camp at the Y. Lil' Donny was on the phone, macking some girl, as usual.

I eased around the small dining area and poured more orange juice in all the empty glasses.

Tate grabbed my hips and forced me down on his lap. "LeQuisha, why don't you sit down? You've been up running around all morning. You cooked all this food and you haven't eaten a thing."

"Mommy never sits down. She's up all the time cleaning and cooking," Dante said, chewing slowly on his fifth piece of sausage.

"Is this true?" Tate turned to face me.

"Yes, it's true. We try to get her to relax, but she never does," Daneisha explained. "All she does is work, go to school, and then come home and do more work. I'm worried about my mom."

"Don't worry about me." I bit into a sausage link. "I'm fine."

Tate whispered in my ear softly. "Yeah, you're fine all right."

I giggled as Tate tickled me in the stomach. I was a little embarrassed when I realized all three of my children were staring at us. The smiles on their faces let me know they were glad to see me in his arms.

I realized this was what I wanted all along. I still loved Tate; I loved my kids. I guess I wasn't being patient enough with him. *It must be hard for him, raised as an only child, to jump into a relationship with a mother of three kids. Shit, I'm surprised he didn't run off like the others.*

Tate managed to stick around and not forget about me. When me and Tate were together, I saw it in his eyes, he didn't think of me as a worthy woman. I knew I wasn't perfect, either. But Tate was perfect to me. Determined to let him see I was just as good as those uppity women he worked with on his job, I let him walk all over me.

I prayed he would come back to me. It was always in the back of my mind and in my thoughts. And he did. Only thing, this time it was going to be on my terms. No way would I put up with that shit from him again. He wasn't going to disrespect my kids or me anymore; otherwise, I would have to let him out of my life for good. Anyways, whatever happened in the past was in the past. He was here at my townhouse now with my kids and with me.

We made love last night over and over again. It was so different from the other times. He took things slow and didn't rush at all. He even went downtown, something he'd never done to me before. I knew a man like Tate wouldn't just eat a woman's pussy if he didn't think she was special to him. I wasn't ready to believe he loved me or suddenly he wanted to propose marriage—I wasn't dumb. *This time, things would be different.*

Going to college to better myself had me reading more. So far, I'd read T.D. Jakes' *Woman, Thou Art Loosed!* Learning why I'd allowed men to walk all over me was a revelation. Right then, halfway through Joyce Rodger's *Fatal Distractions,* I'd learned that the woman kept repeating the same mistake until she believed herself worthy.

I possessed more power than I ever imagined, through God. When I tapped into His energy and strength, I was able to not only overcome, but also accomplish anything positive I set out to do. Going to church every Sunday was helping me, too.

I was even surprised that Tate told the kids he would go to Bethel with us for Sunday service. Unlike me, Tate grew up in the church and always said he was "all churched out" and wasn't interested in going.

Things with Tate were starting to look very good. I wasn't sure if I would even see him again after the way things ended before, but here he was with my kids, having breakfast together like a family. God is good.

Chapter 15
(Tate)

Now, I'm not going to even pretend—I was glad to be getting a piece of ass again. I mean months of celibacy wasn't good for a man. Getting some ass like LeQuisha's again wasn't half bad either. Her pussy felt like sweet whipped cream on my attention-starved rod.

Being involved with LeQuisha meant putting up with all the usual drama and bullshit, along with even more requests than before. Now that I had become somewhat acquainted with her kids, she almost demanded I spend time with them. She never came right out and said that, but it was implied. *No problem,* I liked her kids.

When she came over to my place, she actually left before eleven, which didn't necessarily guarantee me a night of hot, passionate sex anymore.

Sometimes, she just wanted to sit around watching movies, eating popcorn, and talking.

She put a dent in my wallet as well. I kicked in a few hundred dollars to help her with the bills, and I had to take her out on dates. It wasn't bad, since the only thing she wanted to do was go out to eat. Discreet in the places I took her, I didn't want to take any chances running into Glen and Terri. I didn't want Glen riding me about seeing LeQuisha. And for damn sure, I didn't want Terri to go back and say something to Tangy. *What? You thought I stopped kicking it with Tangy. Why would I do a thing like that?*

There's one thing a woman must understand about a man—men are hunters; we like to hunt shit. Being crazy was not a good enough reason for a man to leave a woman alone, especially when the possibility of conquering virginity was at stake. Being crazy just made a brotha a little cautious. See, I was very careful with my words and actions, because a psycho had an excellent memory. She never forgot a thing. Falling asleep in bed alone with Tangy, a brotha might wake up to a Lorena Bobbitt-slicing or something worse. It was worth the risk though, because one thing a man liked better than some good pussy was virgin pussy. A nigga would give anything to be the first to conquest uncharted territory, and that usually meant dealing with young meat. And Tangy had a lot of growing up to do. Still, being with her wasn't so bad. Dealing with the sexual harassment suit, sometimes I needed to forget about my problems. Tangy did that for me. She added a little laughter to my days, because she was a trip.

Believe it or not, I appreciated my relationship with LeQuisha. I was comfortable with a woman who knew me inside and out like a book, and she knew all my hot spots, and how to make me scream for more. That kind of lovin' didn't just happen overnight. It wasn't easy for me to walk away from her either, when masturbating was the other option. Until Tangy started to throw some of that fresh nectar my way, I was gonna stick with LeQuisha. Of course, I was working on new prospects too.

Catching a glimpse of the time, I gathered my materials and headed to the big man's office. The investigation into my wrongful doings was discussed in every office, bathroom, and lounge. Everybody had an opinion, including the custodial crew. It was time to learn my fate as an employee at American Income Life. The harassment suit seemed to go on forever. Feeling like my days were numbered, I checked Monster.com for available positions and prepared a new resumé just in case.

"Good morning, Flo," I said with a smile.

"And how are you this morning, Tate?"

I scratched the back of my head. "Wonderful."

Flo stood up. "Glad to hear it. Mr. Rasher and the others are waiting for you."

I cringed. "Thank you." As I opened the wooden door, my eyes scanned the room. I grabbed a seat next to Glen, my only ally.

Dan clasped his hands together. "Tate, you're late."

"My apologies. I was detained for a few moments. It won't happen again."

"I know it won't." His eyes squinted tightly.

Suddenly feeling uneasy, I started shifting from side to side.

Dan explained that after careful review of the evidence and testimonies from all parties involved, the case was dismissed. (Valerie signed a statement to drop her lawsuit earlier that morning.)

After the meeting ended, Glen walked with me back to my office. He patted me on the back. "I know you're relieved it's all over."

I wiped my forehead. "You just don't know."

Glen crossed his arms. "I could've told you Carmela was trouble, but you never asked me. See, that's what's wrong with you, man—you say I'm your boy, but you don't tell me a damn thing."

I shook my head. "You're right. You seem caught up with your life with Terri; I don't want to bother you."

I opened my mini-fridge and handed Glen a bottle of water.

Glen took a long sip. "I needed that. We're boys; you can talk to me whenever."

Even though Glen sounded sincere, I knew better than to believe him.

"I promise from now on, I'm going to start making smarter choices when it comes to women."

* * *

LeQuisha came over to watch *Jason's Lyric*—for the hundredth time. "Baby, you want some more Pepsi?" she asked from the kitchen.

"Yeah." I pushed the DVD door shut.

She sat down on the coffee leather couch and kicked off her shoes. "Which one are we watching first?"

"Yours."

"Oooh . . . let me get comfortable." LeQuisha laid her legs across my lap.

"It's not like you haven't seen this movie before." I munched on a handful of popcorn.

LeQuisha nodded. "Doesn't matter; Jada's my girl."

I took a deep breath and leaned back. "Yeah, I know."

"And Allen Payne—oh, he's so fine." LeQuisha waved her hand. "Not as fine as you, baby, but he does look good."

I yawned. LeQuisha couldn't keep her mouth shut.

"I can't wait to see the part when—"

"LeQuisha!" I held up my hand.

"Huh?" Her eyes grew wide.

"Are we going to watch the movie, or are you going to sit here and talk the whole time?"

"It's only the beginning. I don't even like this part when they all little."

"Fine. I'll skip ahead." I pressed fast forward on the remote.

She tapped my arm. "Stop it. Right there."

"All right." I cut my eyes in her direction.

LeQuisha looked at me, dumbfounded. "What?"

I twisted my lips.

She smiled. "I'ma be quiet, promise."

"Good." I rested my arm on the couch.

LeQuisha kissed my left cheek, and I leaned back.

After the movie ended, she really could have taken her ass home, because she changed into one of my shirts, snuggled up in my bed, and went fast asleep.

I mean, don't get me wrong—I cared for LeQuisha, and there was nothing I wouldn't have done for her. I just didn't see us having a future together. I still want a newly made family of my own, and I never could've had one with her.

While in bed with LeQuisha, my thoughts of the situation were interrupted by the phone. It rang in the second bedroom, which I had converted into a study. On first thought, I decided not to answer it, but you never know, it could've been my moms calling. I jumped up and ran in the other room to answer it, but it was too late. The voice mail picked up on the fourth ring. Since I was already up, I checked my messages. Glen had called to remind me that he was having the next pre-season football hangout with the boys at his house this Sunday and it was my turn to bring the beer.

The second message was from was Tangy. Her parents, Reverend Newsome and his wife Angela, were in town and would be waiting at Carraba's for me tomorrow at six. I wasn't looking forward to meeting the Good Reverend Newsome. I deleted the messages and returned to bed. LeQuisha's snoring stopped, and I was finally able to get some sleep.

Chapter 16
(LeQuisha)

I *know Tate didn't just beg me to spend the night with* *him, just for him to sit on the phone with some other girl.* He must've been talking to that girl, Tangy. He thought I didn't know about her. Hmmph! He tried to be so slick, turning off the ringer on all three phones in his house so I wouldn't answer it. Little did he know I checked his voice mail at least once or twice a day, so I already knew everything I needed to know.

It wasn't difficult to figure out the pin number to his voice mail once he made the mistake of checking his messages from my house. I pressed the redial button and wrote them numbers down. I wanted to know if he was still seeing that woman from his job, but I never heard a message from that skinny, bald-headed bitch, Carmela, who said he wasn't messing with anymore.

What he didn't bother to tell me about was Tangy, who called him around the clock. I guess he must've been mad at her for a while, because the first couple of messages left were her crying on the phone apologizing for something she did that was so stupid. Well, obviously they must've made up because the messages were all cutesy and lovey-dovey now.

I knew Tate was going to mess around with other women, but things were definitely different than the last time. For one, I knew exactly who he was messing with. Two, I demanded he show me a lot more respect than before. Three, a man was going to be a man. I really didn't expect anything more from him . . . unless he showed me more.

Now, if he were married, then that would be a different story indeed. I wasn't messing with any more married men and allowing myself to be used for sex, so he can leave me all alone, and go snuggle next to his wife. *Don't think so!*

I already did that with Kenny and a few others that shall remain nameless, and I didn't plan to do it ever again. It just wasn't worth it. Me and Kenny were still friends, and we still talked from time to time. But, we were never gonna have sex again.

I didn't know when I went back to sleep, but the bright sunlight shining in my eyes woke me up. Living on the beach did have its advantages, but it wasn't like you didn't have to pay for it.

The toilet flushed, and Tate wandered out of the bathroom buttoning up his striped dress shirt. He plopped down on my side of the bed and gave me a big kiss. "Good morning," he said, his breath smelling of antiseptic.

I smiled. "Good morning."

"Are you planning to sleep in this morning?" Tate straightened his printed silk tie in the mirror.

Damn, my man is so fine. I admired the way his charcoal dress slacks cut around his thick, sexy thighs.

"No." I stretched my arms. "Gotta meet with my advisor."

"Oh yeah. When does the semester begin?"

I sat up in the bed, searching around for my thong underwear. I took it off in the middle of the night, because they cut me in my damn crack. My butt was still sore. "Uuuhh, next Monday." I found my thong in between the sheets and slipped them on. I stripped off Tate's oversized shirt.

Tate came behind me, wrapped his arms around me and nibbled on my ear. "Looks like you're going to be late to your meeting."

"And why do you say that?" I knew full well what he meant. I was feeling his hardness between my legs, but I wanted to tease him anyway. I was still a little upset with him for disrespecting me last night.

He slowly kissed my neck and rubbed his hands all over my body. I knelt down on the bed doggy-style while Tate unzipped his pants. He forcefully entered me from the rear. I held onto the sheets as hard as I could. Tried to steady myself, but Tate grabbed my hips and pumped harder.

A few minutes later, he exploded inside of me. As his cum ran down my leg, I suddenly realized he didn't even bother to put on a condom. *Damn it! This was the second time that happened.*

I needed to buy a CD player, because listening to cassette tapes made me feel like I belonged to the dinosaur age. *Being able to skip to my favorite songs, instead of pressing fast forward would save me a lot of time and frustration.* Installing an air-conditioning system had to be my first priority. Better yet, a new car with air conditioning and a CD player would've done me just fine.

Having struggled for so long, I couldn't wait until my graduation date. The thought of earning enough money to take my children shopping and not neglect a bill that month to cover it would be a dream. For real—most nursing positions started at a salary of $45 per hour, not including time-and-a-half.

My life would've improved quicker if Tate proposed marriage. Forget a wedding, marrying at the courthouse woulda been enough. I didn't need no fancy dress or cake, just Tate.

I used my key to enter Rhonda's apartment. The kids begged to stay the weekend, but I wanted to stop by and check up on them, make sure they didn't need anything. Pee-Wee and Lil' Donny stood in the kitchen making bologna and cheese sandwiches.

"Can I have one of those?"

"Oh hey, Mama," Lil' Donny said.

I put my hands on my hips. "Is that how you greet your mama now?"

Lil' Donny wiped his hands on his shirt. "Sorry." He hugged me tightly.

"Now, that's better." I took a bite of my sandwich then added more mustard. "Where's everybody else?"

Tank told me, "In my room, watching dumb cartoons. Me and Lil' Donny gonna watch *Matrix*."

"Where your mama at?"

Lil' Donny pointed. "In her room."

I knocked on her door. No answer. I went in and

sat down on the bed, waiting for her to come out of the bathroom. I could smell the fragrance of weed in the air. Rhonda, eyes bloodshot, came out rubbing her nose.

"You know you need to lay off that stuff."

"Shut up. Ain't nothin' wrong with it. You used to do it, before you got all high and mighty." Rhonda lit a cigarette.

I scratched my head. "Yeah, but it's still not right. Marijuana kills brain cells, and it fogs up your mind."

"Save me the medical lesson, Nurse Stocks." Rhonda searched through her drawers for a pair of clean underwear.

"Knowing the medical facts wasn't enough for me to quit. The best thing God did was remove the taste from my mouth; now I have no desire to smoke or drink."

Rhonda stood in front of me in her red bra and black panties. The girl never knew how to match her underwear to save her life. I couldn't help noticing how she looked like skin and bones.

"Are you eating right?"

Rhonda laughed. "Not really. I've been so busy lately, I just don't have time."

"Well, you've always been skinny, but—"

"But, nothing." Rhonda slung her burgundy head of weave. "Why are you here? You've been on my case since you got here."

"To check on my children. I can see right now, I need to take them home . . . 'cause I don't want them around you when you like this."

"Whatever. Make sure Pee-Wee and Tank go with them too." She waved her cigarette.

"Fine." I marched out the room. She always did

this. People went out of their way to help her, and she would find a way to fuck it all up. All I knew was she had better not lose that job at Dillard's. I stuck my neck out for her, and my manager hired her on the spot, even though she hadn't stayed on a job longer than a month. Plus I depended on her associate discount; the Lord knew I couldn't afford to buy my kids nice clothes without it.

Lil' Donny shot me a worried look. "What's wrong, Mama?"

"Nothing. Everybody get your stuff together; we're going home."

Chapter 17
(Tate)

With barely enough time to sneak in a lunch hour, I decided to grab a sandwich, chips, and soda from the cafeteria downstairs. I spotted Glen sitting at a table alone, and he waved me over.

"How's it going, man?" Glen asked.

"Don't ask." I took a seat.

"Things are starting to get crazy around here."

"Starting?" I smirked. "I have eight adjusters handling the workload of fifteen. The late hours are killing me."

Glen's cell phone rang. "It's Terri. Hold on."

I finished off the last bite of my turkey and cheese sandwich.

Glen closed his phone. "Sorry about that—wedding calls."

I laughed. "I can imagine."

"I'm looking forward to the wedding; it's the getting there that has me so tired. I mean, how many more meetings and decisions have to be made?"

"You know women want any excuse to get together."

"Terri wants me to sit in on all of them. Then she asks for my input, but when I give it, she gets mad." Glen shook his head. "Man, it's a trip. She's turned into 'Bridezilla.' The coordinator and her stepmother are constantly ganging up on me. I'm sick of it."

"Well, let me ask you this." I folded my arms.

"What?"

"Why have a wedding? I mean, if it's as bad as you say it is. We already know marriage is tough. Why do it?"

Glen smiled. "'Cause you have to give the woman what she wants. And when you love a woman, that's what you do, no questions asked. It takes a level of maturity to get married."

"Then call me immature." I took a sip of Pepsi. "I just don't see myself there . . . not yet."

"You have to decide you're tired of playing the games." Glen gestured with his hands. "Because when it's all said and done, you have nothing left to prove to anyone, except yourself."

Glen moved in closer. "I mean, I don't understand you."

I raised my thick eyebrows. "What do you mean?"

"How did a nerd like you turn out like this? I mean, my dad was a well-known playa—it's in my blood." Glen raised his cup. "But you, I mean your dad was faithful to your mother."

I pondered over the question. "I don't know. I guess I got tired of being the nice guy. Nice guys finish last."

"That's what you need to figure out," Glen said. "You're playing a dangerous game, my friend."

I shook my head slowly. "I must admit—I love having a woman to meet my needs, but balancing it all is difficult. The women are demanding more of my time and, with work, I'm exhausted."

Glen looked at his watch. "I gotta go. Let me give you some advice: Take a break from it all; clear your mind and really think about your future." He pointed at his chest. "As for me, I have no intention of turning out like my dad. I love him, but he did a lot of things I don't agree with. I want to be a faithful husband and a good father to my children." Then he patted me on the shoulder and left.

Just like my boy to share a little advice. It wasn't easy to listen to a man controlled by his woman. *Who did he think I was? His protégé? I have a father. If I needed advice, I'd ask him for it. 'A dangerous game.' Please . . .*

I finished my lunch and headed back to my office. An hour into my work, I got a call from Tangy.

"My mom keeps complaining of a headache, leaving me stuck to entertain my dad." She sighed.

Her parents had traveled all the way from country-ass Alabama to visit.

"You should be happy to spend some quality time with the good ol' Reverend Newsome." I chuckled.

"You don't know how overbearing he can be."

I could sense the frustration in her voice. "And you want me to meet him?"

"Yes. Don't be late; daddy doesn't like it."

What's this girl up to? My phone lit up on line 2.

"Tangy, I have to take another call. See you at the Garden."

"No!" Tangy yelled. "We're meeting at Carraba's now. Don't you check your messages?"

I took a deep breath. "Tangy, in case you hadn't noticed, I'm working. Gotta go. Bye." Then to the call waiting, "Tate Gibson."

"Hey, boo."

"What's up, LeQuisha?" I glanced down at my clock.

"How's your day?" she asked, sounding upbeat.

"Very busy."

"Well, I won't keep you. Are you taking Dante to football practice?"

Fuck! "Is that today?"

"Uh huh. At 5:00."

I closed my eyes. "Yeah, I'll be there."

"Tate, if you can't make it, I'll ask my mom to do it."

"No." I shook my head. "I said I would be there."

"At 4:30. I don't want my baby to be late this time."

She was relentless. I wasn't going to accomplish anything today. Now, I only had two hours to review over fifty files. I rotated in my chair, my thoughts lost in space. A migraine spread from my head and settled heavily on my shoulders.

Okay, I would take Dante to practice, meet Tangy's parents for dinner, then rush back to work. It would take an all-nighter to be ready for my review meeting tomorrow morning.

I got up and leaned on Glady's desk. "How are you doing?"

She smiled. "A lot better than you, I see. Is there anything I can do for you, Tate?"

"I'm glad you asked. I need you to make an appointment with my doctor."

Gladys searched her Rolodex. "Work starting to get you down?"

"Yes." I folded my arms.

"Remember, the Lord never gives us more than we can handle." She looked at the card and dialed the number.

"I'll keep that in mind." I kissed her plump cheek. "I have to step out, but I'll be back later tonight."

Unfortunately, I got Dante to football practice fifteen minutes late. Coach kept the team half an hour late, so I arrived at Carraba's late too.

I spotted Tangy sitting with her parents at a table near the window. I gripped her shoulder blade nervously.

She shifted in her chair. "Tate, meet my parents."

I cleared my throat and stretched out my hand to the tall, stocky man. "It's good to meet you, Reverend Newsome and Mrs. Newsome."

Tangy resembled her mother, who was on the heavy side.

A man can always tell what a woman would look like in twenty years when you see her mother. I unbuttoned my suit jacket and took my seat. "I apologize for running a few minutes late. I had a few loose ends to tie up."

"What do you do, son?" Reverend Newsome asked.

"I'm a senior claims rep for an insurance company."

Tangy grabbed my hand and smiled.

"Do you like steak, young man?" he asked.

I swallowed a mouthful of water. "Oh yes, sir."

Reverend Newsome drummed his chubby fingers on the table. "The last time I was here, Tangy took me to this nice steak house. What was the name of the place, Tangela?"

"Tate, it was Stacey's." She held my eyes as I took another sip." You know, where we went for our second date."

I studied her. I knew she was trying to tell me something but couldn't figure it out. "Yes. They have the best steaks. The meat practically falls off the bone. Did you have the T-bone or the sirloin?"

"I had the T-bone," he announced proudly as his bald head wrinkled.

"Next time, may I suggest the premium sirloin? It's the best item on the menu. We'll have to go there on your next visit—my treat."

Reverend Newsome's grin widened. "Well, I don't pass up a free meal."

Throughout the rest of dinner—I couldn't wait for it to end—Tangy's dad continued to share his likes and dislikes about everything, from government to teenage pregnancy to his prediction of which team would win the Super Bowl. Her mother pretended to be interested, while managing to clean her plate. They both had healthy appetites, nothing like Tangy, who barely touched her plate.

Speeding through traffic, I arrived at American Income a few minutes after 10.

Chapter 18
(Tate)

I walked out of the dressing room to receive a standing applause from the other groomsmen all set for the big wedding day. The only person left was the groom to step out the last dressing room to model his tuxedo. Glen, a Kappa man, he stepped out of the dressing room, while the other groomsmen, who just happened to be Kappa men too, surrounded him in the middle of Mitchell's Formal Wear store.

(I was no Kappa man. The Kappa chapter at JU was very small, and I never felt like I was frat material for a number of reasons. Hanging with Glen made me an honorary member, so I had a hell of a time attending all the parties and functions with him.)

We expressed our congrats to Glen. Then the best man, Sherman, asked the big question I was hoping to avoid the entire day. I could have predicted it, since I was the only single man in the group.

"So, uh, Tate . . . man, when you gon' pop the big question and ask that fine and sexy Tangela to be your wife?"

Everyone grew quiet. It seemed as if the other men in the shop wanted to know as well.

"Soon," I said, straightening the sleeves of my jacket.

"How soon?" bad-breath Kyle asked.

My eyes scanned their faces. "I'm shopping for rings now, as we speak." *Why the fuck did I just say that, knowing I did not intend to get married? If I was, I definitely wasn't planning to propose to Tangy.*

All the attention and whoops focused on Glen were now on me. I felt a little out of place. Peer pressure was a bitch. So many times, I tried to go along with all the other guys and do what they were doing. When they brought their wives, I brought Tangy. I guess they assumed we were serious. I hadn't let any of them even think for a moment that I was still messing around with LeQuisha.

Sherman, Raymond, and Kyle was older than me. If you added in the fact I'd only slept with five women, while their numbers probably ran up in the hundreds, I could subtract another ten years in experience. All three of them were ready to retire their playa cards by the time they decided to tie the knot. Sherman had little room to talk, since his count was steady rising, despite the fact he was married.

We changed out of our tuxedos and headed off to the wedding rehearsal, which was followed by dinner in the multi-purpose center adjacent to the church. It was hard to believe any of us guys had the energy for all the events, considering the slamming bachelor party the night before at the Hilton; and I was suffering from a massive hangover with all the tequila shots the night before. Most of us didn't get to sleep until six in the morning, and Glen's father called to remind us to meet him at Mitchell's at eleven this morning. Since it was mid-September, the weather was hot as a steak on a firing barbecue grill. With only three hours of sleep, I wore a white *And 1* athletic shirt and matching shorts with socks and flip-flops on my feet. Tangy stopped by my condo to grab a pair of dress slacks and a silk shirt for me to change into before the dinner. Dressed in a sleeveless misty blue pants suit, Tangy looked as beautiful as Pocahontas, her long, silky hair flowing down her back. I was actually proud to have Tangy in my arms that night. Her ability to articulate and carry on a conversation about social issues was indeed uncanny.

After the rehearsal dinner, I decided to stop by my place to put my plates of food in the refrigerator and hang the tuxedo in my closet. I didn't want to risk my potato salad getting spoiled or my tux getting wrinkled in the back seat of my car.

I was in my bedroom closet hanging up my tuxedo when I heard the front door open and shut. Tangy must have followed me into my condo, even though I asked her to stay in the car since I was only going to be a minute. She burst into the room and violently kissed and groped me in one single motion.

I grabbed her by the head with both of my hands. "Tangy, you need to stop."

"You know you don't want me to stop, Tate. You want this as much as I do. Now, come on and give it to me. Oohhh." She smiled like a naughty girl and lunged toward me.

I quickly turned left to dodge her.

She lost her balance and fell. "Oh, so you want to do it on the floor, right?" She unbuttoned her top and exposed her black sheer bra that showed her darkened nipples.

"What I'm saying is I don't want it at all." I looked down to straighten up my shirt. "Tangy, get your ass up."

"No, Tate." Tangy crawled over and grabbed both my ankles. "I want you to make love to me."

I snatched her hands away from me, nearly pushing her down on the floor again, and walked into the hallway leading to my living room.

"Let's go." My breathing was heavy as my heart beat faster. Practically thought it would burst through my chest. I waited for her by the door.

She came out a few minutes later, pinning her hair back in place. Her lips were all twisted and her face puffed up like she would explode any minute.

I opened the door, and she marched out with an attitude.

On the drive to her apartment, I anxiously gripped the steering wheel. "You don't understand. I'm not trying to go there with you again."

"What do you mean?" Tangy wore a tight-lipped grimace.

"What I mean is—" I licked my dry lips—"You're lucky I'm still talking to your muthafuckin' ass after that stunt you pulled in your dorm room." I waved my free hand frantically. "You got Sharon busting in, practically calling me a rapist, and you just sat there." I took in another deep breath. "I could have found my black ass in jail somewhere, trying to avoid picking up the soap!"

Tangy didn't want to hear it. She sat on the passenger side with tears running down her face, as if she lost her puppy or something. That girl was a trip; I couldn't wait to drop her off.

As soon as I did, I decided to drop by to see LeQuisha, since I promised her I would after the rehearsal dinner. Probably still pissed at me, LeQuisha had a fit when she found out I wasn't taking her to Glen and Terri's wedding. Being in the wedding party, LeQuisha would've had to sit by herself the entire time, since she didn't even know anyone from either family. I knew the excuse was weak, but it was the best I could come up with at the time.

I tried to call before I got to her place, since I'd arrived a few hours earlier than expected. I hooked up my phone to the charger, but by the time the battery had some juice I was already there. I trudged up to the door and knocked hard both times.

Lil' Donny opened the door without asking who it was. I figured he knew I was coming over, so I didn't think anything of it. Every event that followed from that moment was all a blur. All I knew was, out the corner of my eye, I saw some guy on the couch. At first, I thought my eyes were playing tricks on me.

"Where is LeQuisha?" I asked in a callous tone, my eyes scanning the room.

In the kitchen, I spotted LeQuisha frozen in place, her mouth wide open. She held up her hands. "Tate, don't trip."

The dude rose from the couch.

"Who the fuck is this?" My fists opened and closed rapidly.

"Hey, man." He chuckled. "I'm Kenny."

He reached out his hand, and I knocked it away. My blood was boiling.

"Hey, bruh, you need to calm the fuck down, all right." Kenny poked out his chest.

"Naw." I pointed in his face. "You need to get the fuck out—that's what you need to do."

Kenny sucked his teeth. "I'm outta here." He said a few cuss words and headed for the door.

I felt like I'd been disrespected and wanted to re-claim my manhood, so I followed in pursuit.

LeQuisha grabbed my arm, begging me to let him go, and I swung at her.

Next thing I knew, she was lying on the floor with a bloody nose and screaming. Lil' Donny witnessed the whole thing.

"LeQuisha, I'm so sorry. I didn't mean to—"

"Get the fuck out of my house, Tate. I can't believe you hit me." She lunged at me and started throwing her fists in the air. A few of them hit me, one in the mouth.

I grabbed her arms and tried to calm her down.

Lil' Donny said in a very quiet voice, "Mr. Tate, please leave my mama alone, before I have to call the police on you."

And with that, I was out.

Back at my condo, I drank myself into another stupor. I wanted to forget about everything. I got up the next morning suffering miserably from the biggest hangover of my life. If it weren't for Tangy calling me to remind me to pick her up at twelve, I would have missed the wedding myself. *Without a doubt, I would be better off finding another company to work for, because Glen would never forgive my ass.*

Tangy waited for me, dressed in a crème lace

dress with a matching jacket. She clutched her purse under her arm, and waved, when I pulled up in the circular driveway. I expected the cold shoulder from her as she got in, but to my surprise, I received a warm kiss on my cheek.

"You're late. I thought you'd never make it." Tangy smiled. "What time did you get in last night? I tried calling you, but there was no answer." She rubbed her fingers through her hair. "And also, your cell phone was off; I was worried about you."

I shrugged. "Oh, I'm all right. You don't have to worry about me." I looked straight ahead as I drove on Southside Boulevard to the church.

"Well, someone has to worry about you. You were so upset with me last night. I mean, I just kept thinking you were going to do something crazy, and I wouldn't be able to forgive myself." She reached over and rubbed the back of my neck. "I'm glad you're okay and not mad at me anymore."

I nodded. "I'm not mad at you; I want you to understand I'm not playing games with you no more."

"I know you're not. I'm not playing games with you either. I was serious about what I said last night about wanting to make love to you. My methods were all wrong, though; I'm still embarrassed for my behavior." Tangy opened her purse and powdered her face with a white sponge, and her hands shook nervously.

Stopping at the red light on US-1 gave me an opportunity to put Tangy's nerves at ease. I grabbed a hold of her soft hand and kissed it. I brushed my hand onto her face slightly before the light changed to green. On the rest of the way to the church we didn't say a thing while listening to 92.7 FM. That was the way I liked it. I got tired of women talking all the damn time.

I wondered how LeQuisha was doing. I couldn't feel safe until I was sure the police weren't looking for me. *If my mom knew about this, she would have me arrested. Damn the police. I'm more scared of my moms.*

Chapter 19
(Tangy)

Tate didn't say anything else on the ride to the church. *I certainly wasn't going to keep trying to explain why I acted so stupid last night.* It was obvious he wasn't mad anymore, so I let it be.

An-on again off-again pattern developed in our relationship . . . if that's what you want to call it. If I were to define a relationship, it would be two committed people sharing their lives with one another for an indefinite period. What I had with Tate were two people sometimes sharing pieces of their lives together . . . when he didn't have anything better to do. No one could've ever told me things would end up this way, and I know I was to blame for it all.

Tate was steadily growing tired of me. It was evident from the way he talked to me and how he treated me. I really thought that after he got a chance to meet my parents we would begin to spend more time together, but nothing changed. No matter how many attempts I'd made to apologize for our big blow-up, he kept saying he could've ended up in jail because of me. There was some resentment there, and I understood it. More than ready to do something about it, I tried to mend some old wounds. Because of my undying love for him, I was now willing to make a sacrifice.

Tate was, hands down, the best-looking man in the entire wedding party. The groom paled in comparison, and I never seemed happier to have Tate's arms around me during the reception. We danced all night, and I could see other women staring at him and shooting deadly looks over at me like bullets. Ignoring those hoochies was easy, because I was used to it. Tate possessed everything a black woman could ever want in a man. Built, always well-dressed, gorgeous, had a nice car, and a good job. A man like that with no kids was a good catch. *I know Tate's a good man. I'm not ready to let him go. No matter what.*

After the reception, we hung out at my apartment. (Once I became a sophomore, I begged my parents to let me move out of the dorms. I was glad when Sharon's parents agreed too. As spoiled as she was, she even got them to buy furniture.) I loved my new place, and I'd hoped Tate would see me as a mature woman. Sometimes, he treated me like a child and that angered me. I was determined to prove to him I was a woman.

* * *

"Mama, I'm going to church," Tate said. "I know it's been a long time; I'll be on time. I gotta go now, okay. Bye, Mama."

"When am I going to meet your mother, Tate?" I asked him after he hung up his cell phone.

"Not tonight." Tate smirked.

I popped him on the back of his neck—"I know that."

I sat up on the couch next to him while he thumbed through one of my old issues of Ebony. "But when?" I poked out my lips.

"When what?" Tate didn't bother to look up.

"When am I going to meet your mom and dad?" I put my arms around his neck and kissed him.

"I don't know. Soon."

I frowned. That's what he always said.

He looked at me strangely. "What's your problem?"

"I don't have a problem."

"PMS." He went back to reading.

"I'm not on my period," I snapped. "And you want to know what the problem is?" I turned to face him.

"What?—I thought you didn't have one."

I stood and put my hands on my hips. "Well . . . now I do. You know what, Tate?" I put my face closer to his.

"What?" he asked, making eye contact.

"I'm sick of this."

"Sick of what exactly?" Tate sat up straighter.

"Of this relationship. I want more." I paced back and forth. "Tate, we've been seeing each other for a while now. When are we going to become more than that?"

Tate laughed. "More than what?"

I grabbed my head with both hands. "You're not stupid, Tate; you know what I'm trying to say."

He shook his head. "No, I don't—You're bugging out."

I sat down. "No, no, no." I took a deep breath. "I want our relationship to be about more than an occasional date and phone call; I want us to spend more quality time together."

Tate tossed up his hands. "That's it?"

I nodded. "Yeah."

"Okay."

I smiled. "Yeah." That was easier than I thought. I was glad he agreed because I adored this man.

We watched Saturday Night Live together, and as soon as the show ended, Tate headed home.

Sharon dragged in a few minutes later as I nodded off to sleep. "I wanna get married!" she screamed.

"Shut up, girl." I tossed my pillow over in her direction. "I'm trying to sleep."

"That was the most beautifullest wedding I've ever seen. Did you see my sister, Terri? She was so pretty." Sharon collapsed on top of me. My bones felt like they cracked in half.

"Get off me!" I tried to push Sharon off. "Dang, girl, that hurt."

Sharon laughed as her breathing intensified.

"And you're drunk—go to bed." I pushed one last time and Sharon fell to the floor, now laughing harder than ever.

The Avenues Mall's upscale stores made it worth the long drive to get there. Not as crowded as

Regency, I enjoyed its peaceful shopping atmosphere in the afternoons.

"Why are you smiling so big?" Sharon asked.

"It's such a nice day." I held up a Bohemian top. "You think this will go with the jeans I bought?"

Sharon chewed on her nail. "Uh huh. But, I like this one better." She held up a sexy brown top.

I rolled my eyes. "I'm not wearing that shirt— half my bosom will be exposed."

"Shit." She laughed. "You got to show them babies while you can."

My eyes dropped. "My girls aren't big enough."

"That's when the water bra comes in. I'm telling you, it pushes them up naturally. When we go to Victoria's, you need to try on one."

I held up my hands in surrender. "Give me the damn top. You better be right about that bra too." I looked at myself in the dressing room mirror and pushed up my small breasts with my hands. *Maybe the bra would help.* I decided to try it.

I picked out a few more shirts.

Sharon hummed while we stood in line. "Are you in love with Tate?"

I remained silent for a moment. "Yes, I guess so. Why?"

"Just curious." She kept on humming.

"Curious about?" I circled my finger.

"I saw how close you two were at the reception. Seems like you're in love with him."

"Maybe I am."

"I want you to be careful with Tate." Her gaze was intense. "He doesn't have the best reputation with women, you know."

My smile soon faded. "And Paul does?"

Sharon licked her shiny lips. "Paul and I have an understanding."

"Whatever."

I used my almost maxed-out credit card to pay for my purchase. Trying to keep up with Sharon and Terri was breaking me. *When my Daddy gets my bill, he's going to flip out.* "Are you hiring?"

The skinny blonde-haired girl smiled. "We're accepting applications."

"Okay, can I get one?"

"Sure."

I stuffed the application in my bag and met up with Sharon.

"I hope you didn't get mad at what I said."

I flipped my hair. "No, I'm not mad."

Sharon put her arm on my shoulder. "I'm just looking out for you; I don't want to see you get hurt."

Yeah, right. Sometimes I felt a tinge of jealousy from Sharon, and her negative attitude gave me the impression she didn't want to see anyone happy.

Chapter 20
(LeQuisha)

Two little bacon strips and a few spoonfuls of grits—I couldn't believe that was all my children left for me. I took out a small plate to fix my small breakfast. I needed to leave soon if I was gonna make it to church on time. Ever since I got up this morning, I'd been running around trying to help everybody else get ready. Lil' Donny couldn't find any black dress socks; Daneisha couldn't get her hairstyle right; and Dante didn't want to get away from his Spider-Man game on PlayStation 2 long enough to get dressed.

By the time I got my kids dressed and fed, I was down to five minutes. *Guess we'll be late again.* Had to work extra hard to squeeze into my snug velvet black dress. I slipped on stockings and black ankle-cut boots. I piled some foundation on my face and pulled my hair into a ponytail with an add-on piece that ran down the length of my back. Taking one last look in the full-length mirror on the wall after applying ruby red lipstick, I headed downstairs to eat something—my stomach was performing backflips and cartwheels.

"Daneisha!"

"Yes, Mama."

"I need you to get my black purse and zip-up case with my Bible."

"Yes, ma'am."

I heard the heavy footsteps trotting down the hallway. As soon as I saw Daneisha running down the steps in her lavender dress, I announced I was ready to go.

"Would you keep still!" Lil' Donny exclaimed as he struggled to tuck in Dante's white shirt. But Dante kept on wiggling.

"Dante, be still for a second," I demanded. "Now, come on here; we're already late."

We climbed into my car headed for Sunday service at Bethel.

"Mama, your cell phone is ringing," Daniesha said.

"Hand me the phone, baby."

I turned down my Mary, Mary gospel tune before answering. I chimed in with my standard Sunday greeting. "Praise the Lord."

"You're a hard person to get in touch with."

"You think so?" I asked.

"I know so," Kenny said. "I thought you said you was gon' call me back."

I cleared my throat. "You know I only said that because I didn't want to talk to you."

"You don't want to talk to me? You act like I'm the one that bust up in your crib and acted the fool."

"Kenny, I had already asked you to leave way before that. You knew Tate was coming over, and you deliberately stayed knowing my man was going to trip. And for that, I don't have anything else to say to you. So, quit calling me." I bit my bottom lip. "Go to church with your wife . . . just like I'm trying to do with my kids."

"Be like that."

Next thing I heard was the dial tone. Kenny had a lot of nerve hanging up the phone on me. Here, this man done messed up my relationship, while he had a wife. What did I have? Nothing but "Big Jimmy."

Because we were late as usual, we had to make do with the parking lot in the rear of the church. I checked my make-up one last time by glancing in my rearview mirror. There was very little bruising on my face.

After Lil' Donny escorted Daneisha to her junior class, he walked further down the hall to the senior class, and I took Dante down to his. He gave me a big hug and ran inside.

I looked at my watch and realized I had to hurry to catch the choir. Not bothering to waste my time trying to get a seat in the lower section, I headed upstairs toward the balcony. That usually had plenty of seats remaining. Strutting confidently down the aisle with my head held high, I quickly found an abandoned corner and put my purse and Bible down. I joined in with the choir, clapping and singing louder than ever, determined to get in the spirit. During the prayer over the offering, I felt someone stand next to me. I refused to open my eyes, because I prayed for a big financial blessing. A miracle was more like it.

When I opened my eyes, my jaw dropped. Tate

was standing right beside me in a black suit. I couldn't believe it. He had some nerve showing up at my church; he knew I wouldn't make a scene and curse him.

He didn't bother to say anything, just grabbed my hand, and kissed it. I caught nasty glaring eyes from the other single sisters sitting around me in the church. Probably because they never imagined a man of Tate's status would even notice a woman like me, far more hold my hand. I mean he held a tight grip, too!

We sat down and followed the rest of the service, never saying a word, unless cued by Pastor McKissick, Jr. to talk to the person sitting next to me. About halfway through the sermon, Tate placed his arm around me. I snuggled up close. Somehow, I wasn't mad or angry anymore. The entire situation that night had been blown way out of proportion and a part of me wanted to explain that to Tate. Then, another part of me wanted him to feel guilty for hitting me, regardless of what he thought he saw. Any man would go ballistic. Especially, when I knew Tate was coming over later that night too. Of course, I would expect all hell to break loose, but no matter what, no man had permission to hit me. I wasn't having it!

For weeks, Tate called and left messages saying how sorry he was. After listening to all of Tate's pathetic messages, I believed him. It's not like this was the first time Tate had disrespected me. Need I remind you, I caught him with a woman coming out of his condo at one o'clock in the morning! He never bothered to meet my kids; he never took me out; didn't help me out with my bills; and only bought me one gift for an entire year. No, I wasn't ready to let him off that easy.

Since we got back together this last time, Tate and I were getting along very well. He did more things I liked to do, instead of laying up at his house all the time. Even paid bills. I had no complaints. He spent a lot of time getting to know Dante, Daneisha, and especially Lil' Donny until this recent incident.

I didn't think Lil' Donny was going to be excited to see Tate, like Daneisha and Dante would. They were asking me nonstop when Tate was coming over again. I didn't have the heart to tell them never. I would just say, "I'm not sure."

After service, we walked into the children's area.

Dante ran over and grabbed Tate by the knees. "Hey, Tate." Dante's eyes sparkled.

Daneisha hugged Tate by the waist and smiled. "What'cha doing at our church?"

Tate chuckled. "I'm here to see you guys and your mama."

I caught a glimpse of Lil' Donny as he entered the room with his friends. "What's up, dawg?" Lil' Donny nodded as he slapped Tate on the shoulder.

Church members turned around to see what all the excitement was about. A little girl pranced over and tapped Daneisha on the shoulder. "Who is that man y'all hanging on?"

Daneisha grinned. "Girl, this our daddy."

"Well, your daddy is fine."

Daneisha put her hands on her hips. "Hey, don't try and get fresh with my daddy."

The girl waved her hand. "I don't want him; he's too old anyway."

My mouth drew wide open. I couldn't believe it. What was that daughter of mine thinking, telling such a boldfaced lie in the House of the Lord like that?

Tate used the kids to talk me into going over to his parents' house for Sunday dinner. Despite his offer to drive us over to his parent's house, I declined. I figured it would be in my best interest to drive my own car and follow him in his BMW. I must tell you, checking out my man in his nice car was a big turn-on for me; he looked so professional and GQ-fine all at the same time, okay.

Tate parked in the driveway behind his dad's blue Lincoln, and I parked on the street in front of the house. Dante and Daneisha jumped out and ran to grab each one of Tate's arms.

"Man, it's hot." Lil' Donny followed behind me and unbuttoned his silk shirt to fan in some cool air.

"Well, he actually showed up!" Mrs. Gibson yelled. "And he brought company with him. And who is this young handsome boy?" She opened the heavy-metal screen door and held open her arms to give Dante a big hug accompanied by some sugar.

Dante politely wiped his face when he knew she turned away.

I assumed Tate called his parents on his cell phone to let her know we were coming over. I guess Mrs. Gibson was thrilled to have little kids over, since Tate was her only son, and she didn't have any grandchildren of their own yet.

After all of the introductions were over, Daneisha followed me in the kitchen to help Mrs. Gibson, and the boys stayed in the living room with Tate and his father.

Tate was ordered to bring in two folding chairs, so everybody could sit in the dining room to eat. I mean the food was good. I needed to remember to pack a few plates and load up on that macaroni and cheese before I left.

When dinner was over, Daneisha and Dante went out to play in the fenced-in backyard, and Lil' Donny joined Mr. Gibson to watch some game on TV. I finished washing the dishes and putting them up, when Tate came in and swatted me on my behind.

"Hey, now. Don't be messing with me in your mama's house like that."

"I'm just playing with you, LeQuisha. Besides, my folks play like that all the time. Don't you see how they act around each other? Just like they're on a honeymoon." Tate folded his arms and leaned on the counter.

I walked over and leaned beside him. "I noticed. In fact, I'm jealous. Every woman wants to feel special and loved by her *husband*."

We stood in silence. I guess what I said gave him something to think about. *Maybe it would make him feel guilty about the way he treated me in our own relationship.*

"LeQuisha, I really want to say I'm sorry for hitting you. I don't know what got into me. I saw that dude over there, and I just lost it. I've never done anything like that, and I can promise you it will never happen again."

Aawww. He seemed so sincere. I knew he was sorry, but I actually wanted to hear him say it. Not on the phone either, but in person. "I know you're sorry. I'm sorry too. Kenny should have never been there . . . because there's nothing going on between us. And I can promise you he never will interfere in our relationship again. Tate, you're everything to me, and I don't want nobody else but you—I got mad love for you."

I cried as I spoke. I hated that I broke down like

that. When it came to this man, I didn't hold any-thing back. I was willing to do whatever was necessary to make him love me.

Tate held up my face and gently wiped the tears away. "I love you, too."

My heart melted.

He kissed me softly on the lips, and I kissed him back.

"Oh," he said, "and I have something for you."

You know when Tate reached in his pocket and pulled out a small black velvet box I thought I had died and gone to heaven! He opened the box slowly and it revealed a pair of one-karat diamond stud ear-rings.

Huh?

"That's not it." He pulled out a slender black velvet box. "I got you the matching diamond neck-lace to go along with your earrings too."

"Aaawww . . . you didn't have to." Yes, he did. Better had. Naw, let me stop. "Thank you, baby. I love it." I gave him a big, wet kiss on the lips.

"Uhhh hmmm. Excuse me, lovebirds, but I need to sneak in here for a minute and fix me some of this here root beer soda."

"Mr. Gibson, look at what your son bought for me."

Mr. Gibson bent over and looked at my gifts. "I say, my boy did real good. Real good, son." He punched Tate in the shoulder and walked out with his Big-Gulp-size cup.

On the drive home, I felt like I was riding on cloud nine, with my life headed in the right direc-tion. See, it helped when a woman stuck by her man, even when times got rough. It wasn't easy, but Tate was definitely worth all the trouble.

*   *   *

Tate picked us up late as usual. Dante barely had enough time to change into his uniform and get out on the field to join his team. The early morning dew settled on the grass and made my sandals soggy. Lil' Donny and Daneisha found friends to hang out with, leaving me to find a seat.

I squeezed in on the third row of bleachers. Tate spotted me in the crowd and sat beside me.

We cheered loudly as the team ran out on the field. Dante's position was defensive tackle; I flinched every time another player tackled my baby to the ground.

Tate's cell rang. He answered it and walked away from the bleachers.

Goosebumps rose on my arm. *No, he didn't.* "Who was that?" I asked through clenched teeth.

Tate shrugged. "A co-worker. I have to go there as soon as I leave the game."

"On a Saturday?" My voice went up an octave.

"Yes. We're so behind; I'll probably have to gather a team for Sunday too."

"Yeah, right." I said. I had a hard time believing him.

Tate grabbed my hand. "What? You don't believe me?"

"No, I don't."

He waved his cell in front of my face. "Look. He scrolled the numbers on his phone. See, it's Stanley. He's one of my adjusters. If you don't believe me, you can call him."

I waved the phone away. "Forget it."

"Naw, do it . . . since you don't believe me."

I shook my head. "I believe you."

"You do?" Tate kissed me on the neck. "You sure?" He kissed me again.

I pushed him away. "Yes—now would you stop . . . people are looking at us."

Tate turned his head. "I don't give a damn about them nosy-ass people; I just care about you."

When the game ended, we celebrated the team's win at CiCi's. Then Tate dropped us off and went to work. He promised he would return later to take me to a movie.

If I was going to be in relationship with this man, I had to learn to trust him. I made up my mind, no matter how bad I wanted to, I wouldn't sneak in his cell phone again. Or call to check up on him either. I was a grown woman, and I didn't have the time or the energy to keep up with his whereabouts. *Either he's where he is or he isn't. Eventually, he would get tired of running around. He better hope, I don't get sick of him first.*

Chapter 21
(Tangy)

"Tate. Tate." I sighed as I continued to search through the rest of the kitchen cabinets. "Tate."

I hate it when he ignored me. Oooohh. His place wasn't that big, so I knew he heard me. Finally, I opened the drawer by the sink and found a box of candles. Not one candle inside. Now, I was frustrated. "Tate!" I yelled as loud as I could.

I heard his footsteps approaching.

"It's about time. You act is if I live here or something. Like I can do this all by myself. I mean what are you doing back there when I need you here? Didn't you hear me calling you?"

"Oh." Tate shrugged. "Were you calling me? I swear I didn't hear you. I guess I had the television up too loud."

I rolled my eyes. "Yeah, right."

"Believe what you want, Tangy. I'm here, and all you're doing is flapping your lips. Now what do you want?"

"Okay." I threw my hands up. "Okay."

I needed to relax for a moment. Yes, I was nervous, because this was my very first dinner party. Glen and Terri would come in less than an hour, and Sharon and Paul would probably arrive much later.

Why did I decide to do this? I must have been mad to try to pull this off. I studied Oprah's magazine once more on the kitchen counter. When I read the article, it all seemed so easy. Piece of cake. I probably should've started small, like preparing an intimate meal for two, then move up to a dinner party for six people.

When we went over to Glen and Terri's new home, I was so impressed with the table setting decorated with beautiful flowers and candles.

Terri placed an exquisite set of dishes, one of her many expensive wedding gifts, on the dining room table.

I can't wait until Tate and I get married so I can order the most expensive gifts as well. Of course, I'll ask Terri and Sharon to go with me. Terri was so sophisticated and stylish, her opinion mattered to me.

I felt extremely anxious about hosting a dinner party. Just getting Tate to agree was my biggest hurdle. I begged and pleaded with him for over a week. He insisted I was doing it to try to compete with Terri, and he didn't want any part in it.

See, he had a crazy notion I wanted to be like Terri, which couldn't be further from the truth. Terri and I spend a lot more time together. Moreover, shopped together. We also had the same hairdresser and nail tech. There was no jealousy. I loved Terri, and I wanted to celebrate the news of her pregnancy.

Since, I planned it all for three weeks I wanted everything to be perfect. The smell of pot roast and vegetables warming in the oven was a pure delight. Two warm trays of appetizers were cooling off on the counter. A bottle of Chardonnay chilled in a bucket of ice. The salad was in the fridge. Everything was ready to go, and now I had fifteen minutes to slip into my wine-colored sleeveless dress.

I applied more rouge on my cheeks, let my hair fall perfectly past my shoulders. I gave myself one more glance over in the mirror when the doorbell rang. Tate lit the candles, and I dimmed the lights in the living room.

"Hey, girl. You took long enough," Sharon remarked, forcing her way in.

Damn, I wanted Terri to arrive first, so we could have some time to talk privately. It's okay. *Calm down. Everything's going to work out fine. Just keep your cool, Tangy.*

"Hey, I like this cozy set-up." Sharon nodded. "This don't even look like the same place."

"Thank you. Why don't you and Paul have a seat on the couch, and wait for Glen and Terri to get here."

"Uh huh. I'm hungry. Are those stuffed mushrooms over on that tray?" Sharon picked up three, and shoved them in her mouth. "Oh, these are good. I'm so hungry."

When she reached for more, I snatched the tray. "That's enough. What about everybody else?"

"Screw them." Sharon laughed. "Look at them

over there on the couch talking. They're not think-ing about this food."

"Well, let's wait until everyone else gets here, okay. Glen and Terri should be here any minute." I looked over at the clock on the microwave. *Where was Terri? She should have been here ten minutes ago.* I was be-ginning to think they weren't going to show up, when I heard the doorbell.

I made a mad dash to the door, straightened my top and hair, and then swung open the door. "Hi. Welcome Glen and Terri."

"What's up, Tangy?" Glen said as he pushed past me.

I rolled my eyes.

Terri handed me a bottle of wine and a small wrapped gift in her hand. "Excuse him." Terri laughed. "He needs to get to a bathroom right away."

"Oh. Of course." I hugged Terri and grabbed her arm. "Oh, thank you for the gift. Come on in, mom-to-be. I hope you like everything."

We walked arm-in-arm. Terri looked around but said nothing. She spoke to Tate and Paul, before making her way to the kitchen, where Sharon was eating more appetizers. Sharon offered the tray to her sister.

"These are really good, Tangy," Terri said.

"I'm glad you like them."

"Hey, what about us men over here? We need to eat, too!" Glen shouted.

We laughed, while I picked up the second tray, and like the perfect host, offered it to each guest.

The dinner was a big hit. It didn't seem to mat-ter that the roast tasted bland, because more than half of it was gone. Terri helped me clear the table for dessert and told me I put together a nice table setting. I was more than pleased to receive the compliment.

I convinced Tate to help me serve the chocolate cake I ordered from Publix. I arranged thin slices on a tray. Tate placed the small plates in front of our guests seated at the table having a wonderful conversation in the dining area.

After dinner ended, Tate helped me bring in two chairs in the living room so everyone could have a seat. I went back in the kitchen and took out the last bottle of Chardonnay then I eased around the living room, filling empty glasses.

"Hey, you've been running around all evening. Have a seat." Tate grabbed me on the hips and sat me down on his lap.

I reached over and kissed him softly on the lips. Now, I was more than ready for this party to be over.

An hour later, we said our last good-byes to Sharon and Paul. As soon as Tate closed the door, I embraced him tightly.

"We did it!" I kissed him and buried my head in his muscular chest. "Thank you, Tate, for all your help. I couldn't have pulled this off without you. Do you forgive me?"

"Forgive you for what?"

"For yelling and bossing you around in your own place." I rubbed my hands together. "I was a little nervous and wanted everything to be perfect. Anyway, I'm sorry."

"Don't worry about it." He put his hand on my hip. "So . . . are you ready to go home?"

"Not yet. I want to finish cleaning up. There are a few dishes in here and some in the sink that need to be washed."

"I can do the dishes." Tate started picking up dishes off the table. "It's just a few plates and glasses. I want to get you home before it gets too late. I don't know why you turned down Sharon's offer for a ride."

"Well, it wouldn't be right for the hostess to leave the host stuck with the cleaning." I scratched my head. "Let me go change real quick, and then I'll be out to help you."

"Okay."

I dashed in the bathroom and changed in all but five minutes. "I hope you don't mind, but I decided to slip into something a little nicer."

"What are you talking about?" Tate looked up from the kitchen sink and locked eyes with mine. I could tell by his facial expression, he was surprised to see me standing in a black sexy teddy.

"Do you like it?" I asked seductively.

"Yes, I like it." Tate dried his hands and came over. "I like it a lot." He kissed me for what seemed like an eternity. "Are you sure you want to do this?"

I placed my hands on his rippled chest. "Yes. Absolutely."

"Thank goodness. No line outside." I tossed my full head of hair off my shoulder.

"Right." Sharon whipped her Nissan Sentra in the nearest parking space. "We made it before the lunch crowd." She turned off the ignition, but left Beyonce's "Me, Myself, and I" playing.

I closed my eyes as I sang along with Beyonce's

raspy voice. Until last night, I'd had this unrelenting fear of being alone all by myself. Sharing a night of passion with the man I loved changed everything. Tate reassured me we would be together forever, and I had no reason not to believe him. My stomach tingled inside just thinking about the beautiful love exchange. As the song ended, Sharon and I entered Red Lobster.

Sharon eyed the menu. "So what are you having today?"

"This shrimp salad sounds good."

Sharon hissed.

"What was that for?" I stuck out my tongue.

"A salad?" Sharon cocked her head to one side. "What? Are you on a diet now? You already lost your virginity; now you want to lose weight?"

I put the menu down. "What do you suggest I eat?" I crossed my arms.

Sharon shrugged. "I don't know . . . some meat for starters."

"Okay, you pick something, and I'll eat it then."

Sharon bit her lip as she ran her fingers along the lunch specials. "How about the seafood with pasta?"

"Okay. You're treating, right?" I batted my eyes.

Sharon rolled her eyes. "I guess so."

I smiled. "Good."

As we placed our orders, I couldn't help noticing a group of ghetto chicks sitting directly at a table across from our booth. I frowned. "Oooh. They're so loud."

Sharon leaned in closer. "Jacksonville's finest."

"You said it." I took a sip of Diet Coke.

Sharon bored me with details of her night with Paul, until the waitress came back and placed our plates in front of us. With all of her talking, I didn't get a chance to tell her anything. Good thing, since I didn't want her to know all my business. I couldn't understand how she ended up sleeping with a guy she'd only known for a short time.

"I'm really glad I listened to you." I finished off my last bite of pasta with shrimp. "This pasta was delicious."

"I can tell. I was wondering if you were going to come up for air." Sharon chewed on a cheddar biscuit.

"Girl, Tate bought me this necklace and the earrings to match!"

The ghetto-fabulous woman yelled from the table across from us.

"Everybody ain't able!" The other two women screamed.

I stared blankly in Sharon's direction as she continued to chew on her biscuit.

I whispered. "You heard that?"

"Uh huh." Sharon took a sip of Coke.

"You don't think she's talking about my man?" I asked incredulously.

Sharon shook her head. "No. Are you crazy? Tate wouldn't do that."

I twisted my lips. "Somehow, I'm having a hard time believing you."

"What are you talking about?" Sharon asked.

I sat straight up in my chair. "I'm talking about you. You look nervous. I've never seen you like this before."

Sharon refused to make eye contact. "I don't know what you're talking about."

"Yes, ladies. The next time we get together, I'ma be tellin' y'all I'ma be the next Mrs. Gibson."

Oh my God! I stood up from my chair and ran out quickly. I grabbed my chest. Felt like I was having a heart attack. Maybe I was hearing things. I paced back and forth in front of the restaurant.

Sharon came out a few minutes later carrying a take-out box in her hand. "You all right?" She put her free arm around my neck.

"No." I nodded as my face wrinkled up into a big hard cry. "I can't believe he did this to me."

In the back of my mind, I hoped this to be a simple misunderstanding. *As soon I talk to Tate, this would clear up. I had to be overreacting.*

"I know. I know." Sharon hugged me. "This is real fucked up." After a long embrace, Sharon coaxed me into the car. "Don't worry about a thing, Tan." Sharon clutched the steering wheel tightly. "We're going to straighten this out." She reached for her cell phone and dialed.

I pulled my knees in closer and wrapped my arms around them.

"What'cha doing?" Sharon asked. "Yeah. She's here with me. I got a question for you. Who was that girl you said Tate was messing with before Tangy?"

I ran my hands through my hair. For some reason, I really wanted to believe this was not happening. How totally ironic—the man I gave my virginity to cheating on me with some nasty hoochie. *I could've stayed with Vince if I wanted to deal with this kind of drama.*

"Yep. That sounds like her. Tate ain't shit!" Sharon screamed. "She slept with him last night. That's why I'm so fucking angry! I had better not see Tate. That's all I have to say." She lit a cigarette.

I nodded off. My eyes pried open when I felt the

car come to a sudden stop. Realizing where I was, I knew it for sure when Terri tapped on the window.

Terri opened the door. "Are you okay, honey?" Her eyes looked sorrowful.

"I don't know." I responded as I slowly got out. My knees buckled beneath me as Glen carried me inside their home.

"You really didn't have to do this." I shook my head. Feeling a little disoriented, I closed my eyes.

"Tan, wake up."

I turned over on my side. "I'm up."

"Tate's downstairs."

"What's he doing here?"

"Glen called him." Sharon sat down on the bed. "Told him he needed to go over some paperwork."

"You got Glen involved? That's his best friend."

"And?" Sharon threw her hand up in the air. "Look, Tan. Glen wanted to do it. Actually, he was trying to clear his boy's name, but Tate's so stupid, he admitted everything."

"He did?" My stomach tingled nervously. "What did he say?"

"That he's been messing with LeQuisha, 'cause you were playing games and not giving him any ass."

I grabbed my stomach and shook my head back and forth.

"Don't cry, Tan. I took care of him for you. I cursed his ass out." Sharon laughed. "Girl, he had the nerve to try and defend himself."

"Really?"

"Yes." Sharon put her hand on mine. "Come down and give him a piece of your mind; you need to let him have it."

I rubbed my dry eyes. "No, I can't. I don't want to see him."

"You sure?" Sharon raised her eyebrows in disbelief.

I nodded. "Yeah, I'm sure." I lay back down and closed my eyes as I fought back more tears.

"Okay." Sharon rubbed my arm.

When Sharon closed the door, I knew the relationship was over. *Is this how it happened? One minute you feel like you're on a natural high and life couldn't get any better. Then lunch with a friend could absolutely end it all.* I wish I'd never gone to Red Lobster. It would've been better not to know at all. Now, it was too late. *Or was it?*

Not even caring what I looked like, I jumped out of the bed and ran downstairs as fast as I could. Hearing the loud voices from the kitchen, I stormed in.

Tate stood there waving his keys in the air.

"Tate, can I talk to you for a minute?" I asked as I tried to finger comb my hair.

"I don't know, Tangy." Tate put his hand on his side and pointed with his free hand. "Ask your mob squad first."

I tried to pull him by the arm, but he snatched away.

"Don't put your hands on me, okay." Tate held a tight-lipped grimace.

I felt a sudden yank in my stomach.

"Tate, this isn't between you and them; it's about you and me." I struggled to clear my sore throat. "If you don't want to talk to me now, call me later."

"Fine." Tate's voice was stiff. He fumbled with his keys as he made a quick exit.

My heart stopped beating for one full second. It was over. I knew this to be the final time I would see or ever speak to him. I should've been relieved, but inside I felt like a part of me shriveled up and withered away.

"Sharon, I'm ready to go home." My lips slowly curled into a smile.

"I'll go get my stuff."

Chapter 22
(Tate)

After the hour-long evacuation drill, my body ached all over, and the bed in the cabin called my name offering some sense of relief. LeQuisha grabbed both lifejackets and placed them back in the closet.

"What do you want to do first?" She asked.

I kissed her on the shoulder blade. "Go to bed."

"Sounds good to me."

I untied the back of her top and unfastened her bra. Her full breasts burst freely. I massaged circles around each breast and unbuttoned my shirt. The captain's voice announced the Carnival Cruise Line was now sailing the Atlantic Ocean.

"We're sailing." LeQuisha panted and kicked up her right leg.

I pulled her leg closer and plunged a little deeper. "Yeah, and I'm about to come."

LeQuisha's body trembled beneath mine. Her loud squeal let me know she reached her climax.

Creamy juices flowed all over my dick as I worked harder. I slowed down my pace as my body contracted then pulsated. I wiped the sweat from my forehead. "Damn, girl," I said, trying to catch my breath. "It was good, wasn't it?" LeQuisha asked, still gasping for air. She pulled the sheet over her wet body. "I'm gonna have to look for some clean sheets; we can't sleep on these tonight."

I softly kissed her lobe. "We set this cruise off on the right start; you wanted it to be romantic."

"I know. I know." LeQuisha pinched my nipple. "I've never been on a cruise before. I can't wait to see the Bahamas."

"You'll like it." I massaged my penis as it stiffened.

A knock sounded at the door.

"Get the door, Tate."

"I can't open the door like this."

LeQuisha's eyes dropped down to see my hardness. "Okay." She grabbed a robe and gently cracked the door open.

It was our room attendant making a formal introduction. A young Asian guy. I turned over on my side to admire the ocean view from the bed. *Just the break I needed from work.* Realizing I would never close a decent amount of files to earn a vacation, I gave up and planned a three-day weekend trip for two.

LeQuisha went ballistic when I invited her, and I even went so far to whisk her off on a shopping spree a week before we left. Even though her taste in clothing and hair styles changed, I wanted to make sure she didn't embarrass me by wearing something funky and dying her hair blue, or something worse.

LeQuisha shut the door. She stripped off her white terry cloth robe, revealing the most supple pair of breasts a man would kill to squeeze. "Now, let's take care of your jimmy. I'm a little hungry." She licked her lips.

I sat up against the wall as she angrily sucked on my manhood. *A brotha could get used to this.*

Early the next morning we started on our tour of Freeport.

"You're not listening to a word she's saying!" LeQuisha asked.

"Yeah, I am. But I keep thinking about last night and what's to come when we get back to the ship."

LeQuisha flashed a wicked smile. "Wait and see."

The tour bus came to a stop as the tour guide announced we would be leaving the street market in thirty minutes. As soon as I stood up, I felt my legs give a little. I grabbed the seat in front of me to steady my balance.

"You all right?" LeQuisha asked in a puzzled tone.

"Uh huh." I nodded.

"Good." LeQuisha wrapped her arms around my waist. "I need you to stay healthy for tonight."

"Me too," I chuckled.

Standing in line for cold fruit smoothies, I removed my dark sunglasses to admire the bright bold colors of the stands and surrounding buildings. After taking a sip of my piña colada, LeQuisha dragged me over to a stand to try on straw hats. With my digital camera, I snapped a few shots of her posing in various hats. Purchasing a few jewelry items and two hats for LeQuisha, I grabbed a few T-shirts for my mom and dad. Ten minutes later, we boarded the bus and headed back to the ship.

Later that night, we enjoyed the warm air on the deck for the midnight buffet. I fixed two plates of grilled burgers, fries, and beans and joined her at the table.

"I love this place!" LeQuisha rocked her shoulders and arms to the rhythm of the live band playing island music. "I can't believe we have to go home in two days."

"Don't you want to see your kids?" I shoved a handful of fries in my mouth.

LeQuisha frowned. "Of course. Tate, I'm having a good time; I just don't want it to end."

I leaned in closer, feeling the warmness of her breath. "It's not over yet."

"True." LeQuisha sat back and crossed her arms. The strong winds lifted her small braids in the air. "Anyway, things must be getting pretty serious if we're taking romantic trips together."

I finished chewing my burger. Any man at this point knew what this girl was hinting at. Desperation began to take over. *Relax. Breathe. Just a trap; Don't fall for it.* "What do you mean?"

"Nothing."

"I mean—"

Damn!

—"Tate, we've been together off and on for almost two years now. Don't you want to take things further than this?" LeQuisha gestured with her hands. "Don't you want to settle down with one woman and get married?"

I choked on my last bite. Drinking a couple sips of fruit punch helped clear my throat. "LeQuisha, why did you have to fuck up a perfectly good day with some talk about marriage?"

She turned up her nose. "Dang, Tate, I asked you a simple question. Look, I ain't getting any younger, and I needs to know. I just turned thirty-two, okay. Sorry if you feel like I jacked up your day." She abruptly stood up from the table and left.

I sighed.

When I arrived back at my room, LeQuisha lay soundly asleep. I undressed and slipped in the bed beside her. Knowing this wasn't the last I would hear of this marriage talk, I decided to face it head on.

"LeQuisha," I said, giving her a slight nudge.

"Hmm." She rested her arm under her head.

"Wake up," I whispered.

"For what?"

"'Cause we still have one day left of our cruise, and I don't want you to be mad at me."

LeQuisha shook her head. "I'm not gonna be mad; I'm over it."

"Okay . . . if you say so." I turned over on my side.

"I'm just tired, Tate."

"I know. So go back to sleep."

"No—I mean tired in general." She leaned forward. "Do you know how hard it is to be a single parent? You couldn't possibly know. Not a day goes by that I'm not thinking about how my bills are going to be paid. Or how I'ma tell Donny for the hundredth time that I can't afford to buy him the new T-Macs. Or how I can make fifty dollars worth of groceries last for three weeks." She took a deep sigh. "It's just hard, ya know? And I see you, your black ass don't have a care in the damn world. All I'm saying is . . . I need some help. If you suppose to be my man, then you should want to help me."

"I do help you. I give you money." I raised my voice. "Don't I pick up the kids when you ask?"

"I know, and I appreciate everything you do. Really I do. All I'm saying is . . . I want to know you'll always be there for my kids and me. I want to get married, and if you don't want that, then I'm wasting my time with you." LeQuisha turned away and drifted off to sleep.

I scratched my shoulder while my eyes bugged out—this couldn't be the same woman who would leave her kids in the middle of the night to sleep with me. *Damn! I must be losing my touch.* First, Carmela dropped my ass for Don Juan. Then Tangy bought me a one-way ticket to hell. Now, LeQuisha was sitting here telling me she's wasting her time with me. This was some heavy shit!

Who was I fooling? I'd been trying to mess with all these women, so I could be more like Glen and all them other fools. Now, they're married with children. Even Glen, the playa of all playas, was expecting. *LeQuisha was right—If I wasn't interested in taking this relationship further, then I needed to let her go. Let her find a man to take on a ready-made family. She was a good woman, and she definitely deserved it. Can I find another woman with an ass like LeQuisha? A woman that's willing to give it to me whenever and however I liked it. Can cook. A good mother. Worked hard. Smart.*

The more I thought of it, the more I realized she was just like my moms. I couldn't think of a woman more like Myra Gibson. Did I need to spend the next ten years of my life, only to realize I passed on the right woman? *What about her kids? They're great kids.* I actually liked them. Dante was my lil' partner. He looked up to me. I needed to think hard on this.

The next day, LeQuisha's attitude was pleasant, and we finished off our cruise on a good note. When I arrived back at the office Monday morning, Glen didn't waste anytime busting my chops about her. If I didn't know any better, I would have thought ol' boy was just jealous.

"Hey, all I'm saying is . . . if that's what you want, that's your choice." Glen pointed toward his chest. "But as for me—"

"You chose the snotty, bitchy, think-she's-better-than-everyone-else type." I sat up straighter in my chair. "Not that I want to insult your wife, but I'm tired of you trash-talking LeQuisha. No matter what you think, LeQuisha is a good woman. You don't even know her." He based his opinion solely on the word of Sherman, a man known many times for stretching the truth. Glen held up his hands in surrender. "Touché. Oh, before I leave, Mr. Island man might want to call Tangy."

"I have nothing else to say to her." I raised my pen and jotted down a few notes.

Glen cleared his throat. "You might have more to say than you think. Anyway, the girl's been burning up my phone at home, so do me this favor, okay."

He left. I knew he was pissed.

I spent the entire morning checking e-mails and voice mail. It felt good to be back at work, especially after a short break of rest, peace, and backbreaking sex. Just thinking about LeQuisha's watermelons flopping across her chest made my dick hard. I massaged Big John. I tried my best to wrap up my paperwork, so I could pay my woman a visit.

Damn. *My woman?* Whether I wanted to admit it

or not, LeQuisha gave it to a brotha on the regular. She satisfied me in a way that I really didn't need anyone else but her.

I shut my computer down and tossed a few files in my briefcase to take home and review later that night. I looked down at my watch. Nine. *Not bad.* As I strolled out my office with my suit jacket in arm, I whipped out my cell and dialed Tangy's number.

"Hello."

"Hey. Glen told me to call you. What's up?"

"What do you mean 'what's up'?" Tangy asked in a stank voice I only heard used by other women, never by her. "I've been trying to call you for the past week."

"What about?"

"Not that I want your ass . . . so, don't flatter yourself—I'm pregnant."

I stopped dead in my tracks. Immediately, my mind reversed back to the night I messed with her. Doing the math, it was possible I might be in the clear.

Stupid question, but I had to ask, "From who?"

Tangy sucked her teeth. "Look, I don't know about the other ghetto whores you sleep with, but I've only had sex one time and with one person. And you know the answer to that."

I swallowed hard. "What do you want from me, Tangy?"

"Not a damn thing! I thought you should know."

"Would you calm the fuck down and let somebody talk to your ass." I opened the door to my BMW and slid in my seat. Not wanting to miss her response, I hesitated to start the engine.

She sighed. "Okay."

"Regardless of how things went down between

the two of us, I have no intention of leaving you alone in this situation. Just tell me what you want me to do."

"I don't know what I'm gonna do yet. When I decide, then I'll let you know what I need from you."

Click.

I massaged my temples, trying to relieve the migraine that began to settle in. Knowing I never should have slept with that girl, I was feeling the repercussions of my actions. I felt like shit for having taken advantage of Tangy. I didn't even want to do it at first. Then I used my dick as my brain and hit it. Careful to use a condom the first time, I didn't even bother to put on one the second and third times.

I decided to skip the trip over to LeQuisha's and sped home to my condo. Needing to lay in my own bed, I stayed up half the night thinking about it. More than anything, I wanted Tangy to have an abortion.

It was dark. A light shone down on a young toddler. I recognized him, because he resembled me. I moved closer and tried to touch him. He ran away. I chased him out of the tunnel onto a green lawn. His mother picked him up and kissed him. Another man approached and wrapped his arms around both of them. He put the child down and kissed the mother. The child chased his ball out onto the street. A truck approached in the same direction as the boy. I ran toward him yelling and screaming. The couple was engaged in their kiss. As I stepped on the sidewalk, the truck's horn blew and the boy looked frightened.

I sat straight up in my bed in a cold sweat. Glancing over at my clock, I realized I had two more hours of sleep before I needed to get ready for work.

* * *

The best way for me to handle this situation was to meet with Tangy right away. *No sense in putting things off until later.* Turning down the volume of the radio, I cruised barely at forty-five miles per hour along Merrill Road. Needing to clear my head from a hectic day at work, I didn't look forward to seeing my future baby's mama. Just the mere thought made me cringe.

There was a time when I wanted that, but the feeling only lasted for a few months. It didn't take long for me to realize a few screws were loose in Tangy's head. Her spoiled, wanna-be-like-Terri attitude got on my last nerve. Sometimes, I couldn't stand to be around her.

Why did I do it? I banged my head on my steering wheel as I sat in the parking lot facing Tangy's apartment building. *If only I had a chance to do it over again.*

I felt God's hand on my left shoulder urging me to do the right thing. Having gathered my thoughts together, I knew I would have to marry the crazy bitch if she decided to keep the baby. A little fear crept in as I wondered about the reaction of my parents once they learned the news of my impending fatherhood. Then there was Reverend and Mrs. Newsome. The good reverend already couldn't stand my black ass—this would give him the perfect excuse to try to kill me.

I knocked on the door for the second time. Sharon swung it open with pink rollers in her hair, resembling a she-devil.

"Uhhh mmmm." Sharon frowned, causing her eyebrows to meet. "What'cha got to say for yourself now?" She opened the door barely wide enough for me to squeeze through.

I folded my arms and spread my legs apart. "Where's Tangy?"

Sharon cocked her head to one side. "In the bathroom," she snapped.

A few seconds later Tangy swung the door open and plopped down on the plush couch. Aside from her hair tossed up in a wild mess, she looked quite normal.

"You want me to stay here with you, Tan?" Sharon asked.

"That's okay. I'll be fine."

"All right. Call my cell if you need me." Sharon rolled her eyes in my direction.

"What the hell would she need you for?" I clenched my teeth tightly.

"Damn dirty dog," she mumbled under her breath and left.

"It's nice to see you too," I said.

Tangy smirked.

"Well, you wanted to talk. Here I am."

"Yeah." Tangy folded one leg on the couch. "I'm going to keep this short—I've decided to keep the baby."

I nodded but remained silent.

"And, if you want to have a role in your child's life, it's completely up to you." Tangy rubbed her head. "If not, then that's your choice."

I scratched my goatee. "I respect your decision."

"And?" Her eyes searched for more.

"And if you want to get married, that's cool with me; I really don't want my son, or daughter to be born out of wedlock."

Tangy cast her eyes downward. "I'll have to

think about it. It would help smooth things over with my father if he knew we were being responsible about this. I just don't know how that would work out."

"What do you mean?"

"Tate, I caught you cheating on me." Tangy raised her hands in the air. "I can't ignore that. What are you going to do about her?"

"It's over," I stated simply.

Tangy raised her eyebrow. "Does she know that?"

"Not yet." I rested my elbow on my leg. "But, I'll tell her soon."

"How soon?"

"Tonight."

"Well, after you talk to her, then *I* want to talk to her." Tangy shook her head.

"For what?"

"If we're talking about getting married, then we need to do this right. Tate, I don't have time for no shit. I'm having a baby, and I don't need any added stress." She leaned forward. "If you can't be committed to me, then I don't want your sorry hand in marriage."

I nodded. "Okay."

Chapter 23
(Tate)

Dropping the news to my parents wasn't as bad as I thought it would be. I know my mom almost fell through her seat when I announced my plans to marry. It didn't help that I had never even given my folks the opportunity to meet Tangy. As far as they knew, LeQuisha and I were serious. I didn't give them any reason to think otherwise, since LeQuisha and I joined them for Sunday dinner after church on many occasions. Moms even began to think of LeQuisha's kids as the grandchildren she never had.

When my father asked to speak to me privately, I thought I would shit in my pants. Even my dad found a way to let me know although he was proud of me for doing the right thing, that if my heart wasn't in it, then I should reconsider.

* * *

After I dropped Tangy off, I dreaded the drive over to see LeQuisha. I called earlier to let her know I had something serious to discuss. In the back of my mind, I knew LeQuisha was hoping I would propose marriage. Believe me, I really thought about it long and hard. That was before I knew I had a child on the way. Now, I needed to step up and be a man. *How could I do that by abandoning the mother of my child?* No way in hell was I going to let another man raise my son or daughter. I had to put my personal feelings aside and do the right thing.

Dante practically knocked me down when I came in using my key to LeQuisha's townhouse. "How ya' doin', lil' man?" I rubbed his head.

"Good," Dante said with a huge dimpled smile. "Come see what level I'm on now." He grabbed my hand and pulled me into his bedroom.

A few minutes later, LeQuisha stuck her head in. "Hey, baby." She greeted me with a peck. Her lips felt so luscious against mine. I sure would miss them.

I put my arm around her waist. "Dante, I need to go talk to your mother for a little bit."

"All right. But come back and play with me before Mama says I have to go to bed." He moved rhythmically with the PlayStation 2 controller.

"Sure thing."

LeQuisha escorted me back to her room. She could barely contain her smile. As I entered, I could smell the fragrance of vanilla-scented candles. Alicia Keys' CD played on her stereo system.

LeQuisha disrobed, revealing a sexy red teddy.

I scratched the back of my neck. "Don't you think we should wait until the kids are asleep to get busy?"

She threw back her head and giggled. I could

tell by her movements that she was a little bit tipsy. Looking on her nightstand, I noticed a bottle of champagne and two tall glasses.

"So what did you have to talk to me about?" LeQuisha grabbed my hands and sat me down next to her on the bed.

"I . . . well . . . hold on for a minute." I got up, turned off the music, and blew out the candles.

LeQuisha frowned. "Tate. Why are you spoiling the mood?" She folded her arms.

"Because what I have to say is serious. And it's not about marriage—I know that's what you thought."

LeQuisha tried to look dumbfounded. "What? Tate, I wasn't expecting—"

"Yes, you were. I know you." I took a deep breath. "There's something I need to tell you. And after I tell you, I don't think you're going to want to see me again."

"Oh." LeQuisha quickly put on her robe and stood in front of me. "What is it?"

"I will, once you sit back down." It made me feel a tiny bit nervous having her stand over me—she could land a sucker punch, and I wouldn't even see it coming.

"Naw. Tell me while I'm standing." Her face blew up. "That way I'm ready to kick your ass for breaking my heart, you bastard!"

There was no easy way to say it. I cleared my throat. "I cheated on you since we've been back together—"

LeQuisha slapped my left cheek.

I held it and continued—"And now she's pregnant."

The next thing I felt was a punch in the face.

I forcefully grabbed both of her wrists while she struggled to get free from my grip.

"Get the fuck out of my house!" She screamed. "I hate you. I hate you. Get out!"

"Shhhh," I whispered calmly in her ear. "You don't want to scare the kids."

"You don't give a damn about me or my kids. Let go of me now, or I'm going to scream."

"Okay, I'ma let you go. Just hear me out . . . please."

LeQuisha nodded. "Let me go first."

I freed her arms, and she sat calmly on her bed. "How could you do this and not protect yourself . . . not protect me? I can't believe I trusted you, Tate. I believed in you—in us." LeQuisha sobbed intensely.

I tried to put my arm around her to comfort her.

She immediately scooted away from me. "Don't you fuckin' touch me!"

A knock came at the door. "Mama, you okay?" It was Lil' Donny.

LeQuisha wiped her face and opened the door partway. "Mama's fine, baby. Go back and finish your homework." As she shut the door she said to me, "I know you're not going to marry her."

I shook my head. Feeling a single tear roll down my face, I buried my head shamefully in my hands. All this time I thought playing women was all a game. At that moment, I realized how dangerous the game was.

I got off easy, free from an STD or even AIDS, just a baby. At least a baby couldn't kill me. A minute ago, I thought LeQuisha damn sure would. Two women's lives would forever be changed because of my stupid actions.

"Tate, do you love me?" LeQuisha asked.

"Yes, I do."

She moved closer and stroked my hair. "Then don't do it. You don't have to marry that girl. You can still be a father to your child."

I took in a deep breath. "I can't do that."

"Why not? You don't love her; you love me. Please, don't do this." LeQuisha's voice sounded hoarse.

I held her chin. "I love you. But—"

"But nothing." LeQuisha's eyes welled up with more tears. "I will help you get through this; I'll stand by you."

I shook my head. "I can't ask you to do that."

LeQuisha wrapped her arms around me tightly and cried harder. I held her. What more could I do?

The next couple of weeks seemed to drag on endlessly. Buried in piles of paperwork, my once beloved job now seemed to hold me captive as a prisoner, and I longed for the good old days when I felt in control of my life. With a marriage to a woman I didn't love, a baby on the way, and my sinking career, my ambition dried up along the banks of the St. John's River I passed on my way to American Income every morning.

Gladys greeted me with a dozen messages from complaining customers whose claims went unanswered for months. I spent the first three hours of the morning getting cursed out. One desperate man threatened to walk in and blow up the building if he didn't receive a check by the end of the week. My hands were tied.

For the review meeting, I decided to serve catered lunch for my team. At least I could cheer them up for the first half-hour. Once again, I dropped the bomb that our salary budget had been cut once more, leaving me without the option to replace the four adjusters that quit.

"I came up with an idea to help free our workload," I said, chewing on a buttered biscuit. "Dan agreed to our team taking on interns from the local colleges."

Stanley laughed. "Great. Now we can overwork desperate college students for free!"

I held up one finger. "We're going to pay them. Don't be so negative. What we're selling is real hands-on experience."

"How much are we paying?" Cheryl asked. "And how many do we get?"

"Gladys is working on the paperwork to submit to North Florida and JU, as we speak. I'm thinking we can round up a team of ten to fifteen; that way, every adjuster will have at least one intern. I'll take one, and we can float the remaining six." Luckily, everyone agreed it was a good idea, and the meeting ended on a positive note. Lunch provided by Copeland's didn't hurt either.

As I strutted confidently back to my office, Gladys waved for my attention. She placed her hand over her headset. "I've got Tangela on Line 1."

I faked a smile. "Got it." I put her on speakerphone. "Hey, Tangy."

"I hope I didn't interrupt your meeting."

"No, it's over. What's up?" I read over the intern ads Gladys placed on my desk.

"Well, it's about my meeting with the caterer tomorrow. Are you going to be able to make it?"

"No. I told you I made plans with Glen and the guys. I haven't seen them in weeks."

Tangy sighed. "I can't believe you're doing this to me. Why do I have to make all the decisions by myself?"

"You're not; I already made my choices on the menu. What difference does it make whether I'm there or not?"

"Well . . . for support. I don't want to do this alone. Why can't you just re-schedule with the guys and make me a priority for once?"

The vein in my head swelled. "You know I've been working like a dog lately. Finally, I get a chance to relax and enjoy the company of my friends, who I haven't seen in months, and you have a problem."

Why do I have to continue going through this with her? Doesn't she understand I don't give a damn about a wedding? Dresses, flowers, food, I could care less about. All I wanted to do was show the fuck up and the preacher to say, "Bam—you're married. The life you once had is officially over!"

Tangy cleared her throat. "Okay. Maybe I'm being unreasonable. Promise me you'll come to the next whatever it is."

I leaned back in my chair. "Promise." Having more important things to worry about, I signed off on the ad.

Just then the alarm sounded on my cell phone. *Damn!* I dialed LeQuisha's phone number, and her voice mail picked up.

"Hey, LeQuisha. It's Tate." I took a deep breath. "I'm running a little late. I'll be there in a few."

Chapter 24
(Tangy)

"This is supposed to be the happiest time of my life," I whined.

"I don't know who told you that big fat lie." Sharon smirked. Her cheerful attitude was beginning to annoy the hell out of me.

"Happiness is an emotion that comes and goes," Mama added. "Now if you want peace of mind, then you're going to have to ask the Lord to give you that."

"Amen." Sharon nodded.

Since I never joined a church, Tate and I decided to hold the wedding at Calvary Baptist Church. His family had been members for a number of years. Mama came down to help plan my last-minute wedding, set to take place less than two months after our engagement on June 10th.

Sitting in the church's dark and drafty reception

hall almost made me ill. All these years, I'd imagined myself getting married at my father's church, New Missionary Baptist Church, which was triple the size of Calvary. All two thousand members along with my friends who I grew up with would attend. With Daddy being a well-respected pastor in the community, city officials would have been present, no doubt, to witness Pastor Newsome's only daughter get married in the most beautiful princess gown ever made.

Somehow, my fairytale wedding was shattered when Daddy learned of my sudden engagement to Tate. Not sharing in my fondness or my love for my fiancé, he downright refused to hold the wedding at his church. The pure embarrassment and shame of discovering the daughter who made the promise to stay a virgin until marriage was not only no longer a virgin, but also three months pregnant, nearly caused him to suffer a heart attack. After being hospitalized for two days, the doctors released Daddy, stating he merely suffered from heart palpitations. *At least Daddy would walk me down the aisle and present me to my handsome groom.*

I glanced over the catering menu once more, making sure I didn't leave anything out. "Oh, and I better not forget to order deviled eggs for the appetizer trays," I said out loud to myself. Which was Tate's request, not mine.

Like I should care what Tate wanted. It wasn't as if he cared about the wedding. I felt like my fiancé should be here helping me make these very important decisions. But no, Tate was hanging out with his boys, leaving me to deal with Mama on my own.

"Are you sure on the items you want, Tangela?" Janine asked.

Sitting across the table poised in a two-piece champagne capri set, I felt undressed in my mama-made yellow sundress. I twisted my lips. "Is there anything you think I'm missing?"

"Well, this is only my opinion from receptions I've catered before . . . but . . . I think you're making a huge mistake not to offer a few soul food choices on the buffet."

"I know." Sharon shook her head. "Girl, you need to at least have some potato salad. What about fried chicken? It's far cheaper than steak."

I crossed my arms and pouted. "I don't want my wedding to be another ghetto affair. I want it classy and chic, like—" I cleared my throat—"Like the weddings I see on television."

Mama put her hand on my shoulder. "Need I remind you that you're not working with a classy and chic budget? Tangela, you know if this marriage is going to have half a chance, then you don't need to enter it with a whole lot of debt." Mama scratched her arm. "Your father and I are willing to pay for your wedding and dress. You and Tate are going to pay the rest. Now, there's no need to try and get all fancy and run up that man's bills when you know there's a baby on the way."

"Mama!" I threw my head on the table with my face turning two dark shades of red. "I can't believe you."

Mama chuckled. "What, you think Janine don't see that bulge in your stomach?"

I threw my hands wildly in the air. "I still don't need you broadcasting it to everyone." I stood up to leave.

My mother shot me a glance so hard I almost

felt a pee drop. "I know you're not about to disrespect your mama up in this place."

I sat down slowly. "No, ma'am."

Janine smirked. "So it's settled; I'll replace the steak with fried chicken and add potato salad." She made the changes on the order sheet. "Well, if that's it, ladies, I have to meet with another couple in ten minutes."

Mama pursed her lips tightly.

"Thank you, Janine." Sharon shook hands with Janine and escorted her from the table.

"Don't think I came all the way down here to deal with your attitude, Miss Thang. You either straighten up, or I'll get in my Lincoln and hightail it back to Alabama right now. You know your father isn't even in agreement with this in the first place."

"I'm sorry, Mama. I appreciate what you're doing. Really," I said forcing a smile. "I wish Tate was here to help me."

"Here for what? So you can start a fight with him over something as silly as a menu. Tangela, I didn't raise you to act so selfish. Stop nagging that man." Mama folded her arms. "Hmmm. You ought to be glad he's marrying your behind."

I looked down quickly before Mama could see the expression on my face. *Glad? I would be perfectly fine raising my baby on my own without anyone's help.* It was just like my mama to think I needed a man. Old school. She needed to realize times had changed.

Now that the wedding details were finalized, I needed to handle one more issue. The night before at dinner with Mama, Tate's cell phone rang and he left the table to answer it. I didn't say anything, but I jotted down LeQuisha's phone number while Tate took his shower. All day I anticipated calling that bitch to give her piece of my mind. Now I could finally get the chance.

"Mama, I'm so tired." I held my hand across my forehead.

"You need to get some rest." Mama rubbed my shoulder and stood up from the couch. "I'm cooking up some stewed chicken and rice tonight, so you go ahead and catch up on some sleep before Tate gets here."

I stood slowly. "Okay. First, I'm going to take a shower." Pretending to stagger down the hall to the guest bedroom, I closed the door behind me and started running the shower.

Not wanting to appear to be sinning, while Mama visited, I slept in the guest room. Mama insisted on sleeping on the couch. It was bad enough I moved in with Tate after the semester ended, but I really had nowhere else to go. Sharon moved in with Glen and Terri, instead of going back to Miami for the summer. Good thing, because I needed the support. Being five months pregnant Terri helped me get through the hardest part of my pregnancy, constantly sharing advice and articles.

I eased on the bed and quickly dialed the number. I hoped she would answer.

"Yeah." A teenage boy answered. I could hear the sound of blaring rap music in the background.

I swallowed hard. "May . . . May . . . I speak with your mom?"

"Hold on."

Feeling a yank in my stomach, I held it tightly and squeezed.

Another phone picked up. "Lil' Donny, I got it. Hello."

My heart thumped stronger.

"Hello, LeQuisha. This is Tangela. I'm Tate's—"

"I know who you are. Why are you calling my house?"

I bit my lip. Then cleared my throat. "Because I don't think you should continue to have contact with my husband."

"Your husband? Not yet and maybe never." She snapped.

"We are getting married, and I am having his child," I said defensively. "So you need to stop calling him. Tate doesn't want you; he wants to be with me. Remember, he chose to marry me."

"Hah! Little girl, let me tell you something. Forcing a man to marry you because you messed around and got pregnant don't mean nothing. Yeah, you might be marrying him, but he doesn't love you. He loves me. And he always will." Her voice went up an octave. "And furthermore, you need to talk to Tate, because he's the one calling and burning up my cell phone twenty-four hours a day. He comes to see me. So, I would strongly suggest you talk to your fiancé."

My eyes welled up with tears. "I will." My voice sounded shaky.

"Wait a minute." She paused for a moment. "I'm not sleeping with Tate, if that's what you want to know. I'm not a threat to your marriage. So when it fails, don't blame me."

"What do you mean by that?"

"Tate is only marrying you because you're pregnant. It doesn't take a rocket scientist to know it won't work."

"You're entitled to your opinion."

"No, it's not my opinion; it's the truth, honey. But like I said, don't blame me. And please, please, don't call my house again. Next time, I might not be so nice."

She hung up.

Chapter 25
(Tate)

LeQuisha hung up the phone. Her sniffling let me know she was bothered by the conversation with Tangy. I can't say I blamed her.

I turned to face her. "Are you all right?" I rubbed my hand along her inner thigh. Inhaling my odor reminded me of the sex we both enjoyed less than an hour ago.

"What do you think?" She snapped. "You better tell your little fiancée to quit calling my house. How did she get my number anyway?"

I shrugged. "I don't know."

LeQuisha pointed her finger in my face. "All I have to say is . . . this better not happen again." She scraped her nail across my nose.

"Shit!"

"Awwww, poor baby." LeQuisha pretended to be

sympathetic. "What's the matter? Mama's boy can't take a little pain?" She laughed.

I wiped the blood from my nose. "Ha, ha, hell!"

She folded her arms. "Serves you right."

"Damn! It ain't my fault."

LeQuisha twisted her lips. "It's not your fault, Tate? I wouldn't even be dealing with this mess if wasn't for you." She shook her head. "You know what, I can't do this anymore."

"Do what?" *Here we go again.*

I tried to pull her closer to me, but she snatched away.

"No. I want you to leave. I said I wasn't going to put myself in this situation again, and look at me." LeQuisha snatched the covers away and stood up from the bed. "If you're going through with this marriage, then I don't want you calling or coming over here anymore."

I scratched the back of my neck. "You really mean it?"

LeQuisha rolled her eyes and fought back a tear. "Hell yeah, I mean it."

I got up and started to dress. Nothing was going as I planned it. Barely getting any sex from Tangy, I wanted to at least get one more good fuck out of LeQuisha before I went home that night.

"Okay." With my vision blurred, I struggled to button my shirt. "I'll respect your wishes."

LeQuisha grabbed my arm. "Tate?"

I pulled away from her.

"Tate?"

"What!" I tossed my tie on my shoulder.

"Why are you mad at me? I'm the one sleeping in the fucking bed by myself every night, while you're snuggling up to your soon-to-be wife! You don't give a damn about me, only your damn self."

LeQuisha plopped down on the bed. "Look at you." She turned up her lips. "You ain't shit, Tate Gibson!"

I wished she didn't act like that when her kids were home. "Oh, so I ain't shit, huh?" I put my hand on her face and kissed her on the lips. Closing my eyes, I felt warm tears touch my cheeks. I tongued her harder.

LeQuisha wrapped her arms around my neck and pulled me closer. She unbuttoned my shirt and rubbed her hands over my chest. Unzipping my pants, she pulled out my dick and sucked it forcefully.

"Oh shit."

She worked her lips around my shaft.

I gripped her shoulders to steady myself. Hearing the sound of crashing waves in my head, I bit my tongue as I felt a huge release. "I love you, girl."

LeQuisha turned around so I could enter her from behind. As I pumped her pussy vigorously, she sang that opera shit I loved to hear.

"Aaaaaawwwwwwwww!"

Grappling her thighs tightly, I worked all nine inches in as far as it would go.

"Do it, Daddy," she whispered.

I spanked her ass.

"Do it, Daddy!"

"What's my fuckin' name?" I plunged even deeper.

"Big fuckin' Daddy!" She screamed.

That's what I thought—As long as I served it up

Big Daddy-style, LeQuisha wouldn't give me any more problems.

I left her townhouse and headed home. I drove up to Taco Bell and picked up a spicy fajita combo. As I took another bite of my fajita, my thoughts drifted to LeQuisha. It was only a matter of time before she stood true to her threats. *Was I even ready for all of this?*

Getting married to Tangy was like a damn nightmare that never ended. All of her bitching started to take its toll, and I couldn't stand to look at her, better yet live in the same house with her.

A picture of my son dressed in a graduation cap and gown popped in my head. I wiped my forehead. *Why didn't I use a condom?* Deep regret settled heavily on my shoulders. I had to go through with it.

I passed Mrs. Newsome snoring on the pullout sofa bed and tiptoed down the hall to my bedroom. The light shining from the bottom of the door alerted me that Tangy was waiting on my black ass.

Yep! Sitting on my bed with her arms crossed with an attitude was Darth Vader's sister. "Where the hell have you been?"

"Damn! Can a brother get a 'hello, how you doin', first?" I smiled.

"I'm waiting, you no-good, dirty bastard." Her twisted face resembled the mask from the *Scream* movies.

"I love you too." I chuckled. Her heavy footsteps were on my heels as I headed to the bathroom.

"What'cha getting ready to do?—Wash off the sex?"

I shook my head in disbelief. "You know you're crazy, right?"

"If I'm crazy, prove it." She crossed her arms.

"What do you mean?" I held my hands up. "I don't have time for games."

"Where were you all afternoon and all night? Oh, and before you say out with your boys, know that I called over to Sherman's house, and Peaches told me you weren't there."

I slipped out of my shirt and pants, leaving them on the floor. "So, now you're checking up on me, like I'm your child? Look, I don't need this."

"What do you expect me to do? Just sit around here and act like you're not fucking somebody else?" Tangy sat down on the toilet seat. "Must be screwing somebody, because you're for damn sure not doing it with me." Her tears flowed like the Nile River. "I'm not trying to be a bitch about this; I simply wanted to know where you were. Honestly."

"I'm sorry." I ran my hands through her silky hair. "I was at work."

"Why didn't you answer your cell phone or your line at work when I called? I called you at least fifty times."

"I didn't answer the phone because I had three huge stacks of paperwork on my desk. If I sit on the phone, then I won't get anything done. I have a paycheck to earn; you're not even trying to work."

"I can't work," Tangy said in pure frustration. She held her head up. "Why couldn't you just call me? Don't you even care that I'm carrying your baby?"

"Of course, I care." I kneeled down in front of her. "That's why I'm working so hard; I want my son to have everything he needs."

Tangy giggled. "Don't you mean your daughter?"

I grabbed her hands. "As long as my baby is healthy, I'm happy."

"Good." Tangy kissed me on the lips. "You want me to fix you something to eat? Mama made stewed chicken and rice."

I rubbed my stomach. "Yeah. I'm starving."

That was fucked up, right? Why did I have to lie about being hungry? Lying was becoming second nature, and I didn't even feel the least bit guilty. *Man, I need help.* My life was spinning out of control, and I had no clue how to slow down.

Chapter 26
(Tangy)

"You plan on getting off the couch anytime today?" Tate asked.

I looked up. "What do you care?"

Tate sat down beside me, dressed in a navy suit. "I care because you need to get out of here, breathe in some fresh air." He ran his fingers through my hair.

I snatched away, and embarrassingly tried to finger comb my wild strands. "I look a mess."

Tate laughed. "Well, I don't want to hurt your feelings, but you could use a little work. Do me a favor, Tangy. Call up Sharon today. Go get your hair and nails done. Do some shopping. Hell, here's my credit card."

Tate never offered me his credit card. Not wanting to go in debt, I refused to fill out those credit card applications. I wondered how long it would take before he added my name to his credit card accounts. With all the money he was making, I could probably buy myself some name brand outfits like Terri.

"All right. I'll call Sharon. When should I expect you back?"

"Late." Tate glanced down at his watch.

I sucked my teeth. "How late?"

He kissed me on the forehead. "Don't wait up for me."

"We're newlyweds; we should be spending more time together." I put my hands on my hips. "Why can't you come home early for once?"

"Because we had a wedding that nearly broke me, that's why! We stayed in Vegas for a week. You don't know how that honeymoon set me back." Tate poured a cup of coffee from the kitchen. "I'm down one adjuster who left us with more than two hundred open accounts. My staff needs me."

My stomach rumbled. "I need you too."

"And you *have* me. See ya tonight." Tate rushed to the door.

Here I was getting mad at my husband for working hard to earn a living for our soon-to-be-family. It's not like he was out running the streets or anything. LeQuisha told me they weren't sleeping together, and that woman didn't have any reason to lie to me.

"Wait a minute." I kissed him on the cheek. "Have a good day. I love you."

Tate smiled. "I love you."

I closed the door behind him. Grabbing my shoulders, I chuckled to myself. He's never said that before.

Preparing a pancake breakfast with sausage and

fried eggs, I sat down at the bar to eat. It seemed like no matter how much I ate, I couldn't get enough. Lying up on the couch watching TV all day wasn't helping. The last thing I wanted to do was lose my figure. I needed to get out of the house. The exercise would do me every bit of good.

I dialed Terri's number. Sharon moved in with Glen and Terri, because she could no longer afford to pay the rent after I moved out. She flat out refused to get another roommate.

"Hi, Tan," she answered.

"Hey, what are you doing home today? I was calling to talk to Sharon."

"I took the day off. Sharon left early for a job interview."

I took another bite of my pancake. "Have you made plans?"

"Get my hair done, taking a day off for myself. What about you?"

"I need a touch-up so bad, it's not even funny." I laughed. "I'm going to call Renee and see if she can see me today."

"Okay, try to make it at ten. Then we can have lunch afterwards."

"All right. I'll call her at home."

"Call me back."

I hung up and called Renee. She worked me in for a ten thirty appointment. If I wanted to arrive on time, I needed to get ready. I showered and picked out a pink shorts set to wear. Even though it wasn't a maternity outfit, the elastic waistband gave my belly enough room for comfort, and I still looked cute.

Leaving the dishes in the sink, along with the ones from the day before, I promised myself I would do them as soon as I got home. And wash a few loads of laundry. Then I would vacuum. Since Tate wasn't going to be home until late, it didn't matter.

Spending the day with Terri was the perfect antidote. Complaining about the aches and pains of pregnancy made me feel more normal than weird. I didn't want to tell Tate about the awful gas I experienced. However, Terri completely understood. Having read a lot of books on pregnancy, Terri advised me to avoid spicy foods altogether. "It would help with heartburn as well," she said. Before leaving, we agreed to spend another girl's day next month.

To my surprise, Myra Gibson was at the house when I came home around six.

I followed the sound of the vacuum cleaner in the hallway. Almost startling her, I tapped on her shoulder.

"Baby, you scared me." Mrs. Gibson hugged me. "How you doin'?" She rubbed my belly.

"I'm fine. What are you doing here?"

Mrs. Gibson rested her hand on her hip. "Tate asked me to stop by and check up on you. Since I was delivering some pies over at the Dotson's place just around the corner, over there on Fifth Street, I decided to come on over." She wiped the beads of sweat from her forehead. "Well, since you didn't answer, I let myself in."

A look of embarrassment showed on my face as I tried to explain. "I was planning to do this tonight; I haven't been feeling well."

"That's why I stopped by." Mrs. Gibson frowned. "But you look good to me; I don't see anything wrong with you."

"Tate insisted I leave the house today. I went to get my hair done." I patted my head. "It was looking so ragged."

Mrs. Gibson put her hands on my shoulders. "You don't have to explain to me. I'm here to help whenever I can. You know, I can't have my son living in no nasty house."

I nodded. "Me neither."

"Humph, you could have fooled me." Mrs. Gibson turned the vacuum back on.

I stared up at the ceiling. I wanted to give her a piece of my mind. *What difference would it make?* She probably had already called Tate to talk about me like a dog. Turning in the opposite direction, I went in my bedroom and closed the door. Not even bothering to wrap my hair, I rubbed my stomach as I drifted off to sleep.

Tate rubbed my shoulder and I turned over. The clock read eleven thirty.

"Hey."

"I'm sorry about my mom," he said; "I didn't know she was coming."

"Myra told me you asked her to stop by," I said annoyed.

"No, I didn't." Tate stripped down to his boxers and went in the bathroom.

I sat up. "I think you should ask for your key back; your mother shouldn't be allowed to come and go as she pleases."

Tate stuck his head out. "No. Moms has a key for emergencies. Anyway, she's going to start coming over to clean this place up once a week."

"Oh no, she isn't."

"Why not? You haven't lifted a finger since you've been staying here; don't complain about my moms trying to help out."

"I've been sick. Tate, I don't want your mother cleaning up my house." I folded my arms. "I can do it myself."

Tate growled. "Sure you will."

"Tate," I said stupefied. "This is my house too."

He stood at the door. "If it is, then act like it. Until you can do that, my mom will take care of the cooking and cleaning around here just like she used to."

My jaw tightened. I knew Tate was a momma's boy, but this was plain ridiculous. No way would I put up with Myra meddling in our business, so she could talk about me with her little church group. Those gossiping hyenas needed to get some business of their own to tend to and stay out of mine. Not wanting to end the night on a bad note, I decided to drop it.

"Fine."

"Oh, while we're on the subject, have you registered for your classes yet?"

How did we get on that subject? "No."

"No? So you plan on dropping out your junior year?"

I twisted my lips. "That's what I said—I'm taking some time off until I have the baby."

Tate cleared his throat. "The baby ain't due until January. I know one thing—if you don't plan on going to school this semester, then your ass needs to get a job."

I raised a brow and smirked. "Who's going to hire someone who's pregnant?"

"Plenty of employers." Tate waved his muscular

arms. "Tangy, there are over a hundred temp agencies in Jacksonville. You have one week to find a job."

"Or what? What's going to happen if I don't?"

Tate spoke calmly. "I'm not threatening you. I'm not going to do anything. If you're not contributing to this marriage and household, then you're contaminating it."

"Don't quote me, Dr. Phil. Tate, you're full of shit, and you know it. I fuckin' hate you." I grabbed my pillow and turned over on my side. *Who did he think he was, telling me, I had to get a job? Fuck him. It's not as if he was my daddy. And that damn Myra thinks she's my mother. I'm not having it.* Tate had another thing coming, if he thought he could just tell me what to do.

I heard the shower start and my head ached even more. Struggling to drag myself out of bed, I swallowed two Tylenol pills. Not wanting to see Tate's face, I marched into the guest bedroom.

"So, let me get this right." Sharon pointed her fork at me. "You, a newlywed, are choosing to sleep in the guest bedroom every night, instead of cuddling up next to fine-ass Tate at night."

I crossed my legs at the table. "You make it sound so simple."

"That's because it is!"

"No, it isn't," I said through clenched teeth. "Didn't you listen to anything I've said for the past ten minutes?"

Sharon chuckled. "Oh, I'm listening."

I swirled a piece of lettuce in the dressing. "Then you should understand. You don't even like Tate."

Sharon took another bite of her shrimp. "True. But you married him anyway. All I'm saying is that's your husband. You guys are expecting a baby, and the best thing you can do now is provide a supportive environment for your child."

"Not if I'm the only one doing something."

Sharon slammed her fist on the table. "Would you just listen to yourself? You sound like a damn baby. What's wrong with getting a job like the rest of us?"

"This is about more than a job, Sharon, and you know it. It's about his meddling mother, his long hours at work, and his infidelity."

"Look, I'm not saying your marriage is perfect. What marriage is? The only way to make it better is to take on one problem at a time." Sharon tossed her hands up in the air. "I can't believe I'm giving advice on marriage."

"Tate earns more than enough money to support us." I finally took a bite of my crab cake. It was delicious. (Gene's was known for the best seafood in town.)

"That may be so. Tan, you're a smart girl. If the marriage is doomed like you say, then you need to set up an account for you and your child. Handle your business, girl."

"I guess so."

Sharon swallowed a mouthful of mashed potatoes. "And go back to school; don't give up your dreams for nobody."

My eyes met hers across the table. "You're making perfectly good sense."

Sharon shook her head. "I know. Now, if you come by the bank, I'm sure I can get you an interview."

"What's the best time to stop by?"

"First thing tomorrow morning."

"Okay. I'll be there." I had no intention of going to the bank. *One look at my pregnant belly, and Sharon's manager would run me out of there.*

When the tab came to the table, I politely used Tate's credit card to pay for lunch.

Sharon smiled coyly. "Look at you, big baller."

Chapter 27
(Tate)

I checked my watch. For the first time I was early. I slid into my seat with the table in the corner, with a view of the waterfront. Since I knew the owners at Southern Brewery, it wasn't hard to call in a favor.

Luckily, the crowd filled in slowly. *Tangy shouldn't have a hard time finding a parking space. I for damn sure hope I don't find another dent on my BMW this time either.* Now I bought her a perfectly good car—a Honda Civic—and she had the nerve to be disappointed. This bitch didn't even have a car when I first married her ass. Since she claimed it was too small for her, I reluctantly agreed to let her drive mine.

I knew the real reason—Tangy wanted to act like she had it like that while she fronted to her friends, Sharon and Terri. Especially, stuck-up ass Terri. *Tangy must think I'm rollin' in the cash.* She thought I was going to buy her a more expensive car. Shhhhiiit! Even if I could, there was no way in hell I would.

"Have you been here long?" Tangy kissed me on my cheek.

I didn't hear her come up from behind me—it freaked the shit out of me. I straightened the collar of my shirt. "No."

I signaled the waiter, and the redhead kid came right over. "Are you ready to place your drink orders?"

Tangy grinned. "Yes, I'll have water with lemon, and he'll have a peach sangria."

The redhead nodded. "I'll be back in a few."

After enjoying a good meal and listening to Tangy talk for over an hour, I resisted the urge to have dessert.

"Can we go walk on the waterfront?" Tangy asked. Her big brown eyes widened.

"I was just about to suggest the same thing."

As we walked down the steps in front of the statue of the sailor, I decided to initiate the conversation. I scratched the back of my neck with my free hand. "Tangy, how long do you plan on sleeping in the guest bedroom?"

"As long as I have to." She turned away.

"What kind of an answer is that?" I smirked. *This girl was dumber than I thought.* I prayed to God my son would take after my side of the family.

"A good one." She rolled her eyes. "You don't respect me, so why should I sleep with you? Isn't that what this is really about?"

"Yes. We're married now, and husband and wife

are meant to sleep in the same bed together, and—yes—have sex."

"What about respecting one another's opinions, decisions, and values?"

"I respect you, Tangy; you don't respect me." I snatched my hand away. "I asked you to get a job, and you laughed in my face. You don't clean, cook, or do laundry. I know you're pregnant, but, Tangy, you leave the house every single day. My mom shouldn't have to drive across town to clean up our home."

She waved her hand in the air. "That's not my doing. That's the reason why I leave the house. I'm not going anywhere. Just driving around the block. Not that I have anything against your mother, but sometimes she can be so headstrong."

I smiled coyly. "Moms can be a little bossy."

Tangy laughed. "That's like me being a little pregnant."

I shrugged. "Okay. You got me on that one."

Tangy grabbed both of my hands. "I love you. I want our marriage to work. Really I do."

"I love you too. You're the mother of my child."

She took a deep breath. "Is that the only reason you love me?"

"No, it's not." I held her chin and kissed her. Wrapping my arms around her, I felt my manhood get harder. *Damn. I wish we didn't have to drive back in separate cars.*

I waited for Tangy to back out first. Turning up the radio, the sudden loud bam startled me. When my eyes scanned the parking lot, I saw my BMW filled with a huge cloud of smoke. Tangy's head lay still on the steering wheel, covered with blood.

I jumped out my car. Several people made it to the car before I could. My legs felt so heavy. Barely able to move, I struggled to maintain a steady pace. I couldn't understand it. Only less than five feet, the car seemed more than a football field away. My vision blurred.

Someone grabbed me. "Hey, man, you okay?"

I grabbed my chest as I tried to speak. No air came out.

"I need some help over here! I think he's having a heart attack!"

Grabbing my chest, I slowly forced my eyes open. I caught a glimpse of mom holding my hand tightly.

"Mom." My sore throat ached in the worst way. "What's going on? Where's Tangy?" I asked.

Mom moved in closer. "Baby, you're in the hospital. You went into shock and passed out at the scene of the accident last night."

She rubbed my forehead. "You're going to be fine. Tangy's still in ICU."

I struggled to sit up in the bed.

My mom pushed me back down. "You're in no condition to sit up. Hold on for a second." She tried two buttons on the side of my bed and the third finally worked, putting the top half of the bed in an upward position.

"Thanks." I scratched my coarse head of hair. "I must look like shit."

Myra Gibson crossed her arms. "Now you watch your language young man; I didn't raise you to talk like that."

I covered my mouth. "Yes, ma'am. I'm so sorry. It just slipped out; it won't happen again."

"It better not. I know you don't want me to put you back to sleep." She laughed.

As soon as I tried to laugh, my throat ached.

"Let me get you some water."

My thoughts wondered back to the accident. "Mom, is Tangy all right?"

My mom handed me a cup with a straw. "She's going to be fine. Her parents arrived this morning, and we've been praying for her. I know Tangy's going to come out of this. Tate, she lost the baby."

"Oh," I said in a voice barely above a whisper. Touching my ring finger, my heart sank as I thought about the son that I would never get the chance to hold. "Mom, I need a minute to myself."

"Okay, baby." I'll go wait for your father. She hugged me once more before she left.

Tangy lost the baby. I buried my head with both hands and cried like a small child. Hollered. Screamed. Feeling a yank in my throat, I sat silent, allowing tears to drop on the white bed sheet.

Later that day, I was released from the hospital. Planning to stay at my parent's house, while Mr. and Mrs. Newsome took temporary residence at my condo, I spent a few hours with Tangy in her room. Released from ICU, she was now breathing on her own but had yet to wake up.

I felt compelled to pray for her. I asked God to forgive me for acting like such a selfish jerk. Tangy was supposed to be my wife, and I was treating her like an insignificant roommate. *What the hell is wrong with me?* My mom was right—she didn't raise me to be like this. Judgment weighed heavily on my shoulders.

I looked at Tangy sleeping peacefully, her head wrapped in bandages to help heal the wounds that would eventually leave permanent scars. Her broken left arm sat in a hard cast that took eight weeks to heal. The doctor explained, "The impact of the SUV happened so suddenly Tangy would probably have no memory of the accident." She was immediately knocked unconscious. As soon as they realized the fetus growing inside her womb had no heartbeat, they delivered it stillborn.

I squeezed Tangy's hand gently. Before I left, I made a promise to God—from this day forward, I would treat my wife the way she deserved. I wasn't sure how long it would take Tangy to get over losing the baby.

My mom told me she lost a child before she had me and was devastated by the loss. No matter what, I vowed to do all I could do to help my wife get through it.

Later on that night, Mrs. Newsome called my parent's house with the news—"Tangy opened her eyes". Following the doctor's orders, I took a few days off from work. I sat with Tangy the next day. I planned to spend every minute there until the doctor released her. I picked up a few magazines for her to read once she was up to it. I walked in carrying a vase full of roses surprised to see her awake in her bed.

"Hey there," I said, a huge grin on my face.

"If I didn't know any better, I would think that smile was for me." She forced a grin. Her blue eyes held a hint of a sparkle.

I grabbed her hand. "It's for you. I'm so glad you're awake." I kissed her red swollen cheek.

"I'm going to leave you two lovebirds alone for a while." Mrs. Newsome hugged me and exited the room.

I sat down holding onto her small hand. "Has anyone told you what happened?"

"Yeah." A tear rolled down her face. "I was hit by a car. And . . . and . . . I lost the baby." She cried for a few minutes.

I put my arms around her to comfort her. Not wanting to cry in front of her, I fought back my own tears. "We can have another baby, Tangy."

"I . . . I know." Tangy sniffled. "I loved that baby."

I cleared my throat. "I won't forget him either."

Later that afternoon, I went to the cafeteria to grab something to eat. Tangy had drifted off to sleep, and Mrs. Newsome relieved me of my shift. Still no sight of Mr. Newsome. I wasn't looking forward to seeing the good ol' reverend.

I placed a warm ham and cheese sandwich, a bag of plain chips, and a coke on my tray. I scanned the room for an empty table, and my eyes caught a glimpse of LeQuisha in the far corner. She was talking to another woman. They were both dressed in floral printed uniforms.

I stood at the table. "I thought that was you. How you doin', LeQuisha?"

"Tate." She looked surprised. "I haven't seen you in so long. Have a seat."

I smiled.

"What are you doing here?"

"Tangy was in an accident. I saw the whole thing and went into shock. I was just released two days ago." I took a bite of my sandwich.

"Your face does look a little rough. I'm sorry to

hear about your wife; I hope she gets better real soon."

"Girl, I need to clock in. I'll see you upstairs," the other woman said.

LeQuisha nodded. "Okay."

"Are you working here?" I asked.

LeQuisha laughed. "Now you know I wouldn't be wearing these clothes if I wasn't, but yes, I am."

"True. What about school?"

"Oh, I'm in nursing school now and working the evening shift here. I only have three more semesters left before I'm finished for good."

"You must be taking a lot of hours to get that far."

"Maximum load." She tapped her fingers on her tray. "I'm ready to get out of there."

I chewed slowly. "Well, congratulations. You really did it."

LeQuisha smirked. "Did you think I wouldn't?"

I took a deep breath. "I knew you would. It seems like things are happening quickly for you, that's all."

"Maybe to you," she said, "not to me. I've missed opportunities in my life; I finally feel that I'm heading in the right direction. God is good." She gazed over at the opposite end of the room.

"I know what you mean." I took a sip of my drink.

We sat silent for a moment.

"Tangy lost the baby," I brought myself to say.

LeQuisha held my hand. "I'm sorry."

I rubbed the tears welled up in my eyes. "LeQuisha, I'm sorry for the way I treated you—you didn't deserve it. I wish things could've turned out different between me and you."

She squeezed my hand tighter. "Tate, it wasn't part of God's plan. As hurt as I was, I got over it. I'm fine now. The whole thing brought me closer to God, and for that I'm grateful."

"I can see that."

"I forgive you." LeQuisha leaned in closer. "I respect you for wanting to provide a family for your child. Now you have to help your wife get through this. There's nothing worse than losing a child. I know. I suffered a miscarriage once."

I slowly kissed LeQuisha's soft hand. "Thank you."

"You're welcome." She stood up from the table. "I need to get back to work."

I sat back in my seat. "But we didn't get a chance to talk about the kids."

"They're good. You know they ask about you from time to time. You don't have to be a stranger. Dante would love to hear from you. Next week, he'll start in the third grade." She smiled like a proud mama.

"Man!" I crossed my arms. "Tell him I'll call soon."

"All right, you take care."

I watched as LeQuisha sashayed away and disappeared down the hall.

Chapter 28
(LeQuisha)

My day couldn't get any worse, having to work at the hospital on my day off, when I was supposed to be at my kids' schools, meeting their new teachers. I always prided myself on never missing a year. Now I gotta wait until the first day of school and try to fit in conferences. With my busy schedule, it was going to be tight.

With my children getting so big, I needed to be around more than ever. It wouldn't be long before they would be gone off to college, leaving me all alone—without a man.

Four months ago, I was devastated at the thought of not having a man. I grew up believing I needed a man to help me with my children and all these bills. I wanted a house and—I ain't gonna even lie—some fine brotha to snuggle up to every night.

To tell you the truth, I was doing fine all by myself. Don left me with these kids when he was hauled off to jail.

Then Kenny helped pick up some of the slack, but I truly banked on Tate pulling through for me. Looking back, I realize how stupid in love I was for that man.

All them men ever did was use me and toss me aside like I was nothing. When Tate told me he was going to marry that lil' girl, I wanted to lie in my bed and never wake up. I thought I hit rock bottom. But, honey, I'm here to tell you, the next morning came, and I was happy to be alive. *I may not have a man, but I got my children, my sanity, and a future career. Why should I throw that all away?*

I found my way to Jesus, and was standing ever since. *He's the father I never had, the man I need, and the provider for my household. He takes care of me better than any man ever did.* I was on fire for the Lord ever since.

I was feeling real good about myself until I saw the man that hurt me more than life itself. It took everything in me to keep from cursing him out. I was proud of myself for keeping my cool. With the way Tate looked, it wasn't that hard. His whole demeanor was tore up from the floor up. *What happened to his confident strut?* His soul was lost. *Losing his unborn child and almost losing his wife must've messed him up pretty badly.* All I could do was pray for him.

It was hard. Tate was still fine as wine. I loved him. For two years, I loved that man. Deep down inside, I still wanted him too. He did have the nerve to call me from his job from time to time. Just to talk. Okay, I did let him hit it a couple times too! And he put it down better than he ever had when we was together. Tate licked my cherry until there was no sweetness left. In my mind, I had this messed up fantasy he would beg me to take him back and not marry that girl. He never did.

I already told y'all I wasn't going to be nobody's woman on the side. Not anymore anyway. Been there, done that. Got the T-shirt too. Knowing that kind of situation wasn't right for me or my kids I found the courage to break it down for his behind. Just a few days before his wedding, I asked him not to call my house ever again.

I can't tell you how badly I wanted him to ignore my wishes and keep calling and sneaking over for a quick rump. He never did. No matter how hard it hurt, I had to keep reminding myself it was for the best . . . for all parties concerned. When that lil' girl, Tangy, called my house, she sounded so pitiful. Lord knows, I wanted to burst her bubble, but I decided if Tate were the man for me, he would come back on his own, I didn't have to resort to playing childish games, like she did.

I walked into my townhouse to a whole bunch of commotion in the living room. "Hey, what's all this fuss about?" I asked, my hands on my hips.

"Nothing, Mama," Lil' Donny answered. "We were cheering for the Jaguars—they scored the first touchdown."

"Well, bring your voices down; I got a migraine." I picked up the mail from the sofa table. Flipping through the stack of bills, I tossed junk mail in the trashcan beside me.

Daneisha turned around with the cordless phone up to her ear. "How was your day?"

"It was okay." I caught a glimpse of the red thong underwear sticking out from her hip-hugger jeans. "Are those my thongs you wearin'?" I cocked my head to the side.

The boys burst into a loud uproar of laughter.

"Get her, Mama. Yeah, she's been all up in your drawers!" Lil' Donny yelled.

"She sure was," Dante added.

"Shut up!" Daneisha swung on Lil' Donny and missed.

Dante ran over to me and grabbed my leg.

"Daneisha"—I gave her the evil stare down— "Get off that phone. Change out of my underwear. And I bet' not catch you in them again." I pointed my finger in her direction.

She poked out her lips. "Okay."

"Excuse me." I snapped my fingers.

"I'm sorry—yes, ma'am." Daneisha made a fake smile.

"All right then. I'm going to lay down for a little bit. Make sure this house is clean. First thing tomorrow, I'm taking y'all to the Gateway Mall to get your school clothes." I stopped at the foot of the stairs. "Don't make me have to change my mind."

Dante shook his head. "We won't. We promise."

I turned around and headed for my bedroom.

"Oh, Mama . . . I forgot to tell you some guy named Mike called over here for you," Daneisha said, clutching my bedroom door.

"That's nice," I said in a low voice. I stepped out of my uniform and left on my slip. I didn't feel like changing into a nightgown.

"That's it." Daneisha cocked her head to the side. "Who is he anyway—he sounded handsome?"

I shrugged. "Mike's a doctor at Baptist. He's teaching a course I'm taking."

Daneisha picked up one of my favorite perfume bottles. "He must be smart."

"I guess you could say that, I don't know. I

haven't really talked to him all that much." I walked up behind my daughter. "Do you mind?"

She quickly put the bottle down. "Okay . . . okay. Well, I think you should call him back. Mama, you need a man; you've been so lonely around here. It wouldn't hurt to talk to him."

I rubbed Daneisha's hair. "Maybe I will. But for your information, I'm not lonely. And I don't *need* a man."

"I know that."

"Good. The last thing I want my daughter thinking is she needs a man to fulfill her. And you better not be wanting no woman either."

Daneisha turned up her nose. "Now Mama, that's just nasty."

I shook my head. "Just making sure." I lay down in the bed on my side.

Daneisha kissed my cheek. "Night, Mama."

"Good night, baby."

On our way home from the mall the next day, I felt so exhausted from a long day of shopping. My "dogs" were aching so badly. When I first heard my cell phone ringing, I didn't want to answer it. When I saw my home number show up on my caller ID, I pressed "accept" quickly.

"Hey, sis, what's up?" I asked in a puzzled tone.

"At your apartment, waiting on you to get home," Rhonda responded. "Where you been all day?"

I knew I should've got my key back from her the other night. I know she done raided my refrigerator and closet by now. Not that I don't love spending time with my nephews, but my sister loved to take full advantage of it.

"Girl, I had to take these kids school clothes shopping. You know I don't get paid until the first." *Why did I say that? Oh, that's probably why she there, wanting some money—if she didn't find some already.* Good thing I took Tate's advice and opened an account at the bank.

"Why didn't you call me? You know I would've hooked you up with my discount at Dillard's?"

I rested my arm on my car window. "Because I don't have Dillard's kind of money . . . even with your discount. I went straight to the Northside, so I could get what I could afford."

Trying to avoid the traffic jam on I-95, I made a quick exit. I figured I'd take the Main Street Bridge over to Bay Street.

"I'm almost there, so I'll see you in a few minutes. I hope you cooked dinner. Oh, and put all my outfits back in my closet."

Rhonda growled. "Yes, I did cook. And I only took your red catsuit that you don't even wear anymore since you done got so saved and sanctified."

I scratched the back of my head. "You can have that. And that had better be it. I'm almost there."

I parked my old Honda Accord next to my sister's new one. It was nice, with tan leather interior to match the black exterior. *I ain't been nothing, but jealous of her since she got it. I wish I could figure out how she could afford it.* I know she got her child support check on time every month, but with a new apartment on the Southside, it still didn't add up.

I couldn't wait to graduate and work full-time on a nurse's pay. The first thing I planned to do was start saving for a house. With the assistance the state provided for single mothers, it wouldn't take long. I looked forward to the day when I could buy me a new car . . . instead of driving around in Jacksonville in my hot box every day.

"What you cooked, Auntie?" Daneisha asked as soon as we got in the door.

Rhonda hugged her niece. "Hot dogs and French fries."

"Sounds good to me," Lil' Donny said, rubbing his stomach. "I'm hungry."

"Y'all need to bring these bags in first. And make sure you fix your little brother a plate."

"Yes, ma'am," they replied in unison.

I hugged my two nephews, who were sitting on the couch watching Cartoon Network. Then my lovely sister. I stepped back. "You look like you done lost weight. What? You supposed to be on a diet?"

Rhonda struck a pose like a supermodel. With her tall and slender frame, she was always mistaken for one. "Call it *love,* baby—my man takes damn good care of me."

I rolled my eyes. "Oh, really. When am I going to meet him? Mama told me about Tony Red the other day."

"Very soon." She giggled. "We supposed to be going away this weekend."

"To where?" I asked as I headed to the kitchen to fix myself a plate.

"Miami," she added nonchalantly.

"And what about the kids? You takin' them with you?" I chewed on a soggy French fry and frowned.

"Well . . . that's what I wanted to ask you?" Rhonda batted her deep, dark-brown eyes.

I twisted my lips. "You wrong for that . . . not that I don't love my nephews. But how you just gonna ask me at the last minute like that?"

Rhonda put her arms around me. "'Cause Mama agreed to, but then decided to go on the gambling cruise with her girlfriends. She just told me a few hours ago."

I took a deep breath. "All right, they can stay here."

"Can I borrow a hundred dollars 'til next week? I promise to pay you back as soon as I get my child support check."

My head jerked, and my eyes blinked rapidly. "What kind of a nigga are you fooled up with that can't afford to pay your way?"

Rhonda rolled her eyes. "See, I should've known not to ask you for nothing."

"Yes, you should've." I jabbed the air with my finger. "I just told you—I barely had enough money to buy my kids' school clothes. And I still need to buy groceries."

"Make it seventy-five," Rhonda said. "And you can use my food card to buy your groceries."

I munched on a handful of fries drowned in ketchup. "Fine." I reached in my purse and handed her the money. "Did you pack their clothes?"

She shook her head. "No. I didn't know if you were gonna say yes. I'll be back, and then you can meet Tony Red."

I glanced down at my watch. "How long is that going to take?"

"Less than an hour."

"All right. Stop by Blockbuster and pick up a couple of movies."

Rhonda held out her hand.

I put my hand on my hip. "You better take it out of that money I just gave you."

"Bitch!"

"Takes one to know one. Bye!"

Rhonda showed up about two hours later with her good-for-nothing boyfriend. Tony Red must've thought he had it going on, since he kept bragging about his little minimum wage job as a cook at Applebee's. Something told me this brotha did more than flip burgers. Especially when he flashed a mouth grilled down with gold teeth. *Lord, I hope my sister ain't getting herself in no big mess.* I tried to be friendly, and even went so far as to tell them to have a nice trip.

I did have to give my little sister credit, though—he was fine . . . if you like "red bones." And red bones just happened to be on my menu.

As soon as I came back in, Daneisha handed me the phone.

"It's for you," she said.

"Who is it?"

"Grandma."

"Hey, Mama," I said with an attitude, "I thought you were on the gambling ship."

"Excuse me," the male voice answered.

I twisted my lips. "Who is this?"

"It's Mike Peeples. Remember, you gave me your number last week? I work at the hospital with you."

"Yes." I popped Daneisha on her arm for tricking me. "That's right. I'm sorry."

"That's all right. Are you busy?"

I shook my head. "Not at the moment."

"Good."

I could hear the sound of relief in his voice.

"Why haven't you returned any of my phone calls?"

"Well, I've been busy . . . you know . . . with my classes and work. You know I have three kids, right?" I walked up the stairs to my bedroom for more privacy.

"Yes. We already had that conversation. Remember, I told you I was divorced with two children of my own."

I smiled. "That's right. Two daughters—Tasha and Nicole, right?"

"Yes. So when do you want to get together—that is if you're still interested?" he asked in a deep, husky voice.

I sat down on my bed. "Let me see . . . are you free during the week?"

"Except for Wednesday—But you already know that."

"Why don't we go out for a late dinner after class then?"

"Alrighty then. I'll be sure to wear something nice."

Nice? The man wore a suit everyday. "Okay, I'll do the same." *Maybe that was a hint for me.*

"Wednesday after class, it is. Swell."

'Swell.' He sounded like a nerd. *Maybe that wasn't such a bad thing.*

"Okay. Good night, Mike."

I hung up.

* * *

The kids kept me busy over the weekend. I was hot with Rhonda, because she and Tony Red arrived from their trip late Monday night. I had to get everybody ready for the first day of school. Come Tuesday, just thinking about my date with Mike made me nervous. I ain't ever held a conversation with a doctor longer than five minutes, much less dinner.

I didn't want to get my hopes up high either. Wasn't no doctor going to be interested in me. And I was going to make it clear that I wasn't interested in a sexual relationship either.

For the first time, I dressed up for class. My dark-brown dress helped to hide the few pounds I'd put on. When class ended, I followed Mike to Applebee's.

He greeted me with a kiss. "You look nice."

I smiled. "Thank you."

Once we sat down, I scanned the room as usual. With it being so late, there were more empty tables in our section. It felt intimate and cozy.

"So . . . Mike, where you from?"

He scratched his nose. "You don't waste any time, do you?"

"If you mean, small talk—no, I don't. I'm straight to the point. After all, we're supposed to be getting to know one another."

He held up his glass of wine. "Yes, we are."

"So . . ." I moved in closer.

He chuckled. "I grew up in New Jersey, a white suburb, where I was the only black child—it was rough."

"How was it rough growing up in a lily-white suburb?" I teased.

Mike raised his thick eyebrows. "Well, I didn't have many friends, no one I could identify with. My parents pretty much kept to themselves, so I felt very isolated from the rest of the world."

"Oh, I see. I guess that wouldn't be easy. It's funny." I took a sip of wine. "Growing up in the projects as I did, I struggled to find a place to isolate myself from everybody else, just get away. Seemed like everybody was always in my business."

"Interesting." He gazed in my eyes. "Maybe we're more alike than you think."

My eyes drifted downward as I put my glass down. "No, I don't think so."

"You disagree?" He placed his hand on top of mine.

"Yes, I do. Our worlds would have never mixed. To tell you the truth, I'm surprised you even asked me out to dinner."

"You shouldn't be." Mike winked. "I like you. Your direct approach reminds me lot of my mother—she's a lawyer, you know."

I pointed at my chest. "Your mother's a lawyer— what about your dad?"

"A doctor. That's why I wanted to study medicine."

"A real-life Cosby family." I took a bite into my penne pasta with chicken and vegetables. "This is good."

"Let me try."

I forked up some chicken and pasta and fed him with it.

"You're right. Tasty." He winked again.

All this attention made me nervous. I shifted in my seat. "So I guess that's why you studied medicine, to be like your father."

"Pretty much," Mike said as he sliced his fish perfectly. "I wanted to impress him."

"Did you?"

He wiped his mouth with his napkin. "He's proud of me. Yes. I've learned over the years, it's more important for me to work hard for myself and not do for others—I learned that from my first marriage."

"Do you two get along?"

"Not really, but we're dedicated to making it work for our two daughters."

"That's good."

Before the night ended, I agreed to another date.

Then another.

The more I got to know Mike, the more I liked him. Not sure where it all headed, but the company of a man in my life was something special . . . especially since I never expected it.

Throwing a party for Daniesha turned out to be the worst day of my entire life. First, the temperature was so hot and nobody wanted to stand by the grill long enough to keep the burgers and hotdogs from burning. Then Daneisha invited more people than I gave her permission to. I can see now, I needed to talk with Ms. Fast Behind later on tonight.

I must admit, Mike was a great help, stopping by the store at the last minute to pick up a few items and coming by early to help me set up.

Lil' Donny assigned himself the job of DJ and was doing a good job of mixing old-school jams with new-school. Dante ran around with his cousins having a good time, and as long as he stayed out of my hair, I couldn't have been happier.

"Hell yeah. Now that's what I'm talkin' 'bout—that's my shit!" Mama stepped out in the center of the picnic tables to dance freak-style with her current boyfriend, Leroy.

You could see my face turn bright red in embarrassment.

"Are you okay?" Mike asked as he massaged my shoulders. Standing six inches taller than me, he blocked the sun off my back.

I shook my head. "Would you look at my mama over there? Lord, I can't believe she's dancing like that in front of these children."

Mike laughed. "LeQuisha, I think you should take another look—the kids are dancing nastier than your mother."

I turned around. Sure enough, three girls were grinding up on one boy. And one was my daughter!

"Oh hell no!" I marched over there and snatched up two girls while Mike grabbed the last one. "Daneisha, come here."

She poked out her lips and stormed in my direction. When she caught a glimpse of my tight-lipped grimace, her whole demeanor changed. "Yes, mama," she said, forcing a crooked smile.

I cleared my throat. "I didn't raise you to act like this. Now, you get your act together or I'm going to send all your friends home and just keep family here." I pointed my finger in her face. "Do I make myself clear?"

"Crystal clear." Tears welled up in Daneisha's eyes. "I'm sorry."

My heart melted. From all the stress, I probably overreacted. My children had never given me a moment's trouble. I held her in a tight embrace. "It's going to be all right."

"Why you got my niece over here cryin'?" Rhonda asked.

"Don't go there." I released my grip on Daneisha.

"What you mean?" She put her hands on her hips.

I crossed my arms and stuck out one leg. "Where have you been? I asked you to pick up ice, and it takes you almost two hours to get back here—that's what I mean."

Rhonda tossed her long hair weave. "Well, damn, you clockin' me or something?"

I waved my hand. "Forget it—where's the ice?"

"Right here." Rhonda handed me one bag of melted ice.

"Thank you, Rhonda. I'll put this in the freezer." Mike chimed in. "LeQuisha, can you come with me? I need your help with something."

I glared at my sister. "Sure."

Mike practically dragged me back to my town-house. He kissed me on the cheek. "Maybe you should go lie down for a bit. Leroy and I will finish the grilling, then I'll come get you."

I rubbed my wet forehead. "Maybe I should."

I landed a kiss on his soft lips. He wrapped his arms around me and squeezed me tightly.

"Good." Mike spoke in his deep, husky voice. Take two Aleve for your migraine and get some rest."

"How did you know I had a migraine?"

He chuckled. "I'm a doctor; I'm supposed to know these things."

I smiled. I ran my hands down his deep chocolate-brown arms, wondering what it would feel like to have them wrapped around my naked body. Quickly, I erased the thought from my mind. I reluctantly turned around and headed upstairs. I knew I could depend on Mike to hold down the fort for me. Even though we had only been seeing each other for three weeks, I knew I could trust him. At first, I was intimidated as hell, dating a doctor. I mean, what did he see in a single mother of three children that barely had two nickels to rub together? But I'd learned one thing through my walk with Christ—stop trying to figure things out all the time, just let it be.

Mike took me out to some of the nicest restaurants in town. In two weeks, we'd made plans to spend the weekend on Amelia Island at a Bed and Breakfast. I couldn't wait! Things were happening so fast, but I felt like I'd known him all my life. We could spend hours talking to each other, and he listened to me. The real surprise was we hadn't had sex. Only kissed. The next time I planned to have sex was with my husband, and I meant that.

But do you want to know what surprised me more than anything? Mike hadn't even tried me like that. Never had a man shown me more respect. And that had to count for something. Our kids got along very well. His ex-wife, Marilyn, was a trip, but I could handle her.

After what only seemed like five minutes, I was awakened by strange noises coming from my daughter's bedroom. Well, they weren't strange to me. I slowly got up and walked down the hallway. I tried to listen through the door first, but I smelled this funky odor coming from the room. I burst the door open.

I grabbed my chest and took two steps back. I couldn't believe it. Two bodies jumped up from the bed and dropped something on the floor.

"Rhonda, what the fuck are you doing in Daneisha's room!"

"Nothing," she said. Tony Red scrambled around on the floor, nervously looking for something.

I picked up the crack pipe from the floor, where it landed. I dangled it in my hand. "Is this it?"

Rhonda straightened her skirt. "I can explain."

"Oh no hell you can't!" I shouted. "I can't believe this shit!" Before I knew what was happening, I pushed Tony Red into a wall. "You muthafucka!—you got my sister usin' crack!"

Rhonda wrestled with me as I landed a few punches on that nigga. "Leave him alone!"

Tony Red bowed up at me. "Your sister been usin' crack longer than me." He laughed. "Now what you gon' do?" He pushed me hard in my face.

I went wild and crazy. I jumped dead on his ass. My arms and feet were kicking. I shouted every curse word I knew at him. Out of nowhere, Gayle and Mike had to pull me off him, his face covered in blood. That's when he pulled out his 9mm gun.

"Back the fuck off me, bitch!" Tony Red's face scrunched up, and he breathed heavily. He took two steps closer.

"Hey, man. . . ." Mike moved in. ". . . You don't want to do this."

I trembled in fear. My stomach twisted into a complete knot. My chest throbbed harder.

"Baby, put the gun away." Rhonda tried to reason with him. "This my family—don't you hurt 'em."

Tony Red flashed a wicked smile. "See here, I know what's going on here." He shook his head rapidly. "Y'all muthafuckas got me mixed up with the wrong one—I'll take all y'all asses out. I don't give a damn 'bout your family . . . just you, baby."

Rhonda grabbed his arm. Her crying intensified. "Tony, baby. Don't do it. Let's go, baby. Let's go."

He glared in my direction. "You never did like me, did you?"

I had no clue what he was talking about. I'd only been around him a few times. Paranoia was common with drug addicts. My head shook rapidly. "I . . . I—"

"Shut the fuck up!" He rocked from side to side. "No, you didn't like me. I tried to get you to like me, but your stuck-up college ass thought you was better than me."

I held my gaze fixed on him, not wanting to move a muscle. Tony Red was high, and there was no telling what he would do. Thoughts of my children finding our dead bodies spread out on the floor flashed through my mind. They would never get over this. *Jesus. Jesus. Jesus. Help us, Lord.*

"You see, I love your sister. I loves her. I would do anything for her. That's why I'm gonna marry her." Tears flowed down his face.

"That's right, baby." Rhonda nodded. "I was gonna tell them."

Tony Red bounced up and down. "Well, I just did; now you don't have to." He grinned and then nodded. "Yeah, let's go."

He pointed the gun at Rhonda's head and dragged her out of the room. "Don't make a move or I'll kill her ass."

I held my hands up in surrender. Gayle and Mike took my cue and did the same thing.

As Tony Red and my sister charged down the steps to make a quick exit, I heard two shots fired.

"No!" I screamed as I ran toward the stairs. He stood over my sister's limp body. He smiled at me as he pointed the gun at his own head and fired once more.

Chapter 29
(Tate)

After a rather long day at work, I stopped by Publix to pick up some groceries my mom suggested I get. Since she was doing the cooking and cleaning at my place, the least I could do was make sure she had what she needed. Since the accident, Tangy did very little around the house. Even a simple task such as washing her ass seemed an impossible feat.

"Hey, baby—I mean, honey." No mention of the word baby around her. I took the groceries in the kitchen and put everything away. "Anything special happen today?"

Tangy's eyes were glued to the television. She scratched her wild head of hair. "No."

It amazed me how this rather beautiful woman had transformed herself into a beastly creature. I'm not talking about the scars from the accident, because despite what the doctors said, very little scarring remained. What I was reacting to was this wild-haired, funky-smelling, foul-breathed, same-clothes-wearing freak of nature I called my wife. Fellas, help me out here. I know I said, "Until death do us part," but what about when you bring the dead home? Do you still have to love it?

I sat on the table in front of her attempting to block her view of the television. "Tangy, do you realize you're sitting in the same place I left you this morning?"

No response. Her eyes scanned the room. Anything to avoid contact with another human being.

Grabbing the remote control, I turned the television off. "You wanna go take a shower with me?" I held her eyes. "I've had a tough day, and I could use the company."

She nodded. "Okay."

"Thank you!"

Holding her hand, I escorted her to our bathroom—just in case she'd forgotten where it was. First washing her from head to toe, I waited until she stepped out to wash myself. Making sure, I brushed her teeth, washed her face, brushed her hair, the beast now appeared more tamed in her appearance.

We sat on the bed in silence. Since I had a lot to think about, I didn't mind.

"American is really starting to bug me out. My director refused to replace two adjusters that quit, and our workload has doubled as a result—not that I can blame them for leaving."

Tangy grabbed my hand and caressed it softly. *Contact. That's good.*

"Although, the money is good, I don't see myself moving up in the company any time soon. I don't want to remain a senior rep for the next ten years."

Her big brown eyes lingered for a moment. "Are you thinking about leaving?"

My lips slowly curled into a smile. "Yeah. I'm in the process of putting together a new resumé. I've been searching on Monster.com, and found a few prospects. The position I really want is with a company based in Georgia. How do you feel about moving?"

She took a deep breath. "I'm okay with that; moving is probably a really good idea."

I swallowed hard, as I felt my stomach growl for the third time. The smell of oxtails drifted over to my nose, and I wanted to fix a plate of my mom's cooking. I rubbed my stomach. "I'm hungry. You want me to fix you a plate?"

She smiled. "Yes."

I was even more surprised to see her follow me into the kitchen.

We actually carried on a decent conversation over a late dinner.

After the meal, we both headed off to bed. As I turned off the lamp on the nightstand, I realized my wife definitely needed professional help. Getting her to come back to the world of the living completely wiped out what energy I had left from working a long, tiring day.

Her mother would be here in a few days. Hopefully, she could convince Tangy to see a therapist. If anybody could, it would be Mrs. Newsome; she had a way of getting her daughter to do just about anything.

The next day, I didn't even bother going to work. I called Gladys to get her busy finding a therapist for Tangy. Then I spent a good part of the morning with my job search.

After placing close to fifteen phone calls, I managed to arrange meetings with five insurance companies. I rested my head on the back of my hands, proud of my small accomplishment.

The phone rang, and I checked the caller ID. It was Glen.

"What's up, man?"

"I called your office, and Gladys told me you took the day off," Glen said.

"Yeah. I'm working on this job search thing."

"I hear ya." Glen laughed. "It's starting to get rough. I'm thinking I need to make that move with you."

"Why aren't you at work?" I asked.

"Man, I'm at the hospital. Terri had the baby last night—I got me a little girl."

I could hear Glen sniffling through the phone. My heart sank. "Hey, I'm happy for you, man. Congratulations. What did you name her?"

"Trinity—you know Terri wanted to be all religious and everything. Trinity Love Thomas."

He sounded so proud. I scratched the back of my neck, trying to figure out how Terri could've created a more fucked up name for a girl. "That's beautiful, man," I lied, not wanting to burst the Terri-filled bubble he floated on. "I was wondering—do you know if Sharon called over here to the house to tell Tangy about this?"

"I think she called her when we got to the hospital—why?"

I folded my arms and rocked from side to side. "No reason."

"I better go. Terri's calling." Glen sounded alarmed.

"All right, I'll see you soon. Congrats again, my brother."

"Thanks. Wait until you see her. She's so gorgeous."

I grinned. "I'm sure she is; it's in the genes."

"Right."

I hung up. *That's why Tangy acted so strangely yesterday.* Saying a quick prayer, I asked God to help us get through this. *Only good could come from it all. Maybe leaving this place would be the best solution.* I loved my wife, and I wanted her to free herself of the cocoon she used to hide her pain. Here it was November, and she showed no signs of improving.

When I met Tangy, she was so goal-oriented with her plans to earn a degree in journalism and become the next Oprah. Now, I felt like she was simply wasting away. *In sickness and in health. Did I really think about this marriage thing? Did I take the vows seriously?*

If only I could turn back the hands of time, I probably would have handled it differently. I scratched my chin. No sense in looking back, I had to move forward.

I stood up and stripped out of my athletic shirt and shorts. Tossing those clothes in the hamper, I changed into a clean T-shirt and jeans. I caught a glimpse of Tangy sleeping peacefully in bed.

Kissing her on the cheek, I headed for the door. Noonday service was set to start in less than an hour with Pastor Givens doing the sermon.

For the next few days, I returned home early from work. Having already made up my mind to leave the company, it didn't make any sense for me to continue putting in the long hours. At one point, I used the time to avoid coming home to my wife.

Before I married Tangy, I was guilty of taking advantage of the time to mess with LeQuisha. It wasn't easy to stop going to her place because, to tell the truth, I missed her. I never appreciated her. I used her as a good piece of ass, even though she did possess a "ba-dunk-a-butt," fitted ever so nicely on the shortest little body. Slicing hips, big breasts, curvy, shapely, LeQuisha had a tight package.

Things ended cold with LeQuisha the day before my wedding. She asked me not to call her ever again. I honored her request and stopped. Eventually, I got used to the idea of not having her in my life anymore, until the day I saw her at the hospital. Then those old feelings crept back in my mind once more.

Hearing the news of her sister's murder, I felt compelled to reach out in support. Tangy had no idea I attended the funeral. LeQuisha was all hugged up with her new boyfriend, so I made my words with her quick. After spending some time with Dante, I exited the funeral, not bothering to drive to the cemetery.

It took everything out of me not to call LeQuisha afterwards. I wanted to know how she was holding up. More than anything, I didn't want to interfere with her new relationship.

Shutting down the computer for the rest of the day, I dialed my house number to check up on Tangy, before I headed home.

"How did Tangy's visit to the therapist go?" I asked over the phone.

"I believe it went fine," Mrs. Newsome told me. "She seemed to perk up a bit. She's in the shower now. You want me to have her call you when she gets out?"

I slid my chair over to my desk. "Please. Thanks for coming. You've been a great help."

"That's my only child. Of course, I would be here for her."

I wiped my sweaty upper lip. "For what it's worth, thank you." I hung up.

Later on that night, I surprised my wife with a huge bouquet of flowers, and she rewarded me handsomely in return.

"That's it, baby—honey," I squealed. "Just like that, yes."

Tangy slid down harder and faster on my shaft. I held her petite frame as I groaned with satisfaction.

"Is it good?"

I closed my eyes tightly and nodded. "Uh . . . huh . . . oh shit!" My body contracted and trembled as I released my manly juices inside her.

Her body tingled for a moment, then she collapsed on my chest, breathing heavily.

Tangy shot me a worried look. "You think she heard us?"

Softly kissing her sweaty forehead, I whispered in her ear. "I think so, yeah."

Tangy giggled and covered her face with her hands.

I grabbed her by the shoulders. "Your mama is probably happy to hear her daughter getting her groove on. You know we've both been worried about you."

Tangy slid to my side and rested her arm on my chest. She nodded. "I know. I'm sorry." She became teary-eyed.

I hated to see her like that. I held her face with my hand. "Hey, you don't have to be sorry. I understand."

I slipped my tongue inside as she parted her lips. Turning on top of her, I spread her thighs and rubbed down inside. Licking her raisin-sized nipples, I lowered my head and worked my tongue inside her wet pussy.

Tangy purred with contentment. With each stroke of my tongue, her body jerked. I waited for her to reach her climax to plunge inside.

"Oh!" she screamed.

I put my hand on her mouth and plunged deep. Then fast. I tenderly stroked her breasts, and my dick tingled as she rotated her hips in a circular motion.

Her eyes widened with the stronger level of intensity.

I growled as I swelled up inside her and let out one final thrust. My eyes lingered on her face. The beauty was back. I held her tightly, and she fell asleep in my arms.

"I thought your flight would never get here," Tangy said in a gleeful tone. She kissed me squarely on the lips.

I held her in a snug embrace.

"It's so good to be home, I missed you, honey." She held my face. "Awwww. I missed you, too."

We went over to baggage claim, where I picked up my roller suitcase and garment bag. Having caught the plane as soon as I left my interview, I didn't have enough time to change out of my suit. Being back in the humidity, I drenched my shirt with sweat, and I couldn't wait to get home to shower.

"It's nice to see you back in your old dresses again." I winked in Tangy's direction as I exited the airport onto I-95.

"Baby, this dress is new. I picked it up at Stein Mart yesterday." She ran her fingers through her long, wavy hair.

"Well, I meant your old style of dress. You've obviously shed those extra pounds, and you look good."

"I know you're not trying to say I was fat," she snapped.

I rolled my neck. "No, I'm not. I'm a black man, sweetheart—you know we like it either way."

Tangy stared out the window for a few minutes, refusing to say another word. *My intentions were to set the mood for some lovemaking tonight. Now I fucked it all up!* My eyes still on her, I could tell by her posture she was mad as hell. *Make that one icy cold shower coming up.*

"I don't know why I overreacted," Tangy said turning toward me. "All you did was pay me a compliment, and I completely twisted your words against you. I'm sorry."

Somebody's been taking her medicine. You know that Zoloft, along with therapy, has done wonders for my wife. Very few mood swings, and now a brotha was getting sex on the regular.

I raised a brow and smirked. "So does that mean I'm gonna be able to make a withdrawal from the ATM tonight?"

Tangy slowly kissed my lobe and then whispered in my ear, "You don't even have to wait until tonight."

Hot damn. I bounced in my seat and gripped the steering wheel as Tangy undid the zipper to my pants. At that moment, I suddenly realized I needed a hot shower. *Oh, hell no. If I let Tangy get a whiff of my smelly nuts, she would never give me another blowjob again.*

"Tangy, let's wait until we get home. I got a little something special planned for us." *Not a damn thing, but by the time I got home I would have something romantic in mind. I wondered if there was whip cream left in the fridge.*

Tangy lifted her head up. "Huh? You mean you want me to stop?"

I nodded, trying to think of an excuse. My cell phone rang in time to bail me out. *Whew!* "Hello."

"Tate, I'm so glad I caught up with you. How was your flight home?

I cleared my throat. "Absolutely smooth. Thanks for checking up on me, Edwina."

"I'm doing more than that—we were very impressed with you in the second interview today; we'd like to offer you the job."

I grinned from cheek to cheek. "Really?"

"Really. You will work out our branch in Warner Robins, Georgia as our new claims director. You'll run the entire office of about fifty of our best adjusters, as we discussed today. Let me see here . . . the salary starts at $124,000 a year with all the perquisites of upper management. I believe Donna supplied you with the benefits package already."

"Yes, she did. I'll look over it tonight."

"Tate, I'm going to need your decision within a couple of days. Phil's last day is at the end of the week, and it would help with the morale if you were able to assume his position soon after."

"I understand. You made your intentions very clear today."

She took a deep breath. "Good. I'll be expecting

a call from you, say, within the next forty-eight hours."

"Let me discuss this with my wife, and I'll get back to you tomorrow morning." I glanced at the huge grin on Tangy's face. I already knew what her response would be.

"Even better. Good evening, Tate."

"Good evening, Edwina."

"Oh, did you get the job?" Tangy wrapped her arms around my neck.

I pumped my fist in the air. "Yeah. You're staring at the next claims director at Metropolitan Insurance. I'm going to be the $124,000 man!"

Tangy screamed in excitement. "I knew you could do it. When are we leaving?"

"Damn, are you that anxious to leave Jacksonville?"

She laughed. "I'm ready to begin a new life with my husband, and if that means moving to Georgia, so be it."

Wow! Was I ready to make that move? Leave my parents behind and start all over. A new job, new city, new home. I guess not everything would be new, I would have Tangy. Maybe, we could work on starting a family again. Yeah, my son or daughter—I really didn't care at this point.

When I stopped at the next red light, I reached over and kissed her. "I love you, girl. You're my rock."

"I believe you. Tate, you don't know how long I've waited to hear you say that and really mean it— from the heart." Tangy rested her head on my shoulder as I drove home.

Chapter 30
(LeQuisha)

"Ma, I should be there in twenty minutes. Need me to stop and get anything?"

"Could you stop by Walgreen's and pick up my blood pressure medicine? Oh yeah, and a pint of butter pecan ice cream."

I sighed. "Ma, if you stop eating all that ice cream, then you wouldn't need blood pressure medicine."

"Please," she hissed, "one don't have nothing to do with the other."

I shook my head. "Ma, I'm the nursing student; I should know."

"Are you gonna get my stuff or not?"

I could sense the attitude in her voice. "Yes." I hung up my cell phone and placed it in the tray.

No sense in arguing with her anyway, it's not as if I'm gonna win. Plus, I needed to buy some cold medicine, since my Sudafed packet was nearly empty. First infected with the cold Mike passed it on to me, spending as much time together as we did.

I knocked on my mom's door after I made the trip to Walgreen's.

Ma answered the door. "Damn. You gotta a key, don't you?" She blew cigarette smoke in my direction.

I looked just like her—flat face, thin eyes. She wore a weary existence.

I coughed. "I didn't feel like digging for it." I strolled in to inspect the cleanliness of my mom's place. Just as I thought, dirty as usual—dishes piled up in the sink; junk mail and old newspapers all over the tables and couch; a dingy, white Christmas tree stood limply in the corner with lots of presents for all her grandchildren; and clouds of smoke filled the air.

My nephews ran out of their room. "Auntie Quisha," Pee-Wee said as he gave me a big hug. Tank took his cue and squeezed tighter.

"Hey, auntie babies." I kissed them both on the forehead. "You hungry?" I held up two bags of McDonald's.

"Uh huh." Tank eyed the bags and snatched both of them.

"Hey, give me my bag." Pee-Wee chased after him.

Ma scratched her head. "Now, how you know I wasn't 'bout to cook them kids something to eat?"

They settled at the kitchen table to enjoy their happy meals.

I smiled. "Now you don't have to." Shifting the dust-filled plastic flowers to the other side of the couch, I created a place for me to sit.

She sat down on her recliner and devoured her ice-cream. A distant look appeared on her face. Sometimes, I think she drifted in and out of this world. "I been thinkin' a lot about your sister."

I folded my arms. "Me too."

"Even though she's only been gone for three months, raising these kids been hard on me." She pulled on her floral robe to cover her pink slip.

"Ma, if you want me to take them, you know I will." I adjusted my position on the couch.

She shook her head. "No, it's not that—Jacksonville is a rough place to raise children. Period. Especially in these horrible times."

I nodded as I pulled a piece of Kleenex out of my purse to stop my nose from running.

"It was bad enough when I raised y'all." She took another spoonful of ice-cream. "Shit, I ain't have no help, but I did the best I could."

I sniffled. "Yes."

"Anyway, me and Leroy were talking about buying a house out in Middleburg; the country could do us all some good." She handed me a real estate book.

I brushed off the crumbs and stared at the picture of the small brick home. I pointed at the ad. "It says here the house is on half an acre of land."

She smiled, revealing her gold front teeth. "Yeah. I figure I could plant me a garden." She tugged on her robe. "And the schools supposed to be real good too."

"Probably is."

"Well, what you think about it?" She looked me squarely in the eyes.

I shrugged. "Sounds like a good idea to me."

She rocked in her recliner. "I was thinking . . .

you might want to move out there too, once you finish school—that way I'd be close to all my grandkids."

I folded my arms. Not quite sure where things were headed in my relationship with Mike, I didn't want to commit to anything. Even though we'd only been seeing each other for four months, I kinda felt like this time around, I'd met my husband. Then again, I also felt the same way about Tate, and look where that got me. "I'll think about it."

She lit another cigarette. "You know I'm real proud of you. You the first one in the whole family to graduate from college." She waved her cigarette. "You was always smart—that's why I was so damn mad when you got fooled up with Donny's no-good ass."

"Big mistake." I waved my hand in the air. "But I did get three beautiful children out of it."

She hiked up her skinny leg and crossed it. "Yep. How could I expect more when I didn't set the best example with these sorry-behind men I was messed up with?"

"You had some bad ones," I joked.

"Yep." She puffed. "I can't complain about the last one, though. Leroy been good to me."

"Where is Leroy anyway?" I asked. *Six years later, and they were still* together.

She turned up her pointy nose. "Up there to ABC, I suppose."

I decided to let that one go. I never said he was perfect. For the first time, she managed to find a man with a decent job. Not much to look at, but his niceness more than made up for his overweight build. There was nothing Leroy wouldn't do for Ma. And I respected him because he never laid a hand on her.

"Well, I'm gon' go ahead and use part of the insurance money to put a down payment on that there house."

I stood up from the couch. "I think that's a good idea." I removed my keys from my purse. "All right, Ma, I'll call you tomorrow." I turned around.

"You do that," she said as she picked up the remote control.

"Boys, you want to help your auntie unload all your presents out the trunk?"

Tank nodded. "Sure."

The next evening, Mike and I went to a quiet Christmas Eve dinner for just the two of us at Peking's, a Chinese restaurant. Over these past four months, my taste in dining had risen a notch or two. Red Lobster and Olive Garden were fine, but I no longer considered them elegant dining. My man was treating me to places where the bill sometimes exceeded a hundred dollars.

Mike rubbed my hand. "Cat got your tongue?" His deep, raspy voice resembled the black guy from the show *24*.

"Got a lot on my mind, I guess." I tossed my head to the side. "I went over to Ma's yesterday."

"How is Gayle doing?"

"About the same. She taking Rhonda's death pretty bad." I closed my teary eyes. "She wants to move with the boys to Middleburg."

"Is she purchasing property out there?"

"Uh huh. I can't help but wonder . . ."

"About?"

"How my life would've turned out if I grew up in a different place. Like New Jersey, for example."

Mike scratched his chin. "Funny."

"I'm serious, Mike. Maybe I would be a doctor like you, you never know. And my sister wouldn't have messed her life up using, and she would still be alive." My throat stiffened. I drank half of my glass of water as the tears flowed.

"Hey, you can't do this to yourself." Mike squeezed my hand. "Playing the 'what if' game and rehearsing past events will not bring your sister back."

I nodded. "You're right. I can't accept the fact that I'm never going to see her again. Sometimes when I walk into my house, I get weak in the knees."

"I've been trying to convince you to move. At least talk to the manager about transferring to another unit."

"Yeah." I took a deep breath. "I'm going to ask Randall about it." I forced a smile. "Okay, enough of this. You're paying good money for this meal, and I want to enjoy it."

"How's the pepper steak?" he asked. He wiped his mouth with a cloth napkin.

"Delicious." I swallowed a mouthful of steak and noodles. "Wanna try?"

Mike looked grossed out for a minute. "Sure."

He accepted my spoonful, and I took great pleasure in feeding my man.

He nodded. "Humph, it is good. Wanna trade?"

I held up my hand. "No, you can have that sushi; it ain't for me."

Mike leaned in closer. "You'll never know unless you try." He held my gaze until my lips parted. Okay, *now* my cooch felt a little tingly.

"Are you offering me the sushi or something else?" I asked playfully.

His eyes swept the room. "Maybe . . . it depends on whether you say yes."

I sat back in my chair and folded my arms. "What are you up to?"

Mike's dark full lips tried to suppress a grin. "Nothing."

"Uh huh. I'm not buying that, Mike." I twisted my lips.

The sudden moment of silence forced my stomach to fold into a tiny knot.

"Okay." Mike pushed his sushi tray away. "I don't want your little head to start spinning." He reached inside his suit jacket and pulled out a small black velvet box.

My hands clasped my face. "No."

Mike swallowed hard. "Is that your answer?" He opened the box to reveal a large diamond ring. With my vision blurred, I didn't even recognize the cut. Hell, I just knew it was a ring!

"What is it?" I grabbed my chest.

"An engagement ring, if you accept," he said, shifting nervously in his chair.

My eyes searched the room and I cringed. It didn't take long for people sitting in the restaurant to realize what was happening.

Was this really happening? It felt more like a dream. Did I love this man? Does he love my kids and me that much? Lord, keep me from making a fool out of myself.

My head jerked up, and I blinked rapidly. "Oh, I accept."

Mike got down on one knee and placed the ring on my short ring finger. Our newly formed audience clapped with enthusiasm. A few screamed. One guy stood up and whistled. With open arms, Mike hugged me for what seemed like forever. For the first

time in my entire life, I had nothing to say—Except
. . . I'm getting married!

"Are you sure you want to marry me?" I asked
Mike in the car as he drove me home.

Mike chuckled. "What is that supposed to
mean?"

"I mean . . . we've only been seeing each other
for four months. Are you sure you want to do this?"

"Yes, I'm sure. LeQuisha, I love you; you're my
soul mate. What? You don't feel the same way about
me?"

"Now you know I'm crazy about you. I'm just
surprised, that's all. You're my boo. And I love you."

Mike placed two fingers on my lips. "I feel closer
to you than any other woman. You're real; with you,
there is no guesswork involved. You tell it like it is—I
appreciate those qualities in you. You're a wonderful
mother, and I know you would make a good wife." He
hit the gas and zoomed through the intersection.
"Don't get me started on your cooking."

I snapped my fingers and swung my head back.
"True." I giggled. "A sista can burn, if I must say so
myself."

Mike laughed. "Oh, you can say so."

He pulled his silver Mercedes into my driveway.

I rubbed my hands together. "Seriously, though,
I know I want to marry you, but are we rushing into
this?"

Mike shut off the ignition. "LeQuisha, we're not
getting married tonight; it's an engagement. We
don't have to rush into anything. But I'm confused."

I raised my penciled eyebrows. "About?"

His muscular arm held onto the wheel. "Since
our first date, all you've talked about is marriage.
You've made it clear from the very beginning if I

wasn't interested in marrying you, then I shouldn't waste your time."

I tapped my fingers on the armrest. "I didn't say that."

"Yes, you did," Mike corrected. "From day one, I respected what you said. I have done nothing but keep it in the back of my mind."

I sniffled. "I never realized you—"

"That I paid attention to you? LeQuisha, I'm not like the men from your past. I appreciate you." He held my hand up. "I love you." He kissed it. "I want you as my wife." He landed the next one on my lips.

"Careful." I leaned back. "You might catch this cold again."

Mike moved in closer. "I want to catch more than a cold."

"Hmmmm, I like the sound of that." I wrapped my arms around him and leaped on top of him.

Mike planted sensual kisses all over my neck. I rolled my eyes back as I savored each one. Things got heated in his car.

"Maybe we need to take this upstairs," I whispered.

Mike took a deep breath and paused. "No, I think I should go home." He quickly tucked in his shirt.

My eyes widened as I moved back to my side of the car. "Oh." I responded as I buttoned up my silk blouse.

Mike shook his head. "Don't get me wrong. There's nothing I want more than to take my gorgeous fiancée upstairs and make love to her, but we made a promise to God. I take that very seriously."

I turned up my nose. "I'm embarrassed. And I'm sorry, Mike."

Mike rubbed his hand across my cheek. "Don't be. I expect you to do the same thing when my flesh is weak."

I clenched my teeth. "I don't know if I can; I'm definitely going to pray about it."

"We'll both pray about it. LeQuisha, I'll call you when I get home."

"Okay." As I went to get out the car, I caught a glimpse of Mike trying to hide his hard on. I gave him one quick peck and unlocked the door to my townhouse.

Hmmm. I guess it was harder for him than I thought. I twisted my gigantic ring around my finger. Mike was a good man. Moreover, he wanted to marry me. I closed my eyes tightly. *He not only loves me, but he respects me. I am the luckiest woman in the world—I landed me a doctor, y'all!*

The next morning, I traipsed downstairs for breakfast.

"Yeah, we're in no hurry to set a date," I said, tugging on my headscarf.

"Don't get the wrong idea," Ma responded; "I'm happy. You waited so long. And I like that Mike."

I switched the cordless to my left ear. "I know."

"He's a good man. And he makes good money too."

Lil' Donny put a plate of pancakes, sausage, and scrambled eggs in front of me. "Thanks, baby." I smiled at him. Then to Ma, "It's not about the money."

"Yeah, right." Her voice sounded sharp.

"Ma, believe what you want," I said through clenched teeth. "I'm gonna get off this phone now."

"All right." She sighed. "Well, congratulations."

"Thank you. Bye, Ma." I put the cordless phone down on the table.

"Thank you for this delicious meal here." I took a bite of my pancakes.

"You're welcome, Mama," Lil' Donny said. "Daneisha helped."

I rolled my eyes. "She did?"

"Yes, I did," Daneisha replied as she entered and fixed a plate.

"Where's my baby?"

"In the room, probably still playing that Spider-Man game," Daneisha said.

I forked up eggs and sausage. "Well, go get him. I have something to talk to y'all about."

Daneisha let out a sigh. "All right."

Once I had everyone seated at the table, I decided to share the good news of my engagement to Mike.

Dante's eyes grew wide. "Can I be in the wedding?"

I rubbed his head. "Of course, baby."

"I'm happy for you, Mama." Lil' Donny kissed my cheek.

"Where are we going to live?" Daneisha asked. "I mean, do we have to move?"

I looked at her strangely. "I know you don't think I plan to live here forever, so the answer to your question would be yes."

Daneisha cocked her head to the side. "It's not like I don't want you to get married; I just don't want to lose my friends."

"I would hardly call those hoochies you been hangin' with friends. Personally, I can't wait to get you around some better girls, instead of these fast-behind ones." I rubbed my elbow.

Daneisha poked out her lips. "Mama, that's not right."

I jabbed the air with my fingers. "You better stick those lips back in. And I didn't ask your opinion."

"Mama, I didn't mean—"

"I don't care . . . and this is for all of you." I sat back in my chair. "Our lives are going to change. Although Mike and I haven't discussed it yet, I'm sure we'll probably move into his house. He has plenty of room. We'll still be a family, only a little bigger."

If anything, I expected Dante to struggle with the change. But Daneisha's attitude was becoming more and more unbearable. Nevertheless, I had a trick for her.

Entering our suite, I thought I had died and gone to heaven. I've never stayed in the Walt Disney World Resort, and this three-bedroom suite was nice! My eyes lit up when I saw the fully furnished kitchen, dining room, and living room. The patio had a nice table and chairs, with a large grill for a barbecue.

Mike showed Donny and Dante to their room first. Tasha and Nicole dragged Daneisha to the room they would share together, while I wandered further down the hall to the master suite. Dropping my luggage, I ran toward the bathroom with the Jacuzzi tub and glass-enclosed shower. *The vanity bar stocked with toiletries would last a month.* And the bed! It was a circular king-sized bed. Slipping out of my shoes, my feet sank into the plush white carpet as I lay on the bed.

"So you found our bedroom?"

"Ours?" I turned up my nose. "I thought you were sleeping on the couch."

"Ha, ha. Very funny." Mike playfully pushed me to the opposite side of the bed.

"Ouch." I pointed at him. "Don't make me break a nail."

"No, don't worry. That would be the end of the world." Mike joked.

I rubbed my hand across his chest. "Mike, this is really nice. Who knew Mickey Mouse had it going on like this!"

He rested his head on a pillow. "I know. I bring the girls here at least once a year."

"Well, now we'll do it together." I snuggled up close and inhaled his sweet fragrance.

"Yes, we sure will." Mike kissed me with his full lips.

I closed my eyes and savored the taste. "What are we going to do today?"

"We can stay right here if you want," he said with a wicked smile.

I hit him in the chest. "Seriously."

"Okay. Today's agenda? Let me check my planner." He pulled out his Blackberry.

"You did not plan the entire Disney trip with that, did you?" I scratched my head. (Alphonso, my barber, had edged the back a little too short for my taste. But, Mike loved my close-cropped cut.)

Mike nodded. "Yes, I did. Here it is. We'll check out the Magic Kingdom tomorrow. Today, we'll relax by the swimming pool, and then fire up the grill with some steaks, ribs, and hot dogs."

"Sounds delicious. Where is the nearest store?"

"For what?"

I placed my hands on my hips. "'Cause, I needs to go pick up some things. Now you know I gotta make my slamming potato salad if we're having a barbecue."

Mike sat silent for a moment. "Right. There's an Albertson's on Lake Buena Vista. How soon do you want to go?"

"Before we head down to the pool."

"Sure. I'll tell the kids."

As he stood, my eyes gazed over every inch of his body. At first sight, I didn't think he was my type at all. But I was definitely attracted to him. Muscular and tall, dressed in a tan silk shirt and khaki shorts, his dark calves tightened with each step. Don't let me start on his behind—Lawd, have mercy!

After a hot afternoon lazing around the pool, we settled on the balcony to enjoy some ribs and chicken to die for. Mike was a good cook, and with my skills, the kids ate until their stomachs were stuffed. Especially, Lil' Donny, that boy know he can put it down.

Lil' Donny and Dante settled on the couch watching videos, and I passed the girls in the room gossiping as usual.

I eased my way down to my room, where Mike ran the Jacuzzi tub for two, covered with red rose petals. Locking the door, I removed my tank top and shorts and appeared completely nude for the first time in front of my fiancé.

"Encore."

I raised my thin eyebrows. "For what?"

"That performance." He chuckled. "Strip out of your clothes and slide in the tub again."

Not wanting to be a disappointment, I climbed out of the tub and sashayed around the bathroom, modeling my large assets.

Mike clapped and whistled.

"Thank you."

"No, I should be thanking you. LeQuisha, I never realized you had such a beautiful body to match your lovely face."

My face turned two shades redder. "You know all the right things to say."

"No, I'm serious." Mike wrapped his arms around me as the bubbles rose up on his chest. "I guess I never allowed myself to go there."

I hugged his lower half and parted my lips.

"Now, it's your turn," he said.

I closed my eyes. I could feel his breath on my neck. "To do what?"

"You have to stop me from what I'm about to do."

I felt his hardness in between my legs. "I can't." I moaned as he ran his tongue in my ear down to my nipples. "I won't."

As I spread my legs, Mike rammed his penis inside me. I straddled my thighs around his and rode him like a cowgirl bucking a wild horse. "Uuhhh," he groaned, holding my hips to steady me.

I gyrated in large circles as I moved up and down.

Water spilled out of the tub onto the floor as Mike thrust harder.

"Oh my God," he whispered.

Don't try to call on Him now. I worked him faster as I reached my climax.

Mike lifted me out of the tub, and we collapsed on the bed. He entered me once more and thrust in and out rapidly. We went at it like two animals in heat. It was bad, but "oh so good" at the same time.

He sucked on my breasts roughly, just the way I liked and I moaned in satisfaction. He softly whispered, "I love you, baby." Tears landed on my chest.

I wanted to cry too. As he swelled up inside me, I screamed.

His body contracted once more as he reached his own climax. I ran my hands down his sweaty back as he trembled.

For the first time, I heard the jazz music playing in the background. My thoughts went to the kids in the next room. *I hope they didn't hear us. Then God. Would He forgive us?*

As we lay there panting, I replayed the entire twenty minutes over in my head. I couldn't believe Mike worked me like that. He always seemed so gentle. I never knew a man with better skills in the bedroom than Tate. Not that I compared him to Tate, because there was no competition. By far, Mike proved himself to be a man. And Tate, well . . . he was a boy in men's clothing.

Mike loved and respected me, never asking me to change. In addition, I couldn't take it for granted. He bonded with my kids from the very beginning. I didn't have to place any demands on him. He was willing to do whatever and whenever from the start of our relationship.

Mike rolled over and wrapped his arm around my waist. "I think we need to go to the courthouse next week."

I tried to catch my breath, but my heart wouldn't slow down. "You can't wait either, can you?"

"No, I want you as my wife; plus, I don't want to keep doing this."

I turned around to face him. "Then let's do it. Does Tuesday sound good to you?"

He nodded. "Yep."

I shrugged. "I don't know; you better check your planner first."

Mike sat up and kissed my neck. "Damn the planner."

We didn't marry the following Tuesday, but rather two weeks later when Mike's parents, Dr. Arthur and Jonita Peeples, arrived in Jacksonville. The beautiful wedding took place in a small chapel on the Winterbourne Estate. (I fell in love with that mansion when my mom worked there as a cleaning lady. I was only ten years old, but I always dreamed of getting married there.) Wearing a silk mocha-colored gown covered in lace, Mike complemented me in a matching linen suit.

Dee-Dee was my maid of honor while Mike's best friend, David, stood as his best man. We included all of our children in the ceremony. Daneisha made a beautiful bridesmaid; Tasha and Nicole were flower girls. Lil' Donny was a groomsman, and Dante a junior groomsman.

I relived the details of my wedding as I shared the pictures with my co-workers.

"And then the reception followed in the formal dining room," Penelope said to the other hospital co-workers at the table.

They passed the pictures around in a circle. "LeQuisha, you looked absolutely radiant."

I blushed. "Thank you, girl."

Darla turned up her nose. "Fancy. Now you big time."

"Hardly." I tossed up one hand.

"Looks like it to me. Soon, you'll be too high and mighty to sit at the table with us." Darla turned to her right and pointed at the bourgeois women three tables down. "You'll be assuming your rightful place at the table of the other stuck-up doctors' wives."

I shook my head. "Can you picture me with those women?"

"Actually, I can," Penelop said. "LeQuisha, you don't give yourself enough credit. You're ten times better than all four of those fat cows, except maybe the skinny one who resembles a walking ad for plastic surgery."

We bust out laughing.

I pointed my finger. "True. But, to answer your question, Darla, I'm not like that. If you're my friend today, then you're my friend tomorrow—please . . . men come and go."

"I don't know. Mike's one of the good guys." Penelope wrapped her long nails around her sandwich. "He's not going anywhere."

"I agree," Darla added. "Hmmph. Everybody ain't able; you need to take care of that man."

I tossed up my hand. "Girl, you know I am."

Chapter 31
(Tangy)

"**C**ome on, you guys." I waved both my hands in a wild frenzy. "We're not going to get this done standing around talking."

"Girl, we got all day to get this done," Sharon snapped. "Now, finish telling me what happened to Sonny and Carly—I know he kicked her out, didn't he?"

I took a deep breath and adjusted the scarf on my head. "Yes, he kicked her out, and she went running to Alcazar."

"Uh huh. Carly is such a slut." Terri finished changing her baby's diaper on the couch.

Sharon tossed her head and hand at the same time. "Don't be badmouthing my girl, Carly. She's the only woman bad enough to stand up to Sonny's fine ass."

"That he is." Terri nodded her approval.

"I mean sexy body, gorgeous smile . . . mmm . . . mmm . . . mmm." Sharon caressed her body with her hands. "That man can light my fire any day."

I cleared my throat. "I don't mean to interrupt your little fantasy and all, but I really need to get this packing done . . . before the movers get here tomorrow."

Sharon opened her eyes. "One more minute." She went back to feeling all over herself.

Terri and I looked at each other from across the room and doubled over in laughter.

"Your sister is crazy," I said.

"Beyond crazy," Terri added.

"Okay, I'm done," Sharon said, as she came back to reality. "What do you want me to do?"

"Line those boxes in the bathroom and clean out the cabinets," I told her. "Anything that's already open and could potentially leak, throw away."

"Okay, boss." Sharon disappeared down the hall.

Terri put Trinity in her portable playpen. I admired how motherly she seemed as she patiently arranged the toys inside.

"Terri, could you finish packing the dishes in the sink? That way you can still keep an eye on lil' mama," I said as I tickled Trinity in the stomach. Her laughter was contagious. I picked up her rag doll and teasingly pretended to hand it to her. As soon as she reached out her tiny hands, I snatched it away. She giggled every time. *What a pretty girl!*

An ounce of sadness came over me. I wish I hadn't lost my own baby. Not wanting to drudge up the hurt and pain, I quickly left the room.

"Are you all right?" Terri asked as she stood in the doorway.

I folded my arms. "No, but I will be; don't worry about it."

"I saw the way you were looking at Trinity. I know it's not easy for you to see her and not remember the baby you lost."

"People keep telling me I should get over it." I felt a knot in my throat. "It hurts so badly, I wish I could make the feelings disappear, but they just won't."

"Aawww. Come here." Terri grabbed my hands. "I don't know what it's like to lose a child. I'm so happy with Trinity, if I lost her I would be broken up inside." She closed her eyes and let her senses flow. "Tangy, what happened to you was an accident. You're strong and healthy; you'll be able to have more children."

I shot her a worried look. "I don't know if it's worth trying again."

Terri grabbed both my shoulders. "It's worth it. And you're going to make a wonderful mother, and Tate, a good father. You know this incident brought you two closer together. And for that reason alone, I know your baby's death wasn't in vain."

My gaze drifted up toward the ceiling. Terri was right. If it hadn't been for the accident, Tate and I would probably be heading for divorce court instead of Warner Robins. My state of being was complete misery, and Tate appeared to be my adversary. I hated him and loved him all at the same time. "You know, you're right. Tate and I are practically best friends now. "We joke and laugh with each other all the time."

Terri nodded. "Yes. And when you guys look at each other, I can feel the love between you."

I rocked my head. "Yeah. You know, from now on when I feel myself getting down about what I've lost, I'm going to thank God for what I've gained."

"There you go."

"What's going on in here?" Sharon asked.

"Nothing," Terri responded, "just having a girlie moment."

Sharon hugged both of us. "Well, you know I want in on that."

We embraced for ten seconds.

Trinity cried out from the living room.

"Lord, I forgot all about my baby." Terri sprinted out the room.

Sharon put her hands on her hips. "So are we gonna eat or what? 'Cause you know I'm hungry."

I rubbed my stomach. "Yeah, I'm in the mood for Chinese."

"Cool. Let's go to Pandora Express at the Regency Mall," Sharon said, adjusting her mini skirt.

I rolled my eyes. "You're always trying to sneak some shopping in. We need to get this packing finished."

Sharon straightened her red tank top underneath her blouse, exposing her big bust. "Well . . . for just one hour, then we'll go. I promise."

As we rode in Terri's Mercedes, I thought about my marriage to the man I now loved more than anything. Tate's new job and promotion offered him great opportunities, and I wanted to support him, be the perfect wife. I missed my baby so much. *It will be so exciting once I get settled in with my husband, because I missed him so much. I wondered how Tate was handling being without me.*

"Ooops." I handed Trinity the rattle she threw

down on the floor. Her smile was so huge, it lit up her entire chubby face. I brushed my finger across her cheeks.

"Uh huh." Sharon hissed as she looked at me in the back seat.

"What?" I asked dumbfounded.

"I know you, Tan. You're thinking about it, aren't you?"

"Maybe." I shrugged and glanced out the window. I really didn't want to discuss it.

Terri lifted her sunglasses atop her head. "Before long, Tan will have some babies to complete her family. I can't wait."

"Not too soon, though," Sharon chimed in. "You've got to finish school first. You received your acceptance from Morris Brown yet?"

"Yes. I'm going next week to check out the campus and meet with my advisor. The online program is perfect for me."

"That's great."

I pulled my skirt down below my knees. "I believe this move is going to give me a new lease on life."

"It should." Terri responded. "This traffic is horrible."

"That's why I avoid Arlington Expressway like the plague. You better learn the back roads," Sharon said. "Oooh, there's Burlington, I need to go there."

"No, you don't either." Terri snapped. "Now, what you need to start doing is paying me some rent."

"I know." I wrapped my sweater across my shoulders. "How do you have money to shop when you don't even have a job?"

"Hey, I have a man. All right." Sharon pointed in my direction. "Don't go there."

"A man? Who's the lucky guy now?" I asked.

Terri gripped the steering wheel as we made a sharp turn in front of the mall. "Some deadbeat."

"Ha." I chuckled.

Sharon sucked her teeth. "Is married life everything you thought it would be?"

My lips slowly curled into a smile. "Not at all. I have to admit." I flipped my hair off my shoulders. "I know Tate only married me because I was pregnant."

"Yeah, and your point of bringing that up is what?" Sharon asked.

I took a deep breath. "Despite the fact we married for all the wrong reasons, together we survived it." I waved my hand. "And now we're stronger and closer."

"No love lost, but found." Terri circled the parking lot trying to find an empty space.

"Yeah, something like that." My eyes widened.

"Whatever," Sharon added. "I say it's the medication."

"Sharon." Terri slapped her sister on the shoulder.

Sharon held up both hands in defense. "Hey, I'm only telling the truth. Tan, you used to be so uptight and nervous all the time. You're so much calmer now."

Then Terri added, "The therapy has probably made the biggest difference."

I put my hands on my hips. "I can't believe you guys are talking about me like this. How come you never said anything before?"

"Because." Sharon did a "valley girl" imitation. "You would, like, have a cow or something."

I burst out laughing. "Not funny." I popped Sharon in the back of the head. She ducked down in the passenger seat, so I couldn't reach her. "Forget you."

Sharon continued with her accent more exaggerated. "Yeah . . . like . . . whatever."

Terri giggled. "Leave her alone."

Sharon folded her arms. "I'm getting a little tired of y'all double-teaming me."

Trinity screamed.

"Triple-teaming."

We roared in laughter.

"Okay . . . Okay . . . I'll end by saying this. Not to say hard times aren't ahead, but I'm confident we'll get through them. I'll be the first one to tell you, if Tate and I could make it, then there's hope for all marriages out there."

"Amen," Sharon chimed in.

"And yes, even a ho' like you, Sharon, can eventually land a husband."

"Thanks for the vote of confidence."

Later that night, Tate called as I stepped out of the shower. I searched like a lunatic for a phone. I dialed the number to his cell phone. "Hey, babe. I couldn't find a phone. There are boxes everywhere."

"The movers didn't show up?" Tate asked.

"No, but they called. They'll be here first thing in the morning. I'm not complaining, since I have a bed to sleep on tonight."

"You know I don't like that. Maybe I should call them."

I rubbed my neck. "Tate, you don't have to concern yourself with the movers. I have it all under control. How's it going on your new job?"

"Good. I love being in charge. It's going to take some getting used to. The guy before me ran a tight ship, so the employees are hardworking and dedicated."

I plopped on the bed. "Glad to hear it. Well, I miss you a lot, honey."

Tate breathed heavily into the phone. "I miss you too."

"Uh huh. How much?"

"How much what?"

I sucked my teeth. "How much do you miss me?"

"A lot."

"That's it?" I asked in a sharp tone.

"What do you want me to say?"

"Something sweet and romantic." I sat Indian style on my bed.

"Okay. Give me a sec."

I closed my eyes and smiled.

"I miss you so much my heart aches every time I think of you."

I savored each word. "Babe, how often do you think of me?"

"Damn."

I sensed the frustration in his voice.

"Is this a quiz?" he asked.

"No, but I just want to know."

"Every second of every hour."

"That's so sweet, baby." My heart melted. "Is that like every minute or every hour?"

"It's like I want you to quit asking me all these damn questions."

"Okay." I pouted. "Don't forget I'll be staying

with Sharon and Glen tomorrow night." I rubbed lotion on my ashy legs. "What time will your flight arrive Thursday?"

"Let me see . . ." There was a long pause. ". . . at 9:50. What time is the closing?"

"Not until 1:00, so maybe we'll have time to grab some lunch then."

"Sounds like a plan." Tate yawned. "I have to get up early in the morning, so I'll call you when I get to my office."

"I'm tired myself. I love you, baby."

"Love you more."

He hung up.

I turned up the radio to listen to some jazzy tune playing. Not that I liked it much, but it relaxed my nerves enough for me to fall asleep.

Chapter 32
(Tate)

"Fran, can we go to the next slide, please." I pointed toward the next screen. "As I was saying, as adjusters, when we're handling claims, we must always keep in mind these are clients." I placed one hand in my charcoal dress slacks. My leg wouldn't stop shaking. "It is our responsibility to provide excellent service and satisfy his or her needs, so our reputation remains intact." Nervously, I flipped through my notes once more. "Any questions?"

Tara Lyn, one of the top senior claims adjusters, lifted her hand. "Tate, I have one."

"Go ahead."

Tara Lyn leaned back and crossed her legs. "Say, we're dealing with some jerk, I mean a difficult client who, no matter what we do, is never satisfied."

I suppressed a grin. "Well, that's where I step in;

please don't hesitate to use me as a mediator to resolve major conflicts."

"Really? You would do that?" Ken asked in a doubtful tone.

"Yes, I would."

Tara Lyn cleared her throat. "Let me explain where Ken is coming from—we've never had a director offer to resolve our problems here."

I leaned back and folded my arms. "How were these problems solved in the past?"

Darius shrugged and looked around at everyone else in the boardroom. "We've pretty much been left to our own devices. Then we get yelled at if we didn't handle a claim properly."

I scratched my nose. "No, trust me when I tell you never hesitate to seek out my help or discuss a situation and bat about ideas. And I don't yell either."

I could sense a dark cloud lifted in the air.

"I'm confused though." I brushed my chin. "How is it I've worked here for two months and never knew this?"

Darius spoke up for the rest of the group. "We didn't know if we could trust you like that, man."

I suppressed a grin. "Now you do." My gaze drifted down at today's agenda. "If there's nothing else, this meeting is over. I don't have anything else to discuss."

The senior adjusters all glanced around the room.

"Enjoy your day. Oh . . . and Rebecca, I need to see you after lunch for your mid-term review."

Rebecca saluted as she stood from her seat. "Right, boss."

Tara Lyn approached me. "Thanks for answering my question."

"You're welcome," I responded with a slight grin.

"I heard you would be open, honest, and fair."

My eyebrows rose. "Where did you hear that from?"

Tara Lyn moved in closer. "From my cousin. She worked closely with you at American Income Life. I'm from St. Augustine, and I spent many summers in Jacksonville. After I graduated from Flagler College, I was offered a job, and I've been here ever since."

Was she flirting with me? Or was she sending mixed messages?

My eyes scanned the room. Fran sat close by on the phone.

"I see."

"Anyway, I'm glad you're here. The other guy was such a stiff,"—She laughed—"if you know what I mean."

We locked eyes for a moment. *Okay. Now, I'm not stupid.* To find a distraction, I searched the table for some files.

Tara Lyn rubbed my collar. "If there's anything I can do for you, don't hesitate to ask." She puckered her glossy red lips. "Anything."

"Sure thing." I backed away. "Now, if you'll excuse me, I need to go over something with my assistant."

"Of course," Tara Lyn replied.

I watched as she sashayed out of the conference room. I wasn't even trying to tap that ass. Here at Metro, I had a clean slate, and I did not intend to fuck up my reputation.

I looked down at my watch. It was already 12:00. The meeting went longer than scheduled. Fran helped me gather my materials, and we strolled down to my office.

I caught a glimpse of my beautiful wife standing at my assistant's desk. After all we'd been through, I wanted my marriage to work.

"Hey, beautiful." I kissed her on the cheek.

"Hey, yourself." She frowned. "Did you forget about our lunch date?"

"No, the meeting ran over." I adjusted the boxes in my arms. "Let me drop this off first."

I grabbed my suit jacket and came back out. "Fran, I'm off to lunch."

"Okay, have a nice lunch, you two," Fran teased.

"Thank you," Tan told her.

We held hands as we exited the building. I put on my sunglasses as my eyes squinted from the bright sunlight.

"So where are we headed?"

Tan shook her head, her hair blowing in the wind. "Does Chili's sound good?"

I glanced at my watch. *McDonald's sounded better.* "Uh huh."

After a twenty-minute wait, we were finally seated.

"So how's your day going?" I asked after we placed our lunch orders.

"I'm glad you asked that question." Tan's big eyes lit up as she handed me a piece of paper.

"It says here your internship has been approved at WMAZ Channel 13."

Tan clapped her hands and giggled. "Yeah!"

I held both of her hands. "That's good news. I'm proud of you."

"Thanks, babe."

I released her hands and leaned back to admire

her gorgeous blue eyes. "So, when do you start?" I grinned.

Tan smiled bashfully. "In two weeks. What are you staring at?"

I held her eyes as I took a sip of lemonade. "You."

"Well, you—" She leaned forward. "You are making me nervous. Do I have something stuck on my teeth or something?"

"You're a trip." I shook my head. "I was admiring your gorgeous blue eyes."

Her face turned red. "I keep thinking about getting colored contacts, hazel like yours, so complete strangers will stop asking me if they're mine."

I laughed. "Well, you can't blame people for being curious."

"Right, but sometimes people can choose the worst times to ask, that's all." She drank her water.

"Yeah, I know what you mean."

As the server placed our salads in front of us, I placed my cloth napkin on my lap. "How are you going to balance your classes with your internship?"

Tan crunched on a piece of lettuce. "Well, I plan to work at the news station until 4:00 and take two classes online."

"Online, huh? We didn't have those options back when I was in college. The only thing that came close was correspondence courses."

"A lot has changed since the caveman days; for instance, we have electricity and computers now." She chuckled.

"Ha, ha." I clapped quietly. "That was good."

Tan grinned. "Oh, so you like that?"

I nodded. "Not really, but I applaud you on your effort to be a comedian."

* * *

"Terri's pregnant."

I shook my head. "Again? Damn that was soon."

Glen laughed. "I know. I know. But I'm excited, man."

"How'd this happen?" I took a bite of my apple. "I thought she was on the pill, and you were going to wait a few years."

"Some shit about her mixing them up or something. It took me a couple of days to get over it."

"I would be mad as hell. Women are always pulling some shit like that."

"Yep. Since Sharon moved back to Miami, we've had more time to make one, if you catch my drift."

"Yeah, I hear ya." I took another bite.

"Well, this leads to the reason for my call."

I leaned back. "What's that?"

"Man, these folks at American Income are tripping. I need to make that move. Now I know you like it where you at."

"Hell yeah. Metropolitan Insurance treats me like royalty up in here." I chuckled. "I ain't gonna lie to you, it was a lot of work in the beginning; now that I've settled in, it's much easier than American. A breeze."

"See, that's what I'm talking about. You think you can hook a brother up?"

"You and Terri want that?"

"We talked about it. The way I figure . . . if I could bring in the same amount of money as you do, then Terri won't have to work. She can stay home with the kids."

"I already checked out the real estate in Warner Robins. It's dirt-cheap. With the money we'll make on the sale of our house here, the mortgage would be next to nothing."

I scratched my nose. "Man, it already sounds like you have this thing figured out. Hey, I know Tan would be happy if you guys moved up here. She's desperate for some friends."

"So, what do you think? Can you help me out?"

"Hey, you're my boy. Send me your resumé. I'll be sure to get it in the right hands."

Chapter 33
(Tangy)

I couldn't have asked God for a better life. Getting away from Jacksonville was the best decision for Tate and me. Life in Warner Robins moved at a much slower pace, and I enjoyed simple things like grocery shopping, eating out, and catching a movie from time to time.

Our home sat on a huge corner lot in Royal Gardens, the most posh subdivision, where the husbands worked and the wives stayed home with their children. Driving home from school, I envied those women I saw playing on the front lawn or groups of women power walking with strollers. Desperately, I wanted to be part of it, but for now I had to stick with my education.

I sat on the patio enjoying the view of my pool and the landscaping of trees, flowers, and shrubs. Tate hired a company to design it and once a month someone came out to maintain the grounds. Our elegantly designed, six-thousand-square-foot brick front home made us the talk of the neighborhood. White people just couldn't figure out how a young couple was able to afford such a lavish lifestyle.

One neighbor asked, "Are you a rapper or an entertainer?"

Another neighbor had the audacity to ask me, "Do you play professional sports?"

Many probably speculated Tate dealt drugs, never once thinking my husband held down a six-figure executive job. Plus, the real estate was cheap, and Tate's earnings from the sale of the condominium covered half the cost of our new home.

"Tangela, you haven't touched your breakfast," my mom said, her hands on her hips. I'd invited them over for our Fourth of July barbecue, and some of Tate's co-workers and my friends from school were due to arrive in a couple of hours.

"I don't have much of an appetite." I danced the fork around the plate of grits and ham.

"Are you pregnant?"

"No. How come every time I complain about not feeling well or not being hungry or feeling hungry you think I'm pregnant?"

She waved her hand. "I do not."

"Mom, yes you do."

She sat down at the table. "Well, you and Tate have been married for a year now. Now, I might be a little old-fashioned and what not, but most married people would have a child by now."

"Did you forget that I'm working on earning my degree." I grabbed my mother's coarse hand. "Isn't that important to you?"

"Of course it is, sugar." My mom smiled. "But

you're a wife now, and the only sure way to seal a marriage is with a baby. So don't you wait too long to do it. Otherwise, a man feels like he can walk away anytime he wants to."

"Tate would never leave me."

"Tangela, don't be so naïve—anything can happen." She looked outside the sliding glass doors. "Well, you just gon' sit here, or you gon' help me with this meal?"

"I'm helping." I squeezed her hand. "I'll start with the baked beans."

After I changed into comfortable clothing, I settled into the kitchen and laid strips of bacon on the beans. Mom diced potatoes and a garden salad all at once.

The smell of steaks, ribs, and chicken floated from the barbecue grill outside. Daddy kept Tate occupied with taking turns on the hot grill and sharing boring stories of war, politics, and sports. I felt sorry for Tate, he looked like he was losing his mind.

"Tangela, what are your plans after graduation?" Mom asked as she poured the potatoes into a pot of boiling water.

"I'm hoping the station where I'm interning will offer me a job."

"My baby's gonna be on TV," Mom said with excitement.

I crossed my fingers. "If I'm lucky."

"You better hold your hands in prayer and claim it in the name of Jesus." Mom held a tight-lipped grimace. "Now I didn't raise you to believe in luck, but faith will get you anywhere."

"You're right." I smiled. "What was I thinking?"

"You weren't thinking—that's what's wrong with young people today. Trying to depend on people and high degrees to get them somewhere in life. If only they would drop down on their knees and ask the Lord, He might give it to them." She shook her head. "We live in a faithless society, where gay people want to get married and hold high positions in the church. Can you believe that?" She laughed. "Lord, the end is near. I just hope I get to hold me some grandbabies before it happens."

I raised a brow. How did we end up discussing gay marriages anyway? And, what did it have to do with her having grandbabies?

I was so upset, I couldn't wait to tell my husband about it. "And then she started talking about the last days and how she might not be able to see her grandchildren."

"What?" Tate's eyes widened.

"Yes, my mom is stressing me about this baby thing," I said, as I folded one leg on the bed.

"Did you tell her we want to have kids?" Tate rubbed the fold of my back and kissed my shoulder blade. "We are the ones in this marriage, not your parents; don't let them stress you out."

"I know I shouldn't."

"Okay, so what's the problem?"

I turned to face him. "I'm scared."

"Scared of what?"

"To try again, because you know what happened last time."

"Tan, that was an accident. It will never happen again; you have to get over it."

I shook my head. "I know, but—"

"But nothing." Tate grabbed my arm. "I say we practice tonight."

"Practice what?"

"Our baby-making skills." Tate hopped on top of me. "You know it takes a while to get it perfected."

I purred as he kissed my ear lobe. "Uh huh."

"Yeah." He kissed my neck. "So there's no time like the present, right?"

"Tate, you're not listening to me. You'll say anything so you can get some." Even though he had other things on his mind, I wanted to finish this conversation for once. Not that I didn't want to make love to my man, because Lord knows I did.

"What?" He sat up. "Tan, you're being ridiculous. Is there something wrong with wanting to make love to my wife? Hell, I've had to put up with your horny parents all weekend."

I laughed. "I know. And we can make love, honey; I just want to finish this conversation."

"Damn!" Tate crossed his arms. "Go ahead."

"Thank you." I propped my head on my pillows. "When do you think it would be a good time to start having kids?"

Tate shrugged. "I don't know. What do you think?"

"Definitely after I graduate."

"All right, I agree." Tate jumped on top of me. "Let's get busy."

"Get off me! We're not finished."

Tate looked puzzled. "Oh, I thought we were through."

I playfully poked him in the side. "No, you didn't."

"I did. What else?"

"I want you to understand I plan to have a career and be a mother. I'm not like Terri or these pathetic housewives around here." I turned up my nose. Okay, so I didn't think they were pathetic. I'm sure I said it more out of envy than truth. Having a career meant more to me than anything. I almost screwed it up in the past, and now I was determined to have one.

"I understand." His eyes pleaded with me for mercy. "Now can we do this?"

"Yes, we can." I giggled as he lifted my gown over my head.

Tate's smile revealed his gorgeous dimples. "Finally, I can get some lovin'."

Chapter 34
(LeQuisha)

On my drive home from Baptist Memorial Hospital, I felt dog tired. Pulling the nightshift was tough, but at least I had the next seven days to rest up. Now, I wasn't complaining because working as a nurse offered me the luxuries I had never been able to afford for my children or myself.

The added bonus was my marriage. Mike took good care of me and asked for nothing in return. What more could a woman want? Newlyweds for only a few months, my husband didn't hesitate to bring me breakfast in bed or offer late-night oil massages. Don't get me wrong, I took excellent care of my man, too. You know I always have. LeQuisha won't be out-done, and my latest surprise was going to be a week-end getaway to a Bed and Breakfast in St. Augustine.

My life seemed like a fairytale, and it was taking a while for me to get used to it all. Mike sold his house, and we purchased a two-story home in Mandarin. I'm not going to even lie, it was a pricey neighborhood, and I loved it. Who knew people were living this good?

The boys adjusted very well and made lots of friends. Everyday my house played host to all the kids in the neighborhood, and I was stepping over empty bags of chips and soda cans to get through the family room. I wondered where they used to hang out before we moved in. The only thing I asked was that they pick up behind themselves before they leave. As long as my house remained clean, we cool.

Okay, I pulled up in my new silver Mercedes, and I noticed Mike's car still parked in the garage.

"Baby, what are you doing here?" I asked as I put down my keys and purse on the dresser.

"I called in for a few hours." Mike scratched his goatee. "Look, we need to talk."

Sitting down on the bed, I rubbed his shoulders. "What's going on?"

"It's Daneisha."

Here we go again. That daughter of mine had served up more than her share of trouble ever since we'd moved here. I let out a long sigh. "What did she do this time?"

"Where do I begin?" Mike waved his index finger. "She refused to clean up the kitchen, stayed on the phone with her friends all night, and yelled at Dante for taking too long in the bathroom."

"I don't get it. Daneisha has her own bathroom."

"Have you seen her bathroom lately? It's not fit for a dog to piss in."

I stood up. "I'm going to have a talk with Miss Thang, 'cause she done slap lost her mind." I rubbed one side of my husband's face. "I'm sorry you've had to put up with this."

"Don't worry about it. Besides, it's practice for Tasha and Nicole in a couple more years."

"I'm going to take care of this once and for all. Daneisha!" I knocked on her door as hard as I could.

"What Mama?" She rubbed her eyes.

"Don't you 'what mama' me!" I pushed her on the bed and pointed my finger. "You got a lot of nerve strutting around this house like you some kind of diva princess or something." I opened the blinds to let some light into the dark pit. My eyes couldn't believe what they saw. "I can't believe you got this room looking like this."

Clothes and shoes tossed all over the floor and bed, plates and cups under the bed, some with food still on them; the horrible smell reminded me of a dumpster. "Get your behind up!" I yanked on my daughter and dragged her into the kitchen. "Start in here first, then clean up your room and that nasty bathroom. I know doggone well I ain't busting my butt at work all night for you to sit up here and not take care of this house."

Daneisha poked out her lips. "You act like I'm your slave or something. Shoot, ain't nobody tell you to buy this big-old house anyway."

I popped her dead in the mouth. "Quit talking back to me. And I'm grown; I ain't got to consult you on nothing I do. Now you better get to work before I bust your ass!"

I stormed down to my room, where Mike sat laughing.

I cracked a half smile. "What's wrong with me? I've been so busy working this past week I haven't noticed anything. I'm going to put in a request for the day shift."

"That's not the problem—Daneisha is." Mike rested his hand on my shoulder. "I see now I'm going to have to get a little tougher on her."

I threw up my hands. "Be my guest. A united front always works best. I'm just so surprised, because my kids have never given me a moment's trouble. Until now."

"Well, it's only one out of three," Mike added. "That's not bad."

"I guess so. I wish I knew where all this was coming from."

"You gotta talk to her," Mike said.

"I know I need to. I've been so distracted lately with the wedding and graduation. Then buying the house and moving in, not to mention starting my new position." I rubbed my aching foot. "I haven't spent any real time with any of my kids. And they have always come first."

Mike picked up his keys. "Sounds like you know what you need to do." He kissed me on the cheek. "Gotta run. See you tonight."

After I took a few hours to get some rest and cool my temper, I joined Daneisha in her tiny bathroom. "What's going on with you?" I asked in a patient tone.

"Nothing."

I leaned on the doorway. "Gotta be something . . . because you've never acted this way before."

Daneisha sat down on the toilet and scratched her head. "I miss our old place—I don't like it here." She cried.

I twisted my lips. "Daneisha, we've only lived here for two months; you haven't given it enough time."

"Yes, I have. I want to go back to Arlington." She stomped her foot.

"Well, that's not going to happen. I moved you and your brothers here to have a better life, go to a better school, and make better friends. I've always wanted this for you."

"Mama, you don't understand." Daneisha rocked from side to side. "There wasn't nothing wrong with our old life. These girls around here act like they all that. I don't want to be friends with them."

I put my arm around her. "You know what, these girls may seem that way at first, but you have to get to know them. Maybe you haven't met the right ones. I admit I haven't tried to get to know my neighbors either."

Daneisha looked up. "Why is that?"

I shrugged. "Partly because I've been busy with my work schedule. Maybe I'm a little scared too. I never lived around these kinds of people."

Daneisha sucked her teeth. "So you know what I'm talking about?"

"Yes, I do." I kneeled down beside her. "But we're not going to let the enemy steal our joy. For my next few days off, I'm going to meet some of these mothers, see if we both can't make new friends."

Daneisha laughed. "Okay, then you gon' see just how hard it really is."

"Are you willing to at least try again?" I looked deep inside her eyes.

"Yes."

"Good. Now finish cleaning up this bathroom, so we can do some shopping at the Avenues Mall."

* * *

Driving down I-95, the long, winding road felt like it would never end. Having pulled in overtime, my body dragged like dead weight. *The drive would do me some good, give me a chance to let off some steam.* That damn Darla tried me at work. Just because I was trying to better my life for my children's sake, didn't mean I was trying to be white. I know it wasn't easy for her, now that I was in a higher position than her. But she needed to take her black behind to college. I worked hard for my degree, and I wasn't going to make any apologies for it. *She got one more time to make another smart comment, and I'ma be all over her monkey ass! Better believe that.*

Them boys had better have their behinds at the door when I get there too. Lil' Donny called me at work to ask if they could go to the skating rink. I wanted to say no, but Mike talked me into it. The summer break was almost over, so it made sense to let the boys enjoy it. Besides, they would be going to new schools this year. Lil' Donny was going to Mandarin High, Daneisha to Twin Lakes Middle, and my baby to Greenland Pines Elementary. Ain't no way I would've agreed, if I knew I was going to have to pick them up too.

I ran my fingers through my hair and caught a whiff of the foul smell—my hair hadn't been done in over two weeks. Putting in my earpiece, I pressed the phone number on my cell.

"Dynasty Hair Salon. This is Tina."

"Hey, Tina." I took a deep breath. "This is LeQuisha. How you doin'?"

"I'm hanging in there."

"That's good." My eyes caught a quick glimpse

of my exit on University. Not even checking my mirror, I quickly crossed over two lanes, so I wouldn't miss it. Horns blared loudly in my ears. "Can you check Doris' schedule and see if she can fit me in first thing tomorrow?"

"Hmmm . . . let me see." Tina breathed heavily into the receiver. "Yeah, if you can get here as soon as we open."

"I'll be there. Okay, girl, see you then."

"I won't be here." Tina smacked her lips. "We takin' the kids to Disney World."

"All right then. Y'all have a good time." I smiled as I remembered our stay at the Walt Disney Resort. *Me and my man definitely gonna have to do that again. Maybe this time without the kids.*

I pulled up in front the rink and Lil' Donny, Dante, and two other boys jumped in the car.

"Hey, Mama." Lil' Donny kissed me on the cheek. "Thanks for coming to get us."

"Anytime, baby."

"Thanks, Mrs. Peeples," Tim said.

"Yeah, thanks," Curtis chimed in.

I nodded. "No problem." I drove down Atlantic, and then popped a U-turn. I sat back in my seat. "I thought you said Daneisha was going too."

"She changed her mind at the last second." Lil' Donny changed the radio station to 92.7 FM. The boys rocked their heads to "Lean Back."

Catching a glimpse of Tim and Curtis in the rearview mirror, I laughed to myself. *White boys know they ain't got no kind of rhythm. Well, Curtis was only half-white, but he must've inherited dancing from his mother.*

"She only changed her mind, because C-Mafia

called," Dante sang in a girly fashion. The boys roared in laughter.

"C what?"

Lil' Donny grinned. "C-Mafia—that's supposed to be his street-rapper name—you know, Chris Turner from our old neighborhood."

"No, I don't either."

"Ms. Benton's boys. They lived two apartments down from us."

I shook my head. "Donny, the woman has five sons. How am I going to know all of their names."

"Well, it's one of them."

"The oldest one!" Dante shouted from behind my seat.

I turned down the volume. "What! Ain't that a grown man? I know Ms. Benton had at least two sons out of school already."

"Yep, that old-ass man is—"

I reached over and smacked my son across the lips. "Watch your language."

Tim, Curtis, and Dante snickered.

"Sorry, Mama. What I meant to say was that old guy is going with your daughter."

"I know you lyin'." I put my hand across my forehead. Lord, have mercy on my daughter if what my son said was true. I thought after our little talk things would get better; however, it didn't. Daneisha was acting just as grown as ever.

And she wouldn't do nothing Mike told her to do. The latest incident happened two days ago when Mike asked her to straighten up the living room. Daneisha told Mike he wasn't her father and he don't tell her what the fuck to do. Yes, this came from my own daughter's mouth. I couldn't believe it.

You know we try to do things by the book, mainly how the white people do it. I tried to talk to Daneisha until I almost turned blue in the face. *Tonight, there would be no more talking.*

"Mama." Lil' Donny broke my concentration. I looked over in his direction.

"May I?" He pointed at the stereo.

I nodded yes, and he turned up the volume to blast the radio once more. My foot hit the pedal a little harder, and we high-tailed it back home. My body temperature went from warm to boiling hot all in a matter of seconds. This was the final straw. *Wait til I get home.* I pulled up in front of my house and entered.

Just stay calm. "Daneisha!" I stormed down the hallway and burst into her dark bedroom, where she lay across the bed with the phone glued to her ear.

"Get off the phone." I folded my arms and tapped my right foot.

Daneisha poked out her bottom lip. "Hey, I'ma have to call you back."

I snatched the phone out of her hand. "Who is this?"

"It's me, Mrs. Peeples, Chris. I'm Ms. Benton's son," he said in a respectful tone.

"Chris, how old are you?"

"Seventeen."

"Seventeen, huh." I twisted my lips. "Well, I don't know what Daneisha has told you, but she is only thirteen years old. And she is too young to keep company."

"Mama!" Daneisha screamed in embarrassment.

"What! She told me she was fifteen. I swear . . . if I knew that, I wouldn't be talking to her. I'm sorry. I'm not trying to go to jail."

"I believe you." I stepped out in the hallway. "Now that you know, you don't need to be calling over to my house."

"I promise I won't. Please don't tell my mom about this—she's already looking for a reason to throw me out."

Still, I had to set him straight. "I won't. If I find out you called over here again, then that will be the least of your worries. You hear me?"

"Yes."

I hung up. My head boiled and I felt a migraine coming. Taking three deep breaths, I went back in Daneisha's room.

"Mama, I can explain." She pleaded with her hands up in a defensive motion.

"Oh yeah." I walked down to the family room. "Lil' Donny, say good night to your friends."

Lil' Donny made eye contact with me. He knew what was up. "I'm going to walk them home, Ma. Come on, Dante."

"What?" Dante whined. "Sponge Bob is getting ready to come on."

Lil' Donny grabbed his arm. "We can watch it at Tim's house."

I waited to hear the front door shut. Any second, my head felt like it wanted to explode. Then I grabbed Mike's thickest belt out the closet. Before I could even comprehend what was happening, I marched in my daughter's room and started swinging. "Who the hell do you think you are?" I fired three licks. Immediately, a release of anger escaped through my pores.

"You must think you grown"—Two more licks—"I'm sick and tired . . . of your mouth and your damn attitude." I gave that girl so many chances. Now she had pushed me to the point where she was calling my bluff.

Daneisha ran to the other side of the room. I caught her with one hand and slung the belt with the other. "Mama, please."

I popped her again, this time with the buckle.

"Awgh, Ma . . . Mama!" she hollered. "I'ma do better, I promise." Daneisha began to hyperventilate.

I stopped long enough to catch my breath. I observed the welts all over her body, every one of them deserved. This was the first time I ever had to beat one of my kids. They'd never given me a moment's trouble. But now I could see I had a rebellious preteen on my hand, and I was going to take care of this problem before it got any worse.

I snatched the phone out the wall. "I better not catch you on the phone, watching TV, or out of this house for at least two weeks." I took a deep breath. "Until you start respecting what I say and what Mike says in this house, you're not going to do a damn thang!"

Daneisha wiped snot from her face. "Okay. I'ma do right, Mama, I promise."

"You better." I pointed my finger. "Or the next time, I gonna break my foot off in your ass!"

Once everyone was off to bed, I spread out on the couch, drinking a glass of red wine to help me relax. *What is it with my life!* It seemed like every time I thought I had it under control, something else happened.

Finally, I was living the life I'd dreamed about. I had a good husband, a beautiful home, a nice car, and a good job. Now, I couldn't even find the time to enjoy it or a reason to.

I'm never gonna be happy. I wiped the tears from my face and sank even deeper into the cushions.

Mike came in just as I started to doze off.

"You're sleeping with your glasses on again."

I yawned and stretched out my arms. "That's because I'm not 'sleep; I just closed my eyes for a few minutes."

"Okay."

He landed a wet kiss on my cheek. "How was your day?"

"Don't ask."

Mike sat down beside me. "What happened?"

"Daneisha is what happened. Did you know she was seeing a seventeen-year-old boy? At least that's what he said." I closed my eyes as I told him how I found out from the boys. I shared with him all the events that happened next—blow by blow.

Mike lowered his head. "I can't believe you did that."

"She deserved it."

"Not that." He grabbed my hand. "I'm not an expert, but LeQuisha, you're going about this all wrong."

I stood up from the couch. "What? You're the main one that keeps telling me I need to do something about my daughter, and now when I do something, you tell me I'm going about this all wrong."

"You know I don't believe in spankings. My parents never used it, and I turned out okay." Mike shrugged.

"Mike, you grew up in the suburbs. What kind of real trouble could you have gotten into?" I snapped my fingers. "I grew up in the projects, and where I come from, you get your behind tore up when you're disrespectful and choose not to mind grown folks."

"So you grew up in the hood." His tone was patient. "You're not there anymore. Baby, you're a nurse and what you did is considered child abuse. I will not be a part of that."

"Mike, I know you're not trying to tell me how to raise my children." I put my hands all up in his face.

Mike manhandled me and pushed me down on the couch. He pointed directly in my face. "I consider your children to be my children too. Now, I am the man of this house and there will be no spankings, whuppings, or whatever else you want to call it going on in this house! I could lose my job and practicing license over something like this. I will not be a part of it." He rested his hands on my shoulders. "Are we clear?"

Mike never manhandled me like that before. While I was mad as hell, I couldn't stay that way for long, because he did have a point. What I did to Daneisha is exactly what I have reported other parents for doing to DFC on my job.

I nodded. "You're right." Tears welled up in my eyes. "I'll talk to Daneisha in the morning."

"Great." Mike put his arms around me. "You're an excellent mother. Daneisha is going through a rough period, that's all. She needs a little more time to adjust to all this."

I wiped my eyes. "You're right. She's always been a well-behaved child. I know she can do better."

Mike and I decided we would make some changes in the house. We needed to spend more time with the kids and listen more. *Eventually, Daneisha would come around.*

Chapter 35
(Tate)

To say I was nervous wouldn't even scratch the sur-
face. Yeah, I was happy that my boy started at
Metro Life. Somehow, though, I felt like he invaded
my turf.

Overcome with emotion, Tan and Terri bonded
like old times. The more I thought about it, having
my boy around would do wonders for me too. Now, I
had a partner to hang out with at the sports bar to
watch the Jaguar's games. *What? I know you didn't
think I turned into an Atlanta Falcons fan. Get the fuck
out of here!*

As I reviewed more customer service forms, Glen
stopped by for a few minutes. We greeted each other
with our special handshake.

"You moved in yet?"

"Just about." Glen's eyes danced in circles. "Now
this is what you call an office."

Carrie, the company's interior designer, purchased all of the furniture for my office. I wasn't about to tell him that. The chocolate-colored wood desk and matching tables, filing cabinet, and chairs gave me the masculine touch. Red, orange, and brown were the accenting colors. Even the plush carpet had the same color pattern. The tall windows overlooked the view of downtown.

"It's pretty nice. What can I say?" I grinned from ear to ear. "Man, I'm blessed."

"That you are, my brotha." Glen put one hand on his chest. "Man, I'm not hatin'."

I leaned on the arm of my chair and folded my arms. "So you're not going to have a hard time with this, you know, me being the director and all?"

Glen laughed. "It feels weird, but no, I don't have a problem with it. Hey, I'm just glad to be here."

I sat back down in my leather chair. "Good. Are we still on for lunch?"

"You better know it." Glen gathered his box of belongings. "Well, I better—"

"Sorry to interrupt." Tara Lyn cleared her throat. She stood there in a honey-colored blouse and mini-skirt that showed off her muscular calves.

I relaxed in my seat. "Oh, we're just finishing up."

Glen picked his up jaw from the floor. "Right, I'll . . . uh . . . I'll see you later."

"Okay." I raised my eyebrows. "You'll have to excuse him."

Tara Lyn winked. "I'm used to it; he's not the one I'm after."

"Huh?" Now I was the one clearing my throat.

She waved her hand. "I'm not into married guys."

"That's good." I laughed and wiped my forehead.

"I know I'm getting these reports to you a little late, but I needed to make a few more phone calls first."

I looked over her file. "It's quite all right. I see you managed to close ten accounts last week."

Tara Lyn leaned in closer, revealing her ample bosom. "Well, I aim to please."

My eyes grew wide. I tried to hide my expression in the file. I hoped she didn't notice. The last thing I needed was to give a reason to encourage her. "I can see that."

I heard a tap on the door. It was Glen. "I knew there was something else I needed to discuss with you—it's kind of urgent."

Tara Lyn rolled her eyes in disgust. "Sure. See ya later, Boss."

Glen waited until she left before he spoke. "Are you all right?"

"Of course," I said emphatically.

"Oh, 'cause ol' girl lookin' like she want it bad." Glen wiped his brow.

"Naw, man. She ain't into old married guys like us."

"I didn't say me—I'm talking about you." He moved in closer. "You better be careful, you know what happened last time."

I felt my blood pressure rise. "Now, you know there was nothing to that. Why you gotta bring that up?"

"I know that. Nevertheless, you have to watch your back. No matter what the outcome, some people are still going to think there was. Sometimes these things come back to haunt us. You don't need that."

I held up my hands. "Leave it alone. You're going there, and I don't need you all up in my business."

Glen backed up. "Okay. Hey, I'm your boy. If I don't tell you, who will?"

"I know. I got this," I said in a cocky manner. The last thing I wanted to do was cause some drama on my job. I liked where my life was. In love with my wife, job, and future. No way was I going to mess that up. Thinking back to the promise I made to God at Tan's hospital bed, I knew not to cross that line.

I tossed my keys on the kitchen counter as I entered from the garage. Feeling my stomach grumble again, I pulled out a container with leftover meatloaf and mashed potatoes. Popped it in the microwave for two minutes, and I was chowing down in my bedroom.

Glancing down at my watch, it would be another hour before Tan was home from school. A brotha could relax and be the king of the castle. Flipping through the channels, I settled on watching *Die Hard*.

My thoughts reflected back to work, as I rode on a natural high. Mid-year reports came in, and I had even more productive results than my predecessor did. Those cats up in the corporate office were impressed. The entire office ran smoothly, and it was only a matter of time before I would announce Glen's promotion to supervisor. I promised to help him hit the six-figure mark, once he was able to prove himself. I knew it would anger some of the reps, but I ran the show. In addition, Glen had supervisory experience from American Income. Edwina gave me approval for the change, and that was all I needed.

To celebrate the mid-year's success, I wanted to throw a pool party at the house for my entire staff. Fran hired an event coordinator to handle the details, but I still had to run it by Tan first.

As the running credits ran on the screen, I heard the garage door buzzing. A few minutes later, Tan walked in and put her backpack on the chaise lounge.

"You don't look so good," I said.

"It's worse than you think." She responded and plopped down on the bed beside me.

"Let me help you relax." I massaged her shoulders. "Your muscles are tight." I worked my hands down her back.

Tan moved her head to one side and smiled. "Feels good."

"Wanna talk about it?"

"Not really. I'll just get upset all over again."

"All right." I took a deep breath. Here goes. "Maybe this will help you to forget—I have some good news."

"Oh yeah?" Tan leaned back. "What?"

"My mid-year review was rated a 4 out of 5," I stated proudly.

Tan turned around to face me. "Babe, that's such good news." She hugged me. "I'm so happy for you."

"Thank you. And I'm getting a three percent raise."

Tan's eyes grew wider. "For real?"

I nodded. "Uh huh."

"Congratulations, honey." She brushed her

hand across my cheek. "You deserve it. We should celebrate."

"That's exactly what I was thinking." I grinned. "Except . . . I wanted to do something for my staff; you know, reward them for all of their hard work. I didn't want to be selfish."

Tan stood up. "Right. What do you have in mind?"

"I wanted to have a pool party right here at the house."

"Are you out of your mind?" Tan asked incredulously. "We couldn't possibly have enough room for all those people."

"Yes, we can. Fran's going to—"

"You already started planning this without talking to me first?"

"Of course, not." *This was not going well. Damn. Think fast.* I rubbed her shoulder. "I just thought it was a good idea. If you don't agree, then we can find another location. No big deal." My gaze drifted to the floor as I took an extra long sigh.

"Well . . ." Tan took a deep breath before she proceeded. ". . . I guess we could have it here. I've always wanted to host something at this big house, give the neighbors one more thing to gossip about. Let's do it."

I rubbed my chin. "Naw. Don't worry about it. You have too much going on right now; I wouldn't want to burden you."

Tan grabbed my hand. "Babe, let's do it. I think it's a great idea."

"Are you sure?"

"Positive."

Two weeks later, your boy was chilling by the poolside with a margarita in one hand and my baby in my arms. She was looking sexy as hell in a red and yellow bikini. Since we both worked out at the gym, Tan had a six-pack of her own to show off.

"Baby, I'm going to check on the food. I'll be right back."

I revealed a dimpled smile. "Relax. That's why I hired a full staff today. Everything is taken care of. Why are you trippin'?"

Tan stood nervously. "I just need to check on one thing." She walked away quickly. I noticed her hand on her forehead. She didn't look okay.

I slid in the water to cool off.

"Where are you going?" Tara Lyn asked. She swam up in between my legs. "I came over to talk to you."

Pulling my legs out of the water, I searched for Tan. No sight of her anywhere. "Uuhh. Well, I'm kind of busy."

"If you're looking for your wife, I heard her say something about having a migraine and taking a nap earlier." Tara Lyn rubbed my leg.

I knocked her hand away. "That's not proper conduct, young lady." I looked around to make sure witnesses were in clear view.

She giggled. A group of beautiful women surrounded us.

"Friends of yours?" I asked. "I said you could bring one guest."

Tara Lyn put two fingers on her red lips. "Shhh . . . I won't tell if you won't."

"Hi, I'm Maria." The tall, thin one reached out her hand for a handshake.

"I'm Tate. Nice to meet you."

"Oh, so this is your boss?" the one with curly hair asked. "He's cuter in person. I'm Denise."

They all snickered.

"What's so funny?" I asked, feeling like my manhood was in question.

Maria moved in closer. "Ooohh . . . the things we could do to you."

"Sorry." I backed the fuck up. "Not interested." I leaped completely out of the pool and I went in the house to search for Tan.

Sharon stood in the hallway in front of my bedroom.

"Is Tan in there?"

"Yeah. She has a migraine." She folded her arms. "Having a little fun out there in the pool?"

I shook my head angrily. "It's not what you think."

Sharon rolled her eyes. "Whatever you say, Tate."

Choosing to ignore her comment, I went inside. It was dark and all I could see was a hump in the bed. "Hey, baby, you okay?"

Tan lifted her head and groaned. "My head hurts."

"Awww, why didn't you tell me about this earlier?" I sat next to her. I ran my fingers through her hair.

"I didn't want to ruin your party; you've been so excited about it these past few weeks." She rubbed her forehead. "I'll be all right."

I touched her forehead. It was blistering hot. "No, it won't. Tan, you have a fever. I'm taking you to the emergency room."

She opened her eyes. "No, I'll be fine. Just let me rest, okay."

"I don't think that's a good idea."

Tan grabbed my arm. "Babe, you know I hate

hospitals. I'll go see my doctor in the morning. Now go back to your party. Sharon's here. If I need you, then I'll send for you."

With her insistence, I went back outside—only to end the party early. Fran told the guests my wife wasn't feeling well. Little by little, people made their exit. Some told me they had a good time, and a few offered sympathy for Tan. I thanked them all for coming, tipped the staff, and retired in my bedroom to get some sleep.

By then, Tan appeared well rested and sat up watching TV.

"You recovered quickly, I see." I stripped out of my trunks and wrapped a towel around my waist. My body felt nasty, and I needed to wash my ass.

"Not soon enough," Tan hissed.

I scratched my ear. "Huh?"

"I heard all about you and Tara Lyn and those hoochies in the swimming pool." Tan folded her arms and pouted.

"See, that's why that damn Sharon needs to mind her own fuckin' business." I threw up my hands. "Ever since she's been here, she's getting stuff all wrong."

"What?" Tan pointed toward her chest. "Did you think she wasn't going to tell me about this?"

"No, but I'm sure she exaggerated the situation." I paced the floor. "Probably got you thinking I enjoyed the whole thing. Truth is, them girls caught me off guard. I jumped out the pool as soon as it started."

Tan moved to the edge of the bed. "I don't believe a thing you say. You're probably fuckin' all those whores!"

"What!" I sat down beside her. "I'm your hus-

band. Tan, I know I haven't always been honest with
you in the past, but—"

"But . . . what?" Tan cocked her head to the side.
"From the beginning, you have done nothing but
cheat on me. Don't even sit here and tell me you
weren't messing with LeQuisha when we were married."

"No, I didn't—"

Tan socked me dead in the jaw, and I grabbed it
to stunt the pain.

"You're a lyin' muthafucka! I hate you!" Tan
spat in my face. "You make me sick!" She stormed
out of the room. A few seconds later, she re-entered.
"No, you get the fuck out!"

I held up my hands in surrender. "Come on,
Tan." I rubbed my jaw. "Where do you want me to
go?"

Tan lowered her voice. "Out of here."

I grabbed a pillow and walked out. Turning on
the TV in the living room, I stretched out on the
couch. *Ain't this some shit! It's all Sharon's fault.*
Sleeping in the guest bedroom down the hall, I'm
sure she was laughing herself to sleep. I knew there
was a reason why Glen and Terri refused to let her
stay at their house. *If her own sister wanted nothing to do
with her, why was Tan so willing to take her in?*

In addition, don't even get me started on Tara
Lyn. Monday wouldn't get here soon enough. This
conversation was long overdue, and I needed to stop
it before it went further. Sure, I'll admit a little flirta-
tion raised my ego a bit. Being a married man, the
playa in me reared its ugly head again. But, there was
never any intention to fuck that girl. Like I told Glen
before, I learned my lesson and I knew better than to

have sex with another co-worker, especially a subordinate.

The next day, Sharon returned to Miami. She was nothing but trouble. I had a talk with Tara Lyn.

Tan retreated to the master bedroom from the time she got home and only came out when going to school or her internship at the news station.

How did my life end up this way!

Weeks had passed, and I still got the silent treatment from Tan. Lack of attention, conversation, and sex was starting to wear me down. My negative attitude showed at work, and I felt like I was losing control.

Tara Lyn's agreement to stop flirting only lasted a week. She was back wearing the seductive outfits and dropping sexual hints more than ever.

"You want me to suck your dick?" she asked.

I licked my lips. "Yeah."

"Damn. Suck it harder. Ooohh . . . that shit feels good."

Tara Lyn turned over on all fours. "Fuck me from behind."

I guided myself inside her wet pussy.

"That's it, Daddy."

I smacked her plump ass. "That's right, bitch—who's your fuckin' daddy?"

"You are," she squealed.

Smacking her harder, I pumped in and out more forcefully. "Who?"

"You!"

I grabbed her hair and pulled her face close to me. I whispered in her ear, "Say my fuckin' name."

"Tate."

Smack.

"Louder, bitch."

"Tate!"

I jerked my dick harder and released cum all over my hands. Reaching for the towel beside me, I dried myself off. This was fucked up! No married man should have to resort to this.

While I stood in the shower, my thoughts drifted to Tara Lyn's supple breasts. I imagined her large nipples pointing at me. I started to rub my dick.

As I dressed for work, I tried to force Tara Lyn out of my head. My mom told me, "The Lord will never give you more than you can bear." I hoped it was true, because I felt like I was nearing my breaking point.

I wanted to blame it all on Tan, because she knew it was wrong to hold out on her husband. The worst part—Tan was mad at me for nothing. *I should've had sex with the woman, if I knew I was going to be in the doghouse this long.*

Chapter 36

(LeQuisha)

"I'm afraid Daneisha will serve a suspension for five days," Dr. Wright stated. "How soon can you pick her up?"

"Right now?" I realized I had three more hours of my shift remaining.

"You couldn't possibly expect me to send her back to class?" she asked smugly. "Your daughter struck a teacher with a book. Daneisha should be expelled, considering the number of referrals that have been issued only two months into the school year."

Taking a deep breath, I leaned on the counter and said a silent prayer. "I understand. Don't you have in-school suspension. Is there anyway she can remain at school and catch the bus home?"

Dr. Wright breathed heavily through the receiver. "I'll send Daneisha down to ISS for the remainder of the day."

"I appreciate it."

Being a mother for fifteen years, not ever did I even have one of my children get a referral, far more suspended from school. I'd done all I know to do to deal with this daughter of mine—talked to her, punished her, beat her behind, and took everything away.

When I got home that evening, Mike and I sat down and talked to her calmly. Daneisha apologized for her behavior and even went so far as to write a letter of apology to her teacher.

Mike sentenced her to a month of restriction, and she accepted it with no back talk. I believed she learned her lesson. While she was home during the day, Mike assigned her reading and math lessons to complete at home. Three days had passed so far, and she did a good job, even had the entire house clean. I thanked God my family was back intact.

Taking a two-hour lunch break, I drove home to surprise Daneisha to lunch at Olive Garden. Entering the house, the silence gripped me. I picked up the phone to call Mike at work.

No answer. The voice mail picked up.

I forgot. He's in surgery all day. Damn.

Thinking long and hard, I wracked my brain, trying to figure out where that girl could be. Suddenly, it hit me. I jumped in my car and sped all the way to Arlington, taking every shortcut I thought of.

I pulled up in front of Reesy's apartment. I noticed her car was missing from the spot next to where I used to park everyday when we lived here. I sat in my car wondering what I was going to do next.

* * *

Later that evening, I told Ma what happened. It wasn't easy to talk about, but I needed to discuss it with someone; otherwise, I was going to explode.

"Was she there?" my mom asked.

"Yep." I gripped the phone harder. "I burst up in there with the bat and went to swinging. Since Reesy wasn't there, I whupped Kendall's behind too."

She chuckled. "Quish, you're a mess!"

"I was so angry. Nothing in this world could've prepared me to see my daughter in the bed with that boy." More tears welled up in my eyes. I clutched my chest.

"I know. I know it hurts." Her voice was soothing. "Daneisha has never done anything like this. It's gonna be all right. It's gonna be all right."

"Ma, I just don't want her to end up like Rhonda," I said as I cried harder. "I miss her so much."

"I know you do. Daneisha is nothing like Rhonda."

"I don't know. It seems like it. Ma, she rode that boy like she was a pro. Obviously, this has been going on for a long time, right under my nose." I sniffed. "This is all my fault. I've been so busy with work that I haven't taken—"

"I'm not going to sit here and let you blame yourself. Quish, you are a good mother. A damn good one. Better than I ever was. Daneisha knows better, because you have taught her; there is no excuse."

I shook my head. "I could've done better. Ma, you haven't been here."

"Could've, would've, should've—it's all water

under the bridge. I'ma tell you what to do. Send my fast-ass granddaughter down here to live with me. I'll straighten her out!"

"Ma, you're busy with the boys; I can't add anymore to your plate."

"Shoot, them boys ain't no trouble. Daneisha need to get a good dose of this here country life out here in Middleburg. She won't be able to catch a bus nowhere. You already said she been kicked out of school. I'll get her registered right over here."

As I listened to my mother, she did make sense. I told her I would talk it over with Mike before I made a decision.

Standing outside of Daneisha's room, I heard her crying like it was the end of the world.

Discussing the situation with Mike wasn't easy either. Y'all know I loved my husband. I respected him for wanting to be the man of the house and everything. When it came to raising my children that is where he bit off more than he could chew.

"If we send Daneisha away, she's going to hate us." Mike paced back and forth in front of our bed. "I still think there's another solution to this. We just have to be patient."

"This is where you're wrong. Trust me, I know what I'm talking about. My sister started acting the exact same way. Mike, I can't let Daneisha go down that path." I folded my arms.

He sat down beside me, put his arms around me, and squeezed tight. I placed my head on his shoulder.

"Have you talked to the boys?"

"Uh huh." My voice went hoarse. "Mike, they don't deserve to live in this house with all this chaos.

Lil' Donny wants her gone, and you know Dante—he cries over spilled milk, always wanting to save something or somebody."

Mike laughed. "He's a lot like me."

I punched him in the side. "I know."

After we prayed about it, I could tell Mike changed his mind.

"Well, it's only a temporary solution; I'll go along with it for now"—Mike touched my chin—"if you believe this is best." He landed a wet kiss on my lips.

Savoring every bit of it, I pulled him closer. Being so caught up with Daneisha and work, I realized I had neglected my husband. As he worked his way down south, I rubbed my fingers around his smooth bald head. *I loved this man!*

I allowed my thoughts to wander away from my problems and enjoyed the moment. "Uuuhh . . . baby, that feels so good." Every blood vessel in my head exploded as I released my sweet juices.

Mike licked his lips and raised himself over me.

I squeezed his broad shoulders as he guided himself inside me. Wrapping my legs around his muscular thighs, I met each thrust with a circular jiggle.

Mike moaned. "I love you." He kissed me.

I swirled my tongue in his ear and whispered. "I love you more."

I didn't sleep at all. Only tossed and turned. Even though I knew we made the right decision, I wracked my brain to find a better way to handle this. Daneisha was my only daughter, and I loved her so much. Needing a distraction, I turned on the TV and flipped through all the channels. Finally, I settled on CNN. My eyes felt so heavy. I thanked God for giving me rest and peace of mind about the situation.

The next day, we loaded Mike's car with all of Daneisha's stuff and dropped her off in Middleburg. It was the hardest thing I'd ever done. Knowing I made the right decision, I thanked my mother for taking her in. Part of me knew Ma was doing this for herself. She felt guilty for the way she raised us and wanted to do all she could to make up for it. No matter how much I tried to reassure her, she never believed she did a good enough job.

"What are you thinking about?" Mike asked.

"You already know." I smiled. "I'm going to miss my baby girl."

"Yeah. It won't be the same." Mike leaned back in his seat.

I adjusted my seat belt. "We'll finally be able to enjoy some peace and quiet, though."

"With all the friends the boys have, I'm not so sure."

"I think we're going to have to make some changes." I scratched my head. "I'm going to stop working so much overtime."

Mike's thick lips parted. "I was thinking the same thing."

"After last night, I realized my husband could use more quality time too."

He raised an eyebrow. "Now you're talking."

"Since Tasha and Nicole will be here for the weekend, why don't we drive down to Miami?"

Mike slowed down for the red light. "Okay. I'll set up the reservations at The Fountain first thing in the morning." Mike ran his hand across the left side of my face. "Come here."

I moved in closer to my man.

"I love you." Mike searched deep into my eyes as if he wanted approval to continue. "We're going to get through this." Grabbing my hand, he kissed it gently. He gripped the steering wheel and pressed the gas pedal.

At that moment, I felt more secure than I ever had in my entire life. Having a mother with many lovers coming in and out, I never had a man I could depend on. Donny abandoned me long before he ended up in prison. Kenny never intended to leave his wife, so he used me up, even though I got something out of it too. Still it wasn't enough. And Tate—I stared out the window as my eyes teared all up. Needless to say, I experienced more pain as I set myself up, believing he would marry me and be a father to my children.

Ladies, take heed to my advice—just because a man has a good job, is fine as hell, and puts it down in the bedroom, doesn't mean he's the right man for you. Tate never respected me, and I ignored that, believing I could make him love me. With time, my dumb behind thought I would win this man over by being everything he needed me to be. All along, I was losing the most important person—ME. Without me, I couldn't be all God intended me to be—wife, mother, daughter, and, above all, His child.

As soon as I came to my senses, I bettered my life. Going back to school, dropping all the dead weight around me, and focusing on my children. Then one day that gorgeous black king entered my world.

I laughed to myself, just thinking how Mike seemed to fall out of the sky and land in my lap. I never had to do anything except love him.

Mike faced me. "What's so funny?"

I shook my head and smiled. "Nothing. I'm just trippin'."

Chapter 37
(Tangy)

Once I packed all my belongings, I mustered the strength I could to walk out of the place with my head held high. I was so certain the station would offer me a job after my internship ended. Instead, Pete Hughman hired all but two of us. How humiliating! *It's obvious that jerk never liked me, and I couldn't stand his pot-bellied butt.* I wanted to work as the producer's assistant, and I would've put up with his nasty self to get the job. All that time, I thought Kate and I were cool, and all along, she was talking about me behind my back.

Feeling flustered, I stared back at my reflection in the bathroom mirror. Wiping the tears away, I finger-combed my hair and straightened my collar. On my way down the "Hall of Doom," Doug came out of the lounge, holding a small briefcase. I knew my being fired wasn't racially motivated, since Doug was one of the preppy white guys everybody seemed to like.

"You want me to help you with that?" he asked. "Where's your stuff?"

Doug stepped closer and whispered in my ear, "I packed last week. Let's just say, Pete didn't take to my dry sense of humor."

Doug carried my box and followed me to my car. He invited me to dinner to at The Outback Restaurant. I put my things in the trunk and hopped in his shiny red Mustang without hesitation. It's not as if I could go home and talk to my husband about my bad day. My shamble of a marriage was in trouble.

How could I be married to a man I didn't trust? Tate had done nothing but cheat on me from day one. And he lied to me each time without even feeling a tinge of guilt. I didn't believe anything that came out of his mouth. Doing anything I could to make this man love me, including getting pregnant, got me nowhere. I almost gave up my education and career dreams just to be his wife and mother to his child.

Knowing Tate and I were headed for divorce, I focused more on my internship, believing it would materialize into a future career at the station—that's why I was so pissed.

Doug seemed angrier than I did. He explained how he and the station manager butted heads on more than one occasion.

I punched him in the shoulder. "At least you saw it coming; I had no clue."

Doug ran his hand through his blonde hair. "I'm surprised you got canned too. However, in all honesty, you were the best-looking young thing around there." He rested his elbows on the bar. "I don't care how nice they pretend to be, those evil bitches saw you as competition. That's why you were eliminated."

"You act like this was American Idol." I ran my finger around my martini glass. "I don't know. Maybe. I still think it was my work performance." I told him how Kate kept pointing out my weaknesses. "I thought I showed a lot of growth."

Doug chuckled. "Tangela, you logged in more hours than the rest of us. I told you the real reason. Just accept it."

I shook my head. "No, I can't."

"Can't what?" Doug turned around and faced me. "Accept that you're beautiful?" The intensity in his gaze suddenly made me a little uneasy. "Why don't we finish this conversation at my place? My apartment is only two blocks away."

"Huh?" I felt a tinge of nervousness. I glanced down at my watch. With my vision blurred, I realized I enjoyed a few too many apple martinis. I grabbed my forehead.

"Are you okay?" Doug put his hand on my shoulder.

"Yes . . . no . . . no . . . ." My stomach kept doing flip-flops, and I wanted to vomit.

"Here." Doug wrapped his arms around me. "Let me help you."

I pushed him away. "No, I'm fine. You're pushing up on me, Doug—I'm a married woman."

Doug raised his thick eyebrows. "Happily married?"

I hung my head low in shame, wrinkling my face as my stomach boiled over in more discomfort. "No marriage is perfect."

"We're talking about yours."

"I don't want to discuss it. Regardless, I'm not going to your apartment, Douglaaaaas." Now I knew I was drunk.

Doug stood up. "It's a shame; we could've had a good time together." He walked away.

"Boy, please!" I yelled. Finishing off my drink, I grabbed my purse and stumbled outside. The downpour of rain hit me hard like ice cubes. In no time, my hair and clothes were soaking wet. Wandering through the parking lot, I remembered my car was parked at the station. *Damn!*

With little clarity, I dialed Terri's home number.

An hour later, we pulled up in my driveway. Seeing the lights on in the house warned me Tate was probably up. I was in for trouble. I leaned on Terri for support as my legs felt like they would give out any moment.

"Where the fuck have you been?"

I frowned but didn't answer.

"Well, we—"

"Terri, I didn't ask you; I'm talking to my wife." Tate slammed a glass on the counter. "It's damn near three in the morning!"

Terri held up her hands. "I see you two have things to discuss." She grabbed her keys. "Tan, call me."

I fidgeted nervously with my hands.

Tate moved in closer. "What's going on with you? I can't believe you came in this house pissy-ass drunk!"

Shaking my right leg, I broke out in tears. "Like you care anything about me."

"I'm your husband, and I do care!" Tate bit his bottom lip.

"No, you don't." He was just trying to get on my good side, and I wasn't falling for his lies anymore. "I had a terrible day, and I needed somebody to talk to." I stumbled forward.

Tate held my hand and helped me to the couch. "Tan, we can't go on like this. I miss my wife."

I rubbed his hand. "I've missed you. I'm so sorry. When I got fired today, I thought my whole world was falling apart."

"I understand." Tate hugged me. "I'm here for you. I didn't even know you lost your job."

"Kate stabbed me in the back." I started crying as I gave him the rundown for the third time.

Tate listened intently and comforted me. It felt good to be in his arms again. *I guess he did miss me.* We hadn't talked like this in weeks.

"I don't even want to pick up my car." I buried my head in Tate's chest.

"Where's your car?"

"Back at the station. I went with Doug—I mean . . ." Closing my eyes tightly, I slowly opened to them to see Tate's reaction to my slip up.

"Who the hell is Doug?" Tate scratched his chin.

"He's one of the interns at the station." I tried to remain calm, but my lips quivered. "He was fired too. We went to—"

"Okay, so now this is all starting to make sense."

I rolled my eyes. "What is?"

"Why you're coming home late and drunk. Fuck you!" He pushed me off the couch.

I stood up and balled my fists in anger. "Like you care! You're fucking that bitch, Tara Lyn anyway!"

"How many times I gotta tell you—I'm not messing with that woman!"

"Tate, I don't believe anything that comes out of your mouth."

"This is bullshit!" Tate stormed out.

Falling back to the floor, I wrapped my arms around my knees tightly and wept like a baby.

The next morning, I woke up with a hangover. Promising myself to never have more than two drinks, I vomited in the toilet again. Lugging my aching body back to bed, I pulled the covers over my head and cried myself back to sleep.

Tate knocked on the door to our bedroom, holding two coffee mugs.

I sat straight up. "Come in."

He handed me the yellow mug. Dressed in a tan suit, Tate leaned against the dresser near the window. "Are you cheating on me?"

"No. Are you?"

"I'm telling you this for the last time—I'm not messing around. You have to trust me."

"Well, I only went to the bar to have drinks with Doug."

"Drinks, huh?" Tate closed his eyes and turned his head. "Tan . . . forget it." He tossed his hand in the air. "You tell me what you want to do . . . because we can't continue like this."

I nodded. "I know." I took a sip of hot coffee.

"I'm on my way to work. We'll talk about this when I get home. Are you going to be here?"

"Yes. You want me to bake some chicken?"

"Yeah." Tate kissed my cheek. "No matter what, I still love you."

A spark pulsed through my body. That was comforting to hear. I loved him too. *Do people who love one another get divorced?* Everything seemed so messed up. I really wanted to get past it and start over, just get the hell out of this place.

The ringing phone interrupted my thoughts. "Hello."

"Are you okay?" Terri asked.

"Yes. That was a trip, huh?"

"To say the least," Terri said in a snobbish tone.

Her comment caught me off guard. "Why do you say it like that?"

"Tan, you were dead wrong."

I cleared my throat. "Excuse me."

"You heard me. You had the nerve to stay out all night with some man and then show up at your house drunk—I would never disrespect my marriage like that."

"Terri, he's the one disrespecting me." I pointed at my chest. "Need I remind you, Tate was practically having sex with a bunch of women in our pool?"

"I don't care what he did. Tan, you should have more respect for yourself and your marriage."

"You know what—I'm not up for a lecture this early in the morning." I hung up.

Even though Terri was right, I didn't want to admit it. What was I thinking? I knew better than to put myself in a situation like that. Reflecting back, I could've been raped or far worse. Doug always seemed so sweet. *It just goes to show you never really know people.*

Maybe Tate was telling the truth. Up until that incident at the party, he'd been the perfect husband. It's not as if he was the type of man a woman would just throw away. Not for a tramp like Tara Lyn. Hell no! I wasn't having that. Swallowing a sip of cold coffee, I resolved to end the "Cold War" in the Gibson household and make up with my husband. Besides, I missed him. I was tired and ready to get things back to normal. This feud had gone on way too long. I needed some sex, and if Tate hadn't cheated yet, he might get desperate enough to give into temptation.

Chapter 38
(Tate)

On my drive to work, I took every shortcut possible. I had an early meeting, and I didn't want to be late. Tan was acting like she was already divorced. I couldn't believe my marriage was back in a ditch again. At first, everything seemed so right with this move.

When you build a marriage on distrust, it will never be perfect. No matter what I said or did, Tan would never trust me. Already threatening me with divorce, she left me with no choice but to handle it like a man. No sense in acting like a punk. I wasn't going to beg her ass.

I loved Tan. I wanted to share my future with her and have some kids. Maybe it was too late. Regret weighed on my shoulders like a ton of bricks.

I thought back to the events that happened the day before. I called Tan on her cell phone only to get her voice mail each time. Finally, after the sixth try, I left a message. "I'm sorry I'm going to be late getting home."

I jotted down some notes on my pad for tomorrow's board meeting.

Tara Lyn tapped on the door. "You're the last person I expected to see here."

"I was just about to leave."

Tara Lyn licked her lips. "I was on my way out too." She walked around behind my desk. "So why don't we leave together?"

I leaned back. "Tara Lyn, I don't think so. See, I'm going home to my wife. And you . . . well, I'm not sure where you're going."

Tara Lyn rubbed my arm. "I know you and your wife are sleeping in different rooms."

I moved over. This woman was relentless. I didn't get it. There had to be at least a dozen men that wanted her. Why me? I stood up and grabbed my briefcase. "That's none of your damn business."

Tara Lyn flipped her hair to one side. "I can satisfy you better than she can."

I smirked. "Maybe. But I'm not about to find out."

"What's wrong?" Tara Lyn tried to undo my tie. "I heard you like to do it in your office."

I grabbed her hands and pushed her away. "Oh yeah. Where did you get your information?"

"Carmela—you remember her, don't you?" Tara Lyn laughed. "She's my cousin. I can suck your dick better than her."

Okay. This bitch really is crazy. I went to the other side of my desk and pointed to the door. "Get the fuck out, you psycho bitch."

Tara Lyn looked astonished. "What!"

"You heard me. Get your ass out." I grabbed her arm and dragged her to the door.

"You're going to regret this!" She snatched my shirt and four buttons popped off.

I let go of my grip on her. "I already do." I straightened my shirt.

"Oh yeah. Wait until I tell them how you flirted and threatened my job if I didn't fuck you."

"Tell them whatever you like, crazy lady." I pushed her out and slammed the door. "I don't give a flying fuck!"

The incident seemed more like a nightmare than reality. As upset as I was, I wanted to kick Tan's ass when she came home drunk at three o'clock in the morning. Here I am about to lose my job because I wouldn't fuck Tara Lyn. And she was out fucking some other nigga.

I strolled confidently into my office to pick up the tape and then headed to the boardroom. Fran was already there with Alvin, head of security, and Leonard, the company lawyer.

"Is that it?" Leonard asked.

"Yep."

Alvin sighed. "Okay, let's get this over with."

For the next hour, we sat there and reviewed the videotape of my encounter with Tara Lyn. Since my last fiasco at American Income Life, I learned my lesson and had a security camera discreetly placed in my office.

Once the tape ended, I turned the VCR off.

"As you saw and heard, Ms. Davis threatened to claim sexual harassment after I repeatedly rejected her sexual advances."

Fran nodded. "That's what I observed."

Leonard crossed his arms. "I think it's time we took care of this situation before it gets any worse."

I dialed Tara Lyn's extension.

"Tara Lyn's desk."

She was on the loud speaker.

"Good morning, Tara Lyn. I need to see you in the boardroom immediately."

"What for?" She giggled. "Did you change your mind?"

My eyebrows rose in anger. "No, I didn't change my mind."

"Well, forget you then."

"Tara Lyn, you need to get here within the next five minutes," I said firmly.

"Okay, okay. I'll be there in a minute."

When Tara Lyn walked in she was surprised to see the head of security and Leonard seated at the table.

"What's going on?" she asked.

Leonard raised his hand. "Come on in. Take a seat."

"Okay." Tara Lyn nervously ran her hands through her hair.

"We want to talk to you about last night's incident," Leonard told her.

"Oh." Tara Lyn cleared her throat. "I don't know what he told you"—She glared in my direction—"but he's been coming on to me for months."

My eyes grew wide. "What!"

Leonard looked at me. "Please, Tate." He turned to face Tara Lyn. "Who's been coming on to you?"

"My boss, Tate. He said if I didn't sleep with him, I would lose my job."

I slammed my fist on the table. "That's a damn

lie, and you fuckin' know it." I couldn't believe they were listening to a damn word she was saying.

"Okay. I'm going to ask you to leave," Leonard said.

I laughed nervously. "Is this some kind of joke?"

Fran put her hand on my shoulder.

"No." Leonard signaled to Alvin.

I held up my hands in surrender. "No need. I'm outta here." I wasn't about to let Big Al drag me out like a screaming little bitch.

I gathered my composure and left. Pacing the floor in my office, my palms turned sweaty. It was all over! My career and marriage.

I heard a knock at the door, and Glen walked in.

"Hey, man. What's going on?" he asked.

"I'm about to lose my fuckin' job, and it's all your damn fault."

"Hold on." Glen looked shocked. "What the fuck are you talking about?"

I sat down on the couch, and Glen sat beside me.

"I know you're the one who told Tara Lyn that Tan and I were sleeping in separate bedrooms. Why would you do that?"

Glen's jaw dropped. "Awww man. I'm sorry." He buried his head in his hands. "I don't want to lose my family over this."

Huh? I put my hand on his shoulder.

Glen clasped his hands together. "We've been together a few times."

My facial expression went stone cold. "Who?"

"Me and Tara Lyn. Man, I didn't want to tell you. I don't know what got into me."

The man who warned me about Tara Lyn fell for her trap. What is it with these women? My boy looked messed up as he tried to explain and apologize all at the same time.

Glen pleaded, "Promise me you won't tell anyone about this."

I handed him a Kleenex. "You know I won't. Hey, I forgive you."

He dried his face. "Thanks, man."

My phone rang. It was Fran summoning me.

I left Glen in there to pull himself together and I headed back to the boardroom. Once again, I found my career in limbo over another woman's lies. Suddenly, I felt as if I needed to take a long vacation. Just get the hell away for a while.

Tara Lyn tried to deny my claims, but once they showed her the videotape, she had no choice but to admit the truth.

Fired on the spot, Tara Lyn was escorted out of the building by security. Fran happily volunteered to pack her things and ship them to her address.

Relieved to still have my job and rid of Tara Lyn, I decided to head home to my wife. I stopped at the florist to pick up a bouquet of yellow roses. I had no idea what was in store, but I had every intention to do what I could to win back Tan's trust. With the videotape in my briefcase, I planned to play it for her. A brotha needed actual proof these days. As the garage door whirred open, I prayed my plan would work.

I entered to find my wife in the kitchen preparing a home-cooked meal.

She looked up. "What are you doing home so early?"

I handed her the bouquet of roses. "I couldn't wait to see you."

"Really?" She inhaled the fragrance of the roses and blushed. "Thank you, baby." She pecked me on the lips.

"You're welcome." I couldn't help noticing her new attitude. *Was this a sign of good things to come?*

"Well, dinner won't be ready for another hour or so. I just put the chicken in the oven."

"That's okay. I need to get out of these clothes anyway."

Tan wrapped her arms around my waist. "Take a nap too. You should rest up." She bit her bottom lip.

I raised my eyebrows. "I will."

After I showered and splashed on some cologne, I changed into a pair of jeans and white-collared shirt. Flipping through several channels on TV, I settled on watching *Dumb and Dumber* on HBO. *That Jim Carey was a fool.*

Since Tan was already in a good mood, I thought about whether I should even discuss Tara Lyn and what happened today. Not wanting to spoil the evening, I hid the videotape in my bottom drawer. I figured if the subject ever came up again, I would show her the tape then. I can't tell you how relieved I was. I did feel sorry for my boy, though. I had to give him credit for trying to be faithful in his marriage. Guess the dog reared its ugly head in a moment of weakness. As forceful as Tara Lyn was with me, I could see how he gave in to the temptation.

Once I was sure an hour or so passed, I walked to the foot of the stairs.

"Is it okay for me to come down?" I called down. My voice echoed back.

"I thought you'd never ask."

It was dark downstairs, except for the candle-lights burning in the dining room.

"Take a seat," my wife's voice instructed from another room.

My tongue watered as I eyed the glazed chicken, rice, and other dishes before me.

My tongue hit the floor when Tan appeared from around the corner wearing a white silk gown with a see-through robe.

"You like?" Tan asked in a sexy voice.

"Oh, yes." I grinned. "Very much."

As she came closer I stood up, but Tan pushed me back down in my chair. Facing me, she straddled her thighs on mine. "Are you ready?" Her breath smelled of fresh strawberries.

"Uh huh."

Undoing my zipper, Tan slid down on my shaft. I cupped her ass with both hands, but she pushed them away.

"No touching, big boy."

I wiped my chin. "Okay."

Resting her arms comfortably on my shoulders, Tan slid up and down my penis.

"Uuhmm." I grunted.

She gyrated her hips, whipped her pussy in short rotations.

I felt my dick stiffen as if it wanted to explode. I turned away and pulled back some to lessen the sensation. Didn't want to let it out too early.

She licked her lips seductively. "You like?"

"Oh yeah." I shut my eyes tightly. *Oh, what the hell!* I let go, and released as I heard the familiar sound of crashing ocean waves.

We made love once more on the living room floor. It felt good to hold her soft body in my arms. After some small talk, we built up an appetite for dinner. I didn't mind that my food was cold because I was ready for dessert—I'm not talking about the cheesecake either.

Epilogue
5 years later
(LeQuisha)

Mike and I stayed at the Doubletree Hotel. We brought the girls and Dante to visit Lil' Donny for FAMU's homecoming game. It was hard to believe my son was in college playing for the Rattlers. You wouldn't believe it! I ran into Tom Joyner and Sybil in the hotel lobby. I acted the fool as they signed my memory book.

Dante still played football too. He was the star player on his team. Believe it or not, he stopped being mama's baby and grew into a young man. It was hard for me to get used to, since I didn't want to let him go. I was proud of both my boys. At least two of my children were doing well.

As we headed to dinner, Daneisha called me on my cell. "This baby won't stop crying, Mama."

"Did you change him?" I tried so hard to stay calm when it came to this girl.

"Yes."

"Feed him?"

"Uh huh."

"Maybe he's gassy. Did you burp him?"

"I tried. This boy won't burp."

"Every baby will burp. You need to give it more time. Keep patting him. Then change his position and pat him some more."

"Humph. I'm tired of this."

I pictured her bottom lip poked out.

"My grandson is only a month old. You have a long ways to go."

"When are y'all coming back here?"

"Monday."

"I'm not going to make it 'til then."

"Yes, you will. Why didn't you call Kendall like I told you to? I already set it up with Reesy."

"Because . . . she doesn't have time for me anymore."

"Oh. I see." I looked down at my watch.

"I'm calling Lamium. He's the daddy, and he should be here."

"Don't have that boy over to my house."

"I need some help; you ain't here."

"You heard what I said, Daneisha—don't get stupid."

"Forget you!"

She hung up.

I stared at the phone in pure shock. *No, she didn't!*

I pressed redial.

Mike grabbed the phone. "Don't do it. You said you weren't going to do this."

"Right, Mama," Dante chimed in.

"I know but—"

"But nothing. This weekend is about Donny, not Daneisha. Whatever it is, we can handle it when we get back."

I took a deep breath. That daughter of mine— only the Lord knew what she and that boy were doing in my house.

Daneisha knew I didn't want no gang bangers in my house. The last time he jumped on her, he almost left her for dead in the middle of the street. She didn't have no respect for anybody. I couldn't even believe I gave birth to her. I rubbed my forehead.

"You're right." I crossed my arms and stared out the window. *I can't wait until her Section 8 paperwork comes through. She would be out of my house for good. After the way she cursed out Mike, beat up on Dante, two weeks couldn't get here soon enough.*

(Tangy)

Still trying to catch my breath, I turned over on my side, while my husband jumped in the shower. My husband was an amazing lover, and I wanted seconds. Too bad he had to go to work early this morning.

I napped for another twenty minutes, then showered and dressed in a leisure pants set, before checking in on Bria. She was fast asleep. I was relieved our lovemaking didn't awake her.

I tiptoed downstairs to prepare breakfast. On

my Blackberry, I entered another errand I needed to run before reporting to work. I checked my e-mails too.

After breakfast, I helped Bria get ready for preschool. "Do you want to wear the pink or red top?"

Bria pointed to the red top. "This one," she replied as she messed up her hair with her hand.

"Take your hand out of your hair. I'm not combing it again." I pulled the top over her head. The static cling made several strands of hair stand straight up. Brushing it back in two neat ponytails, I admired her pretty face in the mirror. "You're so gorgeous."

Bria gave a dimpled smile. "I know." She giggled.

"You're a mess." I laughed. "Okay, let's get your skirt on." I helped my daughter with her socks and shoes, before putting on my matching jacket, and heading out the door.

On the way to Mt. Tabor Christian Academy, I stopped by Terri's house to pick up her two daughters. It was my week to car-pool. When I pulled up in the circular driveway, I saw Terri's face appear in the bay window.

Trinity and Catherine ran out the door dressed in blue uniforms. "Hello, Auntie Tan," Trinity said as she climbed in and put on her seat belt.

"Good morning, girls." I helped Catherine adjust her seat belt.

Her hair perfectly combed and dressed in a blue and white athletic suit, Terri stood by the door, Robinson on her hip. "What do you have planned today?"

I looked up, and held up my hands to block out the sun. "A few errands. What about you?"

"Robinson's going to the sitter for a few hours,

while I go to the gym. You want to meet for lunch when I'm done?"

I squinted. "Sure. I should be ready, say, around noon."

"Perfect. I'll call you with the details."

"Okay." I waved as I drove away. I dropped the girls off at school, took care of my errands, and changed into my work clothes. After lunch, I headed into the station for my job as evening news anchor at WGXA Fox 24 in Macon, Georgia. I had a little research to do on my own before we went on the air.

I turned up the volume to the CD player in my navy Volvo. *I am a friend of God* . . . I sang along with Israel. *He calls me friend.* The song instantly put me in good spirits. Having a wonderful career, family, and home, I felt so blessed. Not a day went by that I didn't thank God for my life. All my dreams had come true, even though for a while it looked awfully bleak.

With my stomach doing tiny flips, I couldn't wait until lunch. I'm sure Terri was going to bore me with the details about Glen and the kids. Although, she was happy being a full-time mother, it wasn't my cup of tea. I loved holding down a rewarding job; it made me more complete as a woman. Which allowed me to be a better wife and mother.

I know Terri had some gossip to share as well. Hearing about Sharon's latest deadbeat boyfriend would be entertaining. Living in Miami, Sharon still didn't have her life together. She never stayed on a job longer than a few months and changed lovers just as often.

Parking my car next to Terri's, I glanced at her powdering her nose in the mirror. I got out and tapped on her car window.

"Come on, because I'm hungry," I said.

"Okay, okay. I hope we get a good table this time."

"We will, if you hurry. Now, get your little self out of here."

Terri grabbed her purse, and we entered the restaurant.

(Tate)

"Daddy, push me," Bria said.

"Okay. One more time."

I gave my daughter's swing one big push and watched her soar through the air. Seeing her brought me back to being a child again. Remembering my dad pushing me so high as I tried to reach my hand to the sky. Just once, I wanted to touch a billowy cloud; I imagined it felt like soft cotton.

Bria planted both feet on the ground and ran to the monkey bars.

"Come on!" she yelled.

I grabbed her sandals and followed. Standing at the foot of the slide, I caught her tiny body in my arms as she slid down.

"Who loves you more than anything in the whole wide world?" I asked as I spun her around.

"You do." She laughed so hard.

Releasing her from my grip, Bria traipsed up to the top of the slide again.

"Here I come," she said.

"I'm ready." Once more, I caught her. Spending time with my daughter, I treasured her so much.

The warm weather finally arrived. We went to the nearby McDonald's for dinner. I listened to Bria talk about her dog, Suzy. I enjoyed every minute.

Bria chewed on her last French fry.

"Are you ready to go home?" I asked.

She nodded.

We hopped in my new Jaguar and headed back to my apartment in Buckhead. We sang the alphabet song all the way. I was goofy and exaggerated. Anything to get a laugh out of her. I opened the car door and helped Bria out of the car.

"Whee!" I lifted her in the air and carried her upstairs.

"This is fun."

"Hey, Tate." Keisha greeted. She was my next-door neighbor.

"How you doing, Keisha?" I asked.

"I'm fine."

"I can see that." I eyed her big booty as she sashayed past me. *I know what you're thinking. I haven't tapped that booty yet. But a brotha wanted to holla!*

Once we got to the second floor, I used my key to open the door. Bria walked in ahead of me.

"Can we watch *Shrek 2*?"

"Again? We've seen it once already."

"Please, Daddy."

I put my finger on my chin, pretending to think long and hard. "After you take your bath and get in your pajamas."

Bria shook her head. "Okay."

I ran a warm bubble bath for her. Only having my daughter every other weekend was a crying shame. I wanted to be more involved in her life. Since her mother and I couldn't stand to be in the same room, having a decent conversation was impossible.

I couldn't understand why she hated me so

much, considering she was remarried—to the man she left me for.

My job at Metropolitan Life grew more demanding, and Tan spent all of her time building a career as news anchor at WGXA Fox 24 in Macon. The arguments never ended, and I slept in the guest bedroom more than I slept with her. It was surprising to both of us, when Tan learned she was pregnant. When Bria was born, we decided once more to work harder on the marriage, but it was too late.

Ironic, wasn't it?

Tan cheated on me. When I confronted the two of them, she kicked me out. Divorced my ass, and demanded spousal and child support. That was fucked up!

Don't get me wrong, I didn't mind providing for my daughter. I only thought it was fair I get more time with her too.

Tan refused to listen, much less agree to allow me to see my daughter. In a few weeks, we're headed back to court for the third time. My new lawyer assured me the judge will grant us joint custody.

I continued to climb the ladder at Metro Life, recently promoted to Projects Manager at the Atlanta office. Tan and George reside in my old house in Warner Robins. Signing over the house was part of the divorce agreement. It hurt like hell every time I picked up my daughter from the house Tan and I purchased together.

Nevertheless, I was doing okay. Not in a serious relationship, I went on a date every now and then. Sometimes, I wondered if my life would be any different if I'd married LeQuisha instead?

I don't dwell on my past too long, because I

wouldn't have Bria. She meant the world to me. There were no regrets.

"Okay, Bria." I lifted her out of the bathtub and helped her dress into her pajamas. "Are you ready to watch *Shrek 2*?"

"Yes!" she yelled.

"Who loves you more than anything in the whole wide world?"

"You do!" She kissed me on my cheek.

"You know it."

Teaser Chapter from
Messin' Up
Daneisha's Story

*W*ho *does she think she is?*

She makes me sick. I'll be so glad when I get away from here. Getting my own apartment in Arlington, my old neighborhood, is going to be so good. Lamium says he's going to buy me all new furniture. We already picked it out at Warehouse Furniture. I can't wait.

My man treats me very well. He says when he has saved another twenty thousand, he's through dealing for good. He's going to start him up a barbershop, you know, like the movie. And I'ma be struttin' up in there with my fresh gear and hairdos making all them stank bitches who want my man jealous. I know they be wonderin' what a thirty-year-old man see in me anyway—this good ass pussy, that's what. I got my skills from my mama.

One time, I snuck in her room and watched her fucking her boyfriend from her own closet. Tate had a big dick and he used to make my mama scream. I used to hear her all the way in my room. So I decided to find out how good she really was. I watched her technique and tried it on my boyfriend. When I made him howl at the moon, I knew I had my shit down.

Men been beggin' for this stuff ever since. I used to

*give it away for free. Until my best friend, Kendall, showed
me how I could make a lot of money selling my goodies instead. When I had to move to country-ass Middleburg with
my grandma, it was hard. But I learned how to sneak out
and be back before anybody even noticed I was gone.*

*Once Kendall's car broke down, and we asked these
guys at the club to give us a ride. That's how I met
Lamium. He dropped me off, and I gave him my cell phone
number. My stupid grandma didn't even know I had a cell
phone.*

*Drunk-ass Leroy walked in the laundry room as I was
sneaking in through the back door. He was tipping in the
house too.*

*"Uh huh. Wait until I tell Gayle. You know she gonna
beat your ass." He laughed, showing his big gapped teeth.*

*"Come on, Leroy. You know I'm going to the detention
center if I get in trouble again." I pulled out a stack of hundreds.*

Leroy's pop eyes got big then.

*I smiled. "Yeah, that's what I thought." I handed him
three bills.*

"Now, get out my way." I tried to push past him.

"Not so fast, lil' gal."

"Huh?"

*Leroy pulled down his pants and whipped out his
dark, wrinkled, old dick. No wonder my grandma be eatin'
women's coochies out—her man ain't have shit to work
with.*

*"Won't you…ah…give me a lil' head too?" He
breathed his stank breath in my face.*

*I turned up my nose. "Hell no. You better go buy a
trick with that money I just gave you."*

He shoved my face into the wall. "Suck my dick."

*When the numbness left, my nose felt broken. As blood
ran down, I wiped it away.*

He brushed his dick across my lips. I stroked Leroy's dick to try to get it hard. It was limp.

He slapped me so hard; I could taste the wood and paint on the wall.

"Don't play with me." The look on his face warned me if I didn't do it, the cops might find my dead body in the woods somewhere. It's not like he hadn't killed a nigga before. Served nine years in prison. My grandma knew how to pick 'em.

I put his nasty penis my mouth. It tasted like sweat, dirt, and it smelled like a sewer. I almost gagged.

He swelled up in my mouth. Forced his way down my throat. Pulled on my thousand-dollar weave.

"Yeah." He grunted.

Oh no. It got harder. I pulled back, and he rammed harder. Deeper.

His cum tasted like rotten eggs.

Leroy zipped up his pants and closed the laundry room door.

I ran to the kitchen sink and threw up. As I purged, everything I ate that day came up too.

I'd had it! I packed up my shit and hitchhiked a ride out of Middleburg. I didn't even know Lamium all that well, but I went and stayed with him anyway. My mama found out where I was and dragged my ass back home. She saw the bruises on my face, and told everybody Lamium beat me up. I didn't have the heart to tell her Leroy beat me and raped me. She thought she knew every damn thang.

She tried to get me back in school. Boy, was she mad when she found out I had missed sixty-five days.

More bad news—I was pregnant. And I wasn't having no abortion either. I took that money and got me a manicure and pedicure at the spa. My mama kept me prisoner until I had my baby. Now I can't wait until I get the hell up out of here. Me and my mama don't get along. And I can't *stand Mike's punk ass. Always trying to act like he's my friend and he care about me. His faggot ass lets my mom boss him around all day, and my brothers act like puppets.*

Anyway, my bags are packed and my man is pulling up in his money-green Mercedes. We're going to have a ghetto fabulous life!

I'm still making my money. One thing I learned from watching my mama's stupid ass is to gets mine. Okay. If Lamium knew, he would kill me. But he don't have to know everything.